"I know what you're going to say, Michael!"

Carol's voice was curt. "But I've come out here to marry Laine! I'm not interested in flying back to London! And I'm beginning to wish I'd never met you!" she added.

"For the record, I'm beginning to wish that, too!" Michael's tone was strangely enigmatic. "Well, what shall we do? Take in a show? Go dancing?"

"I'd better go straight back to the hotel," Carol said. "It hardly seems fair to have a good time with Laine lying there in hospital."

Michael reached for her hand. "You're still a free agent, aren't you? Besides, I want to give you something to remember—perhaps with a certain amount of regret." Turning her hand over, he placed her palm against his lips.

WYNNE MAY
is also the author of these
Harlequin Romances

1310—TAWNY ARE THE LEAVES
1343—TAMBOTI MOON
1691—A BOWL OF STARS
1794—PINK SANDS
1875—A PLUME OF DUST

Many of these titles are available at your local bookseller.

For a free catalogue listing all available Harlequin Romances
and Harlequin Presents, send your name and address to:

HARLEQUIN READER SERVICE,
1440 South Priest Drive, Tempe, AZ 85281
Canadian address: Stratford, Ontario N5A 6W2

The Valley of Aloes

by

WYNNE MAY

Harlequin Books

TORONTO • LONDON • LOS ANGELES • AMSTERDAM
SYDNEY • HAMBURG • PARIS • STOCKHOLM • ATHENS • TOKYO

Original hardcover edition published in 1967
by Mills & Boon Limited

ISBN 0-373-01158-X

Harlequin edition published November 1967

Second printing November 1967
Third printing July 1972
Fourth printing June 1975
Fifth printing September 1976
Sixth printing June 1982

CHAPTER ONE

A HERD of footsteps added its contribution to the volume of sound which echoed from one end of the Marine Terminal to the other. It was a solid content of voices, expectant and excited, rising to the acoustic ceiling—ships' sirens, the repressed grating of the cranes in operation outside and this beat and rhythm of so many feet upon the mosaic-tiled floor.

Faces tilted towards the slanting light, coming in through immense sweeps of glass, and they were patterned by the queer, twisting and dancing kind of light which was caused by the sun-splintered waters of the Bay reflecting against the glass.

Carol Tracey felt the stirring of a new adventure, and her hazel eyes scanned the faces which were all about her and her slender fingers clutched at the straps of her travel handbag. Something within her shivered with an exquisite sort of apprehension—until she discovered that there seemed to be no one who answered to the description of, or who even faintly resembled, Laine Mulholland, her pen-friend.

She felt a shaft of fear and her mind went a complete blank for a moment and then, when that blank space had shifted itself, she found herself trying to work out whether she was wearing the correct outfit—the outfit she had told Laine she would be wearing.

For a weakening moment she couldn't remember, and was aware of a suffocating feeling that she had lost her memory. How stupid of her! It was panic, of course, and she paused next to a fantastic flight of steps—the brain-child of some architect, which had sprung to life from a blueprint—and looked down at her neat and sophisicated suit.

Like a diver rising for breath, she struggled to remember. "I'll wear a powder-blue suit," she had written, "but just in case a dozen other girls are also wearing powder-blue suits, I'll wear the brooch my grandmother gave me. You won't be able to miss it. It's antique—a large bow, set with glowing rubies and strung with pearls."

5

Her heart lurched. Had the brooch fallen off? This identity piece of hers? But no, there it was—trembling and glinting on her lapel.

She was seized by an overwhelming urge to go back on board and to seek the safety of the cabin she had known as home during the voyage. But it was too late now to ask herself if she had been rash, so she opened her bag and took out the latest photograph of Laine.

"Miss—Tracey?" Carol knew she had been expecting this. It was a voice she had been waiting for, something she recognised *within* herself, but she had almost forgotten it in the past year, during her pen-friendship with Laine, and yet, even in the act of swinging round to face the owner, she was thinking that she had always known that time would run its inevitable course to the inevitable day when she would hear this voice; but not once had she associated it with Laine Mulholland. That was the strange part about it. If she had any doubts about being here now they were swept to one side.

Her eyes came up to meet those of the man who stood beside her and she felt the sudden acceleration of her heart as their eyes met and was instantly aware of his own look of surprise and awareness.

"Miss Tracey?" His eyes dropped to the brooch.

"Y-yes, but you're not . . .?" Her voice died away. Surely there was some mistake? Some terrible mistake—for the voice did not belong to the man whose picture she held in her hand.

The coloured photograph was an excellent one and in it the man revealed himself to be tall and distinguished-looking, in an artistic and sensitive way. The hair, strong and black and a little on the long side, was wavy and slightly tinged with grey—for Laine Mulholland had made no secret of the fact that he was forty-two to Carol's twenty.

Like Laine, the man who stood beside her now was also tall and lean and tanned by the sun, but he was *young*—twenty-six at the most—and his auburn hair was straight and looked as if it gave trouble by constantly falling across his forehead. His eyes were intensely green and at the moment they were slightly narrowed as he looked down at Carol. Laine's eyes were brown!

"My name is Copeland—Michael," he was saying. "That conveys nothing, of course, except that Laine Mulholland asked me to meet you. I'm sorry I'm late."

Carol's young face was shadowed by the apprehension she felt and her voice, when she found it again, was stilted. "Is—is anything wrong?"

"Nothing to get upset about. Laine is in hospital, but as a matter of fact, he is on the verge of being discharged. He had an accident, by the way, resulting in septic hands."

"Oh, I see. Was it serious? The accident, I mean. Is it going to interfere with his music? You—you probably know . . ."

Michael Copeland cut her short. "No, it's not that serious, but I'm going to leave it for him to tell." Although he smiled, she had the uncomfortable feeling that he was not pleased about having to meet her.

"Where is your luggage?" he asked, dropping his eyes in the direction of her feet, where he apparently expected to find it.

"Just over there, at the exit," she told him. "I—I didn't know what to tell the porter, after it was examined. I'd forgotten all about it, as a matter of fact—looking for Laine. My luggage, I mean."

Suddenly she felt a long, long way away from home and the need to cry, somehow, and she looked down at the photograph and then, for the first time, she noticed that Michael Copeland was also holding a photograph—the last one she had sent to Laine, before leaving England, and he was flicking the edge of it against the finger-tips of his other hand. Her lovely eyes came up to meet his. "It seems silly, doesn't it?" Her voice contained embarrassment.

"Well, it *is* silly," he said abruptly, as if finding her rather useless. "It's the silliest thing I've ever heard of. Here," he gave her the photograph, "you'd better keep it now that I've found you."

There was a moment's stricken silence. The way in which he had said this and the way in which he looked at her caused the hurt to leap into her eyes, and she dropped her long lashes quickly and reached out for it.

It was then that she experienced her first terrible sense of fear and dim awareness of possible exposure to mischance.

Standing there, she looked very young and slim with her shining fair hair which curled inwards at each cheek and lay across her forehead in a soft fringe. She had one of those fashionable faces with excellent bonework, the kind of face that photographed well. Her clothes were also fashionable. The blue suit had come from Tatiana's, and when she had seen it Tatiana had given the skirt and jacket the place of honour in the window. Beneath the display there had been a long, narrow card, royal blue in colour, printed with gold lettering which read: FOLLOW THE SUN TO MEXICO—POCATELLO'S SOPHISTICATED YOUNG SUIT WILL LET YOU TRAVEL MILE-AFTER-MILE WITH DASH AND ELEGANCE.

However, the fine bones, slim figure and the suit designed for sophisticated travel could not hide the fact that Carol Tracey was young and touchingly innocent. She slipped the two photographs into her bag and sighed lightly. She had followed the sun all right—not to Mexico, but to South Africa. Marriage to Laine Mulholland had been the reason.

Michael Copeland was saying, "The Mulhollands have left me quite a bit of explaining to do, one way and another, but suppose we get out to the car? We can't stand here all day."

"Yes, of course." Meekly Carol allowed him to elbow her towards her luggage and then eventually she found herself standing in the acid-yellow sunshine next to his car.

While he busied himself with her cases she narrowed her eyes to examine the modern buildings with their sweeps of glittering glass and mosaic-encrusted façades. For a moment she thought of her first impression of Table Mountain as they had docked at Cape Town and of those white and golden beaches seen from the ship—the fantastic blues and greens, the mournful cry of the gulls—and she felt vaguely sick. This should have been the final wonderful experience —her arrival in Durban and her meeting with Laine.

Michael Copeland opened the door for her, but she hesitated. "Get in," he told her, and then he stood watching her as she slipped into the red-upholstered seat of the cream car because, of course, there was nothing else she could do. She heard the door close her in with an expensive thud and although she did not turn her head as he walked across the parking area in front of the car and round to the driver's side, she was aware of him—disappointed in him.

8

Sunshine spilled into her lap and the car was warm from the sun and smelled of metal, well-cared-for leather and carpet. Michael Copeland lowered his long length into the seat beside her, but he did not start the engine. There was a short silence, and then he lit a cigarette and sat staring straight ahead. Finally, without looking at her, he said, "Do you want my advice?"

Dreading something, she said, "No, thank you." Her voice was a tight whisper.

"Well, I'm going to give it to you, regardless," he replied, "whether you want it or not. Get back on that boat and go back to England. If you were my sister, it's what I'd insist upon. In fact, I'd carry you back to that telescopic gangway and . . ."

This took her breath away and she said quickly, "Well, I'm *not* your sister. Your advice is quite uncalled for!"

He swung round and looked at her. "You're just a kid," he told her. "A stupid kid. What did your people have to say about this crazy set-up? Or have you run away?"

"I didn't run away," she said hotly, "and they know everything."

She did not tell him that there was only her grandmother, who had now thankfully given up the London house and was happily settled in an exclusive home for elderly folk. This, Carol had discovered with shock, had been her grandmother's secret desire for some time. She did not tell him about her father who was somewhere on the lower slopes of an extinct volcano in the remote province of Cuzco. There were just the two of them in her young life, her grandmother and her father, but it was none of Michael Copeland's business.

"And they were satisfied?" His voice was incredulous.

"Yes. Quite satisfied." Again she refrained from telling him about her father's last letter, which was in her handbag at this very minute.

"Carol," he had written, "as you know, Laine Mulholland has been writing to me for some weeks now, so that I could get to know him, as well as possible under the circumstances. Well, it seems to me that he has a good home to offer you and that he has grown more than just a little fond of you. I can't bring myself to use the word love. That will have to come, I suppose, but I'm sure that you appear to have thought things over for yourself, according to your

9

letters, and that you have the confidence that your feelings for each other will grow when you actually meet. But can you be sure? That is what I keep asking myself. You're not yet twenty-one. I want you to promise me that if you find you cannot go through with the marriage you will use the money which I have arranged to be settled to your account and go back home.

To what? Carol asked herself when she had read her father's letter. "There seems to be little else I can do—being so far away," he had gone on, "and it seems incredible that the child I knew at ten has now reached the age when she wishes to spread her wings and to marry. How time has flown—and yet believe me when I say that I never meant to stay away so long. Too late, I'm beginning to realise that I put myself first, after your mother died, in my desire to get right away from it all. I will blame myself if things go wrong for you, child. You have never had me to give you any sort of guidance, have you? I will feel that I have failed you."

Michael Copeland was easing himself back into his seat. "And you?" He let out a long breath. "A man of *forty-two*. How old are you?"

Carol took her lip in her teeth. "Really," she thought, "this Michael Copeland is doing his best to upset me," but she said. "In eight months' time I'll be twenty-one."

"So you're twenty?"

"Yes."

"A kid of twenty—and Laine Mulholland is taking advantage of the fact!"

"One can't go on being a—kid." Her voice was soft.

"I noticed all the luggage," he was saying. "All your London glad-rags. You're expecting to hit the high spots with Laine Mulholland, no doubt? You know, of course, that his mother has money—quite apart from the fact that, in his own way, he's doing all-rightee!" The green eyes travelled over her suit—the one designed to follow the sun, Carol thought bitterly—and her voice went up. "For your information, Mr. Copeland I *know* what to expect. Also, for your information, money had nothing to do with it." She felt tense with pent-up emotion.

"In that case . . ." He started the car.

"You still haven't told me where I'm going. In fact, you've told me nothing at all about the things I'm supposed to know." She was more disturbed than she cared to admit to herself.

He reversed out of the parking lot and she watched him, tilting her face very slightly in his direction so that he would not be aware of her scrutiny.

She was conscious of his immaculate suit, the creases down the long length of his legs were like twin razor blades. His white shirt was perfectly laundered.

He gave her the back of his coppery head as he swung the wheel. "Under the circumstances, you're booked in at a hotel. You will stay there for tonight." He moved his position. "Unfortunately, Mrs. Mulholland is away, but she is expected back tomorrow. I'll be in town myself—until tomorrow. I'm to take you to meet Laine at the hospital today and again you'll visit him this evening. Tomorrow I'll take you to your future mother-in-law's home where I understand you are to stay until Laine is discharged from the hospital."

They were driving away from the modern buildings—leaving them behind along with the deep, unfathomable waters of the bay—and the ship! If only Laine had been next to her. If only things had gone according to plan. If, if, if. Carol wondered what had happened to his hands, but was too proud to ask the man beside her.

The hotel overlooked the beach front and the warm Indian Ocean which washed and pawed at the coarse yellow sands. Everywhere there was colour—moving patterns of red, green, violet, blue—brought into an overwhelming confusion by brightly beach-clad people, expensive cars, sun-umbrellas, shop windows which had been fabulously garnished with beautiful things and the lights of advertising signs, flickering on and off in the bright sunlight.

On one side were the tall buildings of hotels and luxury flats and, on the other, the sea which was an expanse of shadowed blues caused by the currents and white-crested waves. Between the two lay the Marine Drive, with its palms, pools, aquariums and places to eat, and over everything there was the peculiarly exciting smell of the sea, the sun, sun-tan oil and a hint of hot cooking oil coming from the casual drive-in eating places.

Carol watched Michael Copeland as he concerned himself at the hotel reception desk on her behalf, and then she saw her luggage being whisked away by a page in livery and was aware of a little lump in her throat. The attractive set of blue leather cases (containing her so-called London glad-rags) had been her grandmother's parting gift.

"I'll see you to your suite," Michael said, coming back to her, "but come and sign the register first, will you? Oh, by the way, these are the orders of your husband-to-be, so you have nothing to worry about. Just settle back and enjoy it all—while it lasts." He spoke well, pronouncing his words with absolute care as though he had become used to people patiently and eagerly listening to the magical tone of his voice.

"Thank you." To hide her embarrassment, Carol made a show of looking about herself with calm, interested eyes. In any case, she was feeling a little better now that something was happening. It was only natural that she should feel strange. After all, even if Laine *had* been the one to meet her it would have been the same—to some extent. All the letters, and even the photographs, would have been flimsy material, at first, on which to base a meeting.

The lift took them to the fourth floor and as she stepped out of it her heels again sank into luxuriously piled carpeting. Even up here, in the corridors, there were exquisite displays of flowers in great copper containers and in flower-encrusted china jardinieres.

A silver-grey door was opened for them by another page and they stepped into the small foyer of the suite. Michael slipped his hands lightly into his jacket pockets and stood watching her with a patient, detached air.

With his brow slightly raised and a faint but sarcastic smile about his lips she knew what he was thinking. He was thinking that *this* would suit the little gold-digger from London, wouldn't it?

She turned to face him, anxious to shake him off now that she was settled under Laine's wing at last—for, of course, this was the result of Laine's concern for her while he lay useless and hurt in hospital and while his mother was away. Here she would be safe until she was taken to Laine's mother and until Laine was discharged to manage her affairs and to take her to his home.

"Thank you for everything you've done," she said, and it was her turn to sound curt now.

"I only hope that everything comes up to your—er—expectations," he said, removing his hands from his pockets and turning to watch the page fidgeting around until he was ready to be tipped. He turned to Carol again, with that faint detestable smile wrinkling his tanned forehead a little. She noticed how the corners of his mouth turned up. He had quite a way with him, she thought, this Michael Copeland. But it went wide on her. He was too good-looking for his own benefit. With his green eyes, tanned skin and insolent manner he reminded her of a secret-agent type in a film. Mentally she clicked her fingers. That was it! Michael Copeland was aware of this, of course. Deliberately she turned away from him, dismissing him, but all the time she was wishing that he would go so that she could sort herself out. She knew an intensity of longing to look at Laine's photograph again.

The suite was out of this world. Stretching before her was a thick, geranium-red carpet, lime-green silk curtains and bedcover and pink-shaded lights.

"You've forgotten something." When she turned he was grinning at her, one brow raised a little higher than the other. One side of his well-shaped mouth lifted in what she supposed was intended to be a smile, but was just a deepening of the ripple of his cheek. He looked, for all his well-groomed appearance and town ways, as though he spent a lot of time in the sun. In fact, he was so deeply and evenly tanned that he might well have looked swarthy but for those intensely green eyes.

"And that is?" Carol's voice was cool.

"You're not quite free of me yet!"

"Oh?" It was an irritable little sound.

"I have the introductions, all round, to make. At the hospital. At the Mulholland home. Or had you forgotten? So you're going to have to put up with me." He smiled then, a slow easy grin, and then looked at his wrist-watch. "I'll give you an hour and then I'll take you to tea somewhere. By that time the nurses will have finished with your boy-friend and I'll take you to the hospital."

"Thank you." Again she wondered what else she could do. "In that case, I'll be downstairs—in an hour." Their eyes lingered.

"By the way," he told her. "Laine also overlooks the Marine Parade and the sea, just as you do. You're quite close to him. That should set your heart thudding."

She was amazed to hear this. "It does." Her voice was sarcastic, and then in a small whisper she asked, "And you? Where do you . . . ?"

"Oh, I have a flat. I'm hardly ever in residence these days, but it's there, anyway, overlooking the Bay. From my picture windows I'll be able to look out on your ship."

"It's not *my* ship. I've left it. For good, I might add."

He shrugged his shoulders. "In an hour, then."

When he had gone Carol stood looking at the silver-grey door for a moment, then she crossed over into the main room, the deep pile of the carpet absorbing her footsteps. On the way to the balcony she paused to look in at the bathroom, shining and impersonal with only the trace of a past perfume to show that it had ever been used. It might even have been the perfume of some cabaret star from England, she thought with amusement.

From the balcony there was a breathtaking view, and she stood there thinking about Laine who was somewhere on this same Marine Drive, overlooking the sea. The sound of the city floated upwards and the wind from the sea caught her silky hair and blew strands across her cheeks and along her mouth. Once again she found herself struggling in a whirlpool of emotion, and then, because she still carried her bag, she opened it, allowing the wind to have its way with her hair and took out Laine's picture.

The man in the photograph wore tan-coloured corduroy slacks, a golden-yellow waistcoat, and a tapestry-blue cravat was tucked in at the open collar of his tan shirt. Only Laine, with that special brand of good looks, could get away with such clothes, she thought, but for one swift moment, which seemed to thrust itself against her taut young body, Carol felt appalled at what she had done.

Turning slowly, she went through the open glass doors, deciding on the way that it would not be worth while changing her suit. She opened her bag and slipped the photograph back inside.

Although it was getting hot, her thoughts ran on, the suit was not a heavy one, so she opened a case and delved into its satiny depths for a crease-resistant blouse. If it *did* become too hot she told herself that she could always remove her jacket and feel cool in the short-sleeved blouse. Then she creamed her face and carefully applied new make-up, examining her face in the long mirror which was fixed to the wall above an equally long dressing-table. Her wide hazel eyes stared back at her and she fought back a sigh. It was so quiet here, by herself, and she glanced at her watch and saw that there were still ten minutes to go.

Michael Copeland was waiting on her in the formal lounge, but he did not see her come in, and Carol watched him as he paced restlessly, stopping only to examine one of the large oil paintings of the Cape mountains which dominated one section of the room. Then, as though sensing her eyes upon him, he turned, and the air between them seemed held fast for a moment. She noticed the taut line of his cheek and the set look about his mouth, but the look was gone in an instant and he smiled faintly, walking towards her in that loose-limbed way of his. "So? You didn't run away?"

"I told you, I don't run away." She could not resist a smile.

"That remains to be seen." He closed the distance between them and stood looking down at her.

"I want to thank you again," Carol's voice had become stiff with sarcasm now, "for giving me *such confidence* since I arrived."

He gave her a long, almost leisurely look. "You must have had a great deal of confidence to get you here in the first place. Anyway, how do you feel? Found your land-legs yet?"

"Yes, thank you."

He bowed very slightly. "Ready for tea?"

"I suppose so."

He took her outside to where his car was parked, and as they drove along the Parade next to the sea Carol was by no means unaware of being so close to him, but she resented this awareness and kept well over on her side.

"I'm taking you to see the monkeys," he said suddenly, breaking the silence.

"That sounds like fun." She still had not forgiven him, and her voice was cold.

"Oh, it is." His voice was dry and he seemed to be having a private joke at her expense. "You'll see monkeys where you're going. Did you know that? This is just to break you in. It will not be uncommon for you to see monkeys on the tea-tables eating the remains of food before

15

they're chased off, but not before scattering food and crockery with a crash. The very brave often bear away a serviette or a tea-cloth."

He took her to the Riverain, which was an hotel overlooking a river. The river spread itself out in a lagoon before it linked up with the sea in the distance and on the aquamarine water a man was driving a speedboat while a girl, behind the towing-line, skied skilfully across the wake, her body at an angle of forty-five degrees. In the shallows, her scarlet bikini disappeared as she sank slowly and expertly into the water. The boat swung round and came back for her.

Carol stopped to study a notice, tacked on to a gnarled tree, which read: KINDLY CLOSE YOUR CAR WINDOWS. WE ARE NOT RESPONSIBLE FOR DAMAGE CAUSED BY MONKEYS.

"Why the notice?" she asked. "Are they *terribly* wild?"

Michael watched her with something like cool amusement while some monkeys fought and squabbled loudly over peanuts, a little way off.

"No—just grabbing, like some girls. Monkeys can show great cunning when they decide that they want something. But sometimes they slip up. The very thing they thought they wanted, and which they thought they had procured for themselves, turns out to be the beginning of the end for them. Often the beginning of captivity."

Once again she had the impression that Michael Copeland was aiming his barbed remarks at her, and she found herself floundering and knew that her face had flushed.

He pointed to a place beneath a red-and-white canvas awning. "Come," he said, "let's buy some peanuts for our grabbing little friends, shall we?" and with a feeling of hopeless despair Carol followed him to the little stall where an elderly Indian was selling peanuts for that reason.

Somehow Michael Copeland made her feel so wretched that she could not even find her temper being involved at his double remarks.

When he had bought the nuts he gave her the packets. "Have one to eat," he said.

"You said that you were buying them for the monkeys."

"I know I did, but I want you to keep a packet for yourself. I want to show you how even cunning monkeys are often outsmarted." She followed his lazy smile in the direction of an old man near by who was busy chewing

16

nuts, in the peculiar way some old people have of chewing, while several monkeys gazed at him with pleading eyes which darted first to the brown paper packet and then to his remote old eyes. Several of the little creatures had outstretched hands, the long tapered and exquisitely shaped fingers ready to grasp out.

Life flowed back into Carol and she laughed softly. "Oh, poor little monkeys! Don't ask *me* to eat peanuts in front of them."

"Poor little monkeys," scoffed Michael. "Serves them right, greedy little devils. They never get enough."

Carol opened a packet and very cautiously handed over some nuts, backing away a little when the monkeys came too close.

The sea sent its breezes to them up on the hill and it swept her hair across her eyes and her cheeks, mingling it with her smile, for she was enjoying herself now. She lifted the hand, which held her bag, to free her eyes from the tangled hair. At first Michael Copeland stood looking on in that amused fashion of his, then he took a packet from her and joined in, laughing outright at some of the outraged antics of the monkeys.

"Let's have something to drink," he said when it was all over, and after he had disposed of the empty packets in the receptacle provided. "What's it to be?"

"Tea," she told him, pointing to a table. "Look, there's a table in the shade." The gardens blazed with colour, brash and impudent beneath the caress of the sun. The roar and wash of the sea could plainly be heard in the distance. A small scarlet-and-silver aeroplane skimmed the blue water, almost tipping the white froth of the waves as they turned over and thumped down on the beach.

"There's an airport near by," Michael explained, "and if there was time we could go for a flip."

She questioned him with her lovely eyes. He seemed to have thawed towards her. "Oh, I'd love that," she said, thinking that each moment with him during the last half hour or so had been a minute point of pleasure.

"I'm not like you think, you know," she said on an impulse. "I mean—I'm not a—grabber, greedy and cunning."

"Aren't you?" His mocking eyes met her own, then flickered over her lovely and expensive suit, and, looking at him, she felt a sudden sense of grievance.

"No," she said stiffly, "I'm not!"

"What did you do in London? What work, I mean?"

"Hairdressing," she told him, "and I did part-time modelling, sometimes."

He threw back his head and laughed and she stared at him, outraged. Nothing made sense to her any more and she clenched her jaws together while he looked down at her from his tall height. "That makes sense, anyhow," he said.

"Really? Well, I can't tell you how relieved I am to hear that, because I was just thinking that nothing makes sense to me. Might I ask in what way?"

"I knew a model once. What a girl! All *she* thought about was feathering her own nest." He looked deeply into her eyes and she knew that he was mocking her—testing her—and she felt a fierce, slow fury rise up, especially when he added, "*This* girl hooked herself a prince and is, I believe, on a cruise round the world. You models certainly get around, I'll say *that* much for you!"

She moved away from him and started walking towards one of the terrazzo-topped tables. When she was seated on one of the white-enamelled cast-iron chairs she frowned in the direction of the Bluff which provided an olive-green backcloth to a long line of buildings that reminded her of jagged teeth. She did not turn her head as he joined her, but when she thought he was not looking, she moved slightly so that she could study his face and then was suddenly unnerved when he looked up at her.

"How did you come to—find Laine Mulholland?" he asked, and her face was immediately set in that "here-we-go-again" expression. Her hazel eyes danced with tiny electric flames. The Indian waiter came for their order and when he had given it Michael turned back to her. "Well?"

"I knew his second cousin—Monica Rich. Monica gave Laine my address. At first my grandmother was furious, but she simmered down. We corresponded for a year, and I got to know Laine very well in that year."

"If he says anything more," she thought, "I'm going to put him in his place!"

"What did your grandmother have to do with all this?" His voice contained curiosity.

"Well, we lived together. She brought me up, after my mother died. She's my father's mother. My father is in

18

Peru and I haven't seen him since I was ten. That was when my own mother died."

"I see. Now we're getting somewhere," he said.

Carol sat back in her chair. Tucked neatly into one of the branches, directly above her head, was a loudspeaker relaying pop music, and as she listened to the tortured writhings of the jangling instruments and the voices fighting for precedence she thought that, deep down, the music was just a reflection of her own thoughts, but she tried to remind herself that this wouldn't last—this cross-talk between herself and Michael Copeland.

She looked across the table at him. He seemed at home wherever he was, just as though everything and everybody belonged to him, she thought resentfully. When his eyes swung quickly in her direction she had no time to drop her own and she realised that they were gazing upon each other with confusion, as though they were no longer the same two people who had met in the Marine Terminal only a few short hours ago. Wildly she looked away and scanned the tea-gardens in sudden sweeps almost as though she might be seeking a way out.

The tea arrived and she managed the cups with hands that shook quite visibly, spilling a little of the golden liquid in both saucers.

When he passed her the sugar bowl her eyes flew open with shock as she felt the shiny little thing slip from her fingers and fall to the table. Helplessly she watched it tip itself to one side and then fall over, almost as if it were in league with the Devil himself, releasing the tiny white grains in a glittering miniature avalanche. She bent her head so that her hair fell across her cheeks, hiding her face from Michael Copeland—but he did not have to see it.

He accepted the cup from her and then, stirring his tea, began to explain a little about the city, pointing out things of interest to her. "Behind the modern skyscrapers of the seafront," he told her, "are mosques and minarets of the Muslim and the Hindu Temples. People from abroad find the atmosphere exciting and exhilarating. I wish we had time to take a drive there, but time is running away from us." He looked at his watch. "In a few moments we'll have to leave—to go to the hospital."

Immediately she lifted her hands to her windswept hair, pressing the golden wings against her cheeks. "Don't

19

panic," he told her, and his voice was nasty again, "there's a powder-room here. You can apply your war-paint."

She stood up, lifting her bag from the table. "You're *enjoying* yourself, aren't you? At my expense!" Before he could say anything she was running from him, but not before she had seen that he was smiling in the easy manner of a man who was not affected by heated rejoinders.

In the powder-room, she took out her comb, and when she had finished with it she picked up her lipstick, uncapped it with shaking fingers and began to apply colour to her lips. A great hurt spread itself over her and for a frantic, beating moment she thought of her father—somewhere out there in Peru.

After all these years she vaguely remembered her grandmother reading her father's letter. "From the plane I saw a wonderful sunrise of the Andes, although there were clouds in the sky. Possibly this accounted for the spectacular beauty. We arrived, in the clouds, at Lima. Some of the peaks of the Andes were covered with snow. Cuzco, eleven thousand feet above sea-level, is damp and cold." Even as a small girl of ten she had been aware of the great distance which now divided her from the father she loved.

Her grandmother had kept all of his letters in some kind of jewel-encrusted antique box and before she had left for South Africa Coral had gone through them, from beginning to end. Her grandmother had kept them all in strict order, right from the first one received up until the last letter to arrive at the London terrace house before it was sold. The box had gone, with her grandmother, to the home for elderly folk.

Her father had written of guides taking him to see towns and ruins—ruins, where llamas were sacrificed and the Incas foretold the future by the size of the animals' hearts.

At this moment her own heart felt ready to burst and she turned her head to look through the windows. A ship was anchored against the rim of the horizon, between sea and sky, waiting for permission to enter the harbour, and she felt a longing, a yearning for the father who had left her. The longing was so intense that it left her feeling weak and wretched. The vision of her father, as she remembered him at ten, rose before her—tall, slightly built, with hazel eyes very much like her own. However, even at the tender age of ten she had been aware of the light which had been extinguished from them when her mother died.

Carol had been more hurt for her father than she had been for herself, but she longed now to be able to give herself up to a flood of belated tears as she sat here after all the years which had gone before, when she had felt as alone and abandoned as an unwanted kitten.

All the time her father had been writing home about Spanish-style houses built on Inca walls, churches with solid silver altars, marvellously outlined mountains and beautiful valleys, she and her grandmother had been alone in a house of memories.

It was not easy remembering, at this minute, and it was costing her a lot of heartache just sitting here getting lost in the past. She knew she must get up and go back to Michael Copeland who, in turn, would take her to Laine— Laine who, like her father, had written about the sunrise and the sunsets, the swimming-pool—just off the veranda —the Valley and the hills embracing it, the tourists who visited his curio shop and who had tea and cold drinks on the long veranda with its rough stone pillars holding up the roof. Laine had at least sent for her to share these things.

As she went back to join Michael Copeland, Carol kept seeing herself in some new way and felt a shock of discovery. She was away from her grandmother now, whose one fear was that her granddaughter would get "linked up with the riff-raff". As a result, for all her fashionable clothes and the odd hours spent modelling, Carol had led a sheltered, rather commonplace existence. The wonder of it was that she had been allowed to take this voyage into a strange country—but then it had suited her grandmother's purpose, and to give the old lady her due she had believed that everything was working out for the best. The girl who floundered about inside the fashionable clothes was having to think for herself, only now she would have to think *twice*.

CHAPTER TWO

A LIFT took them to Laine's private ward and they paused at the tremendous white door, which was closed. Behind that door, thought Carol, was the man whom she had come from England to marry. This was not the way in which she had visualised their meeting, and she felt the chill of the building with its endless corridors and walls of glass separating it from the warmth of the sun and the colour of the sea. Michael knocked lightly on the door, which was so shiny that she could see their reflections in it—vague and slightly blurred—and then she stood, as though in a dream, while he pushed the door open and stepped to one side for her to enter.

Her eyes travelled to the centre of the ward to meet those of the man who was sitting up in bed and his own brown eyes held hers for a moment before he turned to place the book he was reading on the white locker next to his bed. When he looked up again he was smiling, and Carol moved slightly towards him and stood waiting while Michael allowed the door to swing to. The chill she felt was not imagined.

Laine Mulholland was just like his photographs—lean and with a well-shaped head and sensitive face. He was tanned and had the kind of appearance that went with good creams and after-shaving lotions. His dark hair was brushed back from his forehead in small crisp waves and above each temple silver wings had been carefully combed so that they stood out, each silver thread caught and placed until it played its part in drawing attention to the final result.

There was only one way to describe Laine's mouth. It was a decidedly tender mouth and yet, for all that, Carol was aware of a hint of sullenness in its make-up; a kind of disdainfulness, perhaps? There seemed to be a forced look of eccentricity about him, she thought, and then pulled herself up, discarding such critical thoughts.

"Carol!" As soon as he said her name Carol found herself moving automatically towards the bed, but for a moment she didn't know what to say or when to say it. When she finally found her voice, she said, "Laine! I've—

I've thought about this moment so often—but never like this." She drew a steadying breath in an attempt to hold back the fear and disappointment that welled up within her.

From his hospital bed Laine Mulholland had become a stranger to her, and this stranger substituted for the Laine who had been her companionable pen-friend for the past year.

Laine looked down at his bandaged hands. "I'm sorry about this. It was a silly thing to have happened, and I've cursed myself for every type of fool under the sun." He sounded vaguely on the defensive, somehow, thought Carol.

"But it's not *your* fault," she said quickly, and then looked around at Michael Copeland who was standing there, near the door and forgotten for the past strained moments. Michael had his hands in his jacket pockets, thumbs on the outside, and he was looking at Laine Mulholland, but whatever was going on in his mind was neatly barricaded up by those dark green eyes of his.

"Sorry, Mike," Laine was saying. "How are you, old chap?"

Michael removed his hands from his pockets and turned on that smile of his, which began with a mere lifting of the chin and left his eyes looking amused.

"How's the patient?" he asked, looking at the bandages. "Well, it's the right girl, is it? Take a look at— Grandmother's brooch."

"It is the right girl and she's quite, quite beautiful, isn't she?" There was a sort of triumph in Laine's voice. "And so young—Mike?"

"Dangerously young," Michael replied in a flat voice.

"Mike, old chap, pull up a couple of chairs, will you?" Laine had not appeared to notice the remark.

As she sat down on the chair which Michael had placed beside Laine's bed, Carol laughed softly and said shyly, "I —I honestly don't know about being quite, quite beautiful —and *dangerously young*—but I *do* know that I'm—really quite, quite nervous, Laine!"

Michael remained standing. "I seem to have run out of cigarettes," he was saying, patting his pockets and not looking at them. Then he looked up and grinned, "That's a corny one, I know, but anyway—I'm going down to the hospital kiosk."

When he had gone there was a confused silence before Carol started to say something and discovered that Laine had started to say something too, and they both ended up laughing uncomfortably. "Go on," he said. "You were about to say?"

"I was going to ask how it happened—your accident, I mean."

"That's a very good question," he smiled ruefully. "I've no idea, to be perfectly candid. It just—happened. I —I suppose Mike has told you about it?"

"Well, no, he hasn't." There was a young nervous tension about Carol. "He told me about your hands turning septic, that's all. He said he would leave the final telling to you."

Laine laughed very softly. "He had a good point there. However, we won't discuss it now. Our meeting has been hashed up enough as it is, don't you agree? I'm practically on the verge of being discharged, you know. Bandages come off—and *stay* off, tomorrow."

"Will there be—scars?" Instinctively, she knew that this would be important to Laine Mulholland. He would want to hide any scars.

"Nothing to speak of," he answered, and his voice was curt. "I've told you—it was nothing really. By the way, I must apologise for Mother being away from home. It will just be for tonight. She'll be back tomorrow, of course. She went away for a few days and wired me here, at the hospital, asking whether you could put up in town until tomorrow. Fortunately Mike was in town, and so the rest was easy. I contacted him. He's organised everything. He's my 'stand-in'—you might say. Mother loathes meeting people, by the way. At the docks and airports, I mean . . ."

"Please don't worry about anything." A little later Carol found herself describing her suite at the hotel, stressing again just how comfortable she was, and after that they spoke a little about Monica Rich, the second cousin Laine had never met, and they were still discussing her, in a stilted fashion, when the door opened and Michael Copeland walked in.

His mouth looked set as he placed some cigarettes and a packet of fruit on Laine's locker. Then he handed Carol a box of chocolates, and as she took it from him, murmuring her thanks, she kept her lashes lowered so that the restlessness in her eyes would not be seen.

The immense windows in the ward looked right across the sea. Along the Marine Parade a long, never-ending string of cars shone in the sun and gave the impression that they were wavering beneath its warm rays. The beach was a yellow ribbon, polka-dotted with brilliantly coloured sun-umbrellas and the people beneath soundless puppets performing in the sun.

It seemed a strange place to have a hospital, and Carol wondered whether Laine was made more impatient to get out when he saw that carefree life going on out there.

"I'm allowed up, of course." It was almost as if he had read her thoughts. "I go for walks, in my dressing-gown, and quite enjoy a walk to the entrance gates."

On their way in Carol had noticed the flower-sellers at the gates and as she had looked at the lighthearted hues of the blooms, bunched together and glistening with drops of water, waiting to be transferred from their place in the sun into the cool tranquillity of the sick wards, she had wondered whether she should buy some for Laine—but had decided against it.

Michael had little to say, during the whole visit, and conversation remained strained and uncomfortable. When it was time for them to leave he said, "Well, cheerio, Laine. I'll bring——" he hesitated and then went on, "*We'll* come along again this evening."

"Good! I'll be looking forward to it." Laine's smile was a sweet tender thing. He seemed such a gentle person, thought Carol, and yet, looking at his mouth again, she was aware of a hidden temper. Was there something self-willed and knavish about Laine's make-up?

"I'll also be looking forward to the visit," she said, and something told her that she had merely said this with the object of reassuring herself.

Michael did not speak, going down in the lift, and now that they had left the ward he was smoking. Their eyes, green and hazel, met through a haze of smoke. At ground level he stood back to allow her to leave the lift and then followed her along an endless corridor to where enormous plate-glass doors reflected the resplendent beauty of great, shallow concrete basins spilling out a mass of colour-washed blooms.

Outside, the sun beat down on Carol's blonde hair, bringing out its lustre, and she kept her eyes down, watching the toes of her elegant shoes and holding her chocolates to herself, like a small girl. She was only half aware of Michael touching her elbow as they crossed the Parade to where his car was parked. No longer were the people merely small figures, with jointed brown limbs, to be observed by bystanders from behind hospital windows. Instead, their laughter was something to be enjoyed; something to be heard above the roaring, hooting traffic. In the background there was the sound of the sea and the shrieking, laughing noises of the children from the swings in the park. Overhead, some sea-gulls circled, crying.

When Michael held the car door open for her Carol was afraid to blink her eyes. He fitted the key, but before he switched on he said, "Well? There you have it. You've just met the man who's going to help himself to your youth—Carol!"

"Don't," she whispered, huddling herself to herself. "Oh, *don't!*"

He started the car, and then as he twisted round to reverse out of the parking space he laid his arm along the top of her seat and, for a moment, his fingers accidentally touched her neck, just beneath her hair, and she felt her teeth come down on her lip and moved away from him.

"It's practically lunch-time," he said, concentrating on the lunch-hour traffic. "How time flies."

"Yes, I was going to ask you," she stammered miserably, "will you have lunch with me—at the hotel?" She was thinking about his flat and the possibility that he might have to fix himself something to eat, unless he was going out somewhere.

"I don't know that it's a very good idea—but all right." He changed down and drew up at a robot.

"Carol," he said, using her name now with ease, but not looking at her, "I know a man. He has fabulous connections——"

Instinctively ,she held her breath. "So? What has that to do with me?"

26

"It has everything to do with you. If anyone can, *he* will be able to get you back on that ship before it leaves again." He turned to look at her, and then his expression became cold and his green eyes were serious. Although it looked as though it was made for smiling, his mouth was hard. The traffic light changed and he turned away from her.

"There's no need," and then because she couldn't bear it any more she added, "Stop it! Please stop it. I wish you'd mind your own business."

He narrowed his eyes against the sun, which was dazzling on the widely curved windscreen. "You're way out of your depth," he told her. "Just now you won't be able to get back. And you'll go under. Can't you see that? Or is the thought of the Mulholland money too much for you?"

"Oh, how *dare* you! How can you say that?"

"Well, money's the key to a good life. Any fool knows that."

"I'm not interested in the Mulholland money, as you call it."

The car slowed to a halt in front of her hotel. "That's a stroke of luck," he said, changing the subject, "a parking space almost at the front door."

During lunch he seemed relaxed, although aloof. He asked her about the voyage and what she had thought of Cape Town, and her answers came out absently, born of the moment, but it was the stillness that followed each answer that gave indication to the struggle which was taking place within herself.

After the meal Michael fixed his eyes on the tip of the cigarette he had just taken from his silver case. "I'm going back to my flat for a pair of bathing-trunks," he said. "Coming?"

It was impossible to imagine that the slightest idea of an ulterior motive prompted him, but she said, "No."

He was apparently unperturbed, but their eyes clung together. "Okay. Then I'll call back for you and we can go to the beach. I'll leave it to you—if you want to swim—well, all right. *I'm* going in, anyway."

"There's no need to worry about me," she told him. "You don't have to keep me amused, just because Laine asked you to meet me. You've quite done your bit—more than your bit, I should say."

He ignored her remark. "I'll get the receptionist to call you from the desk when I get back."

Alone in her suite, Carol felt too afraid to even try to analyse her feelings, and as she opened the case where she knew her bathing-suit to be, her one longing was to be rid of Michael Copeland and for this time in her life to be over and done with. She even found herself longing for the time when Mrs. Mulholland would have left Laine's home and she and Laine were happily married. It was unfortunate about Laine's accident, whatever it was. If it had not taken place then Michael would not have met her to stir up this feeling of unrest and uncertainty in her. What right had he to do this to her? She shut the case with an explosive movement, giving vent to her feelings. After all, even from his hospital bed Laine had looked the same to her—just as she had imagined him to look. So nothing had changed. Even in his pyjamas Laine had retained that "arty" look about him, as though his mind and imagination were chiefly concerned with his artistic pursuits. The photographs could have deceived her—but they hadn't. Laine was a very attractive man and it could have been the reverse!

She kept trying to think of all the pleasant things she had noticed about Laine Mulholland all the time she was changing. There was his voice, she thought. In a way he had the punctiliously beautiful voice of an ecclesiastic. There was his smile . . . and his mouth. It was only natural that, meeting the way they had, there had been a certain amount of strain and tension. After all, their meeting was supposed to have been so very different—a laughing, breathless kind of thing, surrounded by luggage, porters, the turmoil in the Customs shed, and yet, for all that, an intimate, secret, exciting event.

When she had thrust her slim hips into well-cut slacks she chose a bright yellow mandarin-type shirt, and beneath these garments her bathing-suit had a damp sticky feeling because she had used it constantly on the ship. She did not dare to use the scanty bikini which she had brought to wear in Laine's pool—*after* they were married. (Her grandmother would have had a fit if she had known about it!) She could not help knowing, with a secret delight, that her body was going to tan beautifully.

28

The telephone startled her out of these girlish thoughts and the receptionist stated, in a very efficient voice, that Mr. Michael Copeland was downstairs waiting on her.

Michael had changed into gaberdine slacks and a white T-shirt and was carrying a rolled striped towel. When he saw Carol he smiled and, with a certain feeling of relief, she smiled back. If only he would keep off the personal side of things, she thought, she could bear all this, and then an inner voice immediately struggled to make itself heard. "Bear all *what*? What is this all about?"

"We'll walk," he told her. "It's not far."

The sea breeze tugged at her hair, outside, and the sun seemed to be sliding its warm fingers over the exposed parts of her body, caressing her, like a lover, and she tilted her face to it, closing her eyes.

"Hey, look out!" Laughing, he caught her around the waist, and she blushed, wondering what he would think of her if he knew about the lover part. "Do you want to be run over? You very nearly walked into a car. Do you know that? You might say I saved your life!"

It was then, as he pulled her to him, that she had her first intimation of their mutual attraction, but it was too vague to seem dangerous. He was laughing down into her eyes, and her voice, when she answered him, was breathless. "I was enjoying the sun. It was like a—caress."

"Lucky sun," he said, grinning down at her, his green eyes admiring, and then he said, "I don't suppose you can swim? I mean you *Londoners* never see the sun, do you?" She knew that he was teasing her and she said, "Well, you have a lot to learn. *I* used to think that lions roamed around your streets. I *can* swim, as it so happens. Do you imagine that English girls are just a lot of pale-bodied creatures who've never learned to swim?"

"Yes," he said, taunting her, "with goose-pimples. By the way, this is the beginning of the winter season, but I don't see any goose-pimples on you. I think you'll enjoy our winters here."

"Oh, I am! I'm going to love Durban."

"You won't have time for that, dear girl."

"Why not? Laine isn't so far from Durban. He told me that in his letters."

29

"Not so far as the jet flies, of course, but far enough!" She looked up at him, frowning at his words. He just loved filling her with unrest!

The water was marvellous. She watched him running in rhythm with the pounding surf, sending up sheets of white spray with his feet, before he turned sharply and made his way into the breakers. She was struck by his easy style as he dived under and then began to surf, catching the waves, as they turned over, with the superb precision which was to send him shooting up the beach.

"Come on," he called, coming for her, and there was no time to think of anything now but these moments together. When they had finished splashing about they walked back to their belongings carelessly heaped on the sand beneath a striped umbrella which, for no good reason at all, he had hired. In its pool of shade he draped a towel about her shoulders and playfully jerked her towards him and for one breathless second he held her close and she knew that, to him, her skin would have seemed warm and scented.

They lay on the sand, a little to one side of the umbrella because they were too young to be refugees from the sun, and listened to the thumping breakers vibrating the sand beneath them until it was time for them to go back and shower and change for dinner.

Secretly, the sun had shifted its position and a wind, which the hour before sunset had decided to rustle up, was beginning to have its way and it blew sprays off the heaving wave-tops.

"You can't possibly go back to your flat and cook," said Carol, ignited by the sun and the magic of everything and throwing all prudence to the winds. "If you have no other plans, will you come back to the hotel for dinner? My table is for two, after all."

"It is, after all . . ." he agreed, smiling, "but I'll come only on one condition."

"And that is?"

"That is—I pay for myself. Meals for the 'stand-in' can hardly be expected to come under Laine's expense account!"

She flushed. "Oh, you're always so sarcastic about everything, aren't you?" She was furious with him, and then she noticed that he wasn't listening to her. Instead he was looking at a girl who was coming out of the water, holding a dripping bathing-cap by the straps.

"Excuse me, just one moment," he was saying, and then he was moving across the sand with a lithe, contained stride. She watched him put an arm about the waist of the girl who, startled, swung round to face him.

From where she stood, Carol noticed that the girl had red hair and her wide mouth had a cleft under the lower lip, and for a moment she seemed to be outlined against the darkening sea which was beginning to have a faint night smell about it now—heavy and salty. Then she flung her arms about Michael's neck and stood talking to him in this fashion while the sea sucked and lapped restlessly about their feet. In turn, he slowly closed both arms about her waist, linking his fingers loosely about her back. Carol was amazed by the girl's apparent lack of inhibition and felt her muscles tighten as she saw Michael drop his arms and turn in her direction.

From his attitude, and from the attitude of the red-haired girl, it was quite obvious that they were talking about her, and even at a distance, Carol could see that they were arguing and she was able to see the lovely face collapse into an expression of resentment. Then she watched, with a kind of nervous apprehension, as they began to walk towards her.

Michael made the introductions and he seemed to be choosing his words with care, as if they might trap him as well as Maxine Mason—for that was her name.

Maxine Mason was not so young as she had appeared from a distance, and as a result she was poised and, even in her black bathing-suit, sublimely certain of every movement and gesture. Her swim had done nothing to destroy her gorgeous hair, which was arranged to appear careless and studied at the same time. It looked as though she spent a small fortune keeping it that way and the result conveyed the sense of charming raggedness, although, in some mysterious way, it gave no effect of untidiness at all, but rather to increase that of Maxine being well-groomed— even on the beach.

After the introduction, there was a long cool silence and Maxine's elegant back was tense, then she said, "You're a *long* way from home, aren't you?" Carol had the sensation of being subtly challenged and felt an odd sense of uncertainty.

"Well—yes," she agreed, "I suppose I am, rather. I've —I've come out to South Africa to be married."

"Maxine knows all about that, don't you, my sweet?" Michael spoke mildly enough, and he was smiling, but there was a glint to his eyes which Carol did not know how to interpret. Maxine made no effort to hide the flame of annoyance which he had lighted in her. "I *should* do, shouldn't I? And *you* should, too. Anyway, my sweet, I have to be on duty at six and the old dame has been in a nasty mood all day, so I'd better be getting back. When are *you* going back, by the way?" She looked questioningly at Michael.

"I'm going back tomorrow, after I've taken our friend here to the home of her mother-in-law-to-be. When will I be seeing you again?" His well-lined eyebrows lifted a fraction and a faint, mocking smile crossed his face.

"Oh, don't be so feeble!" she snapped. "Why do you bother to ask? I thought you knew! I'll always be around —unless I'm finally licked, of course."

"Don't be so bitter." Michael's voice was teasing, but sympathetic. "It spoils that lovely mouth of yours." Suddenly he put one arm under Maxine's knees and swung her off the ground. "Shall I cool you off by throwing you back into the sea?" He grinned down at her.

"Put me down, you idiot!" Maxine kicked her long legs. "I'll bite you, Michael!" Then, as suddenly as he had lifted her into his arms, he placed her feet back on the sand again. "Tell me, when did you last see the patient?"

"I saw him yesterday, as a matter of fact. In the afternoon." Maxine turned to Carol. "You were there this morning. You must have felt half delirious with joy—or didn't you?"

Carol was dismayed to find that Maxine's green eyes were as frankly prying as a child's as they raked her face and, for some unknown reason, she did not know how to handle this situation, so, playing safe, she smiled and said, "I was half delirious with nervousness. That's one thing I *do* know!"

Michael stooped to remove his cigarettes from his shirt pocket and straightened up. He shook one free of the pack and offered it to Maxine, then took one for himself and hung it on his lip. After flicking his lighter he held it out for Maxine, who drew back.

"What about," she hesitated, "Carol?"

"Oh, Carol doesn't smoke," he said easily. "I'm getting to know all her vices, but smoking is not one of them." Maxine held the cigarette down at her side and raised her brows, and the fragile amber-green eyes, which went so well with her hair, were again frankly curious. Slowly she brought the cigarette up to her lips and waited on him to light it for her, then she said, "I see. I see." She blew smoke in the direction of his face and it was obvious that she had done so intentionally.

After Maxine had gone, Carol's eyes searched Michael's face anxiously and he looked back at her, one eyebrow lifted. He was smiling.

"Poor Maxine," he said, "you've upset her apple-cart. Did you know that?"

"I've never felt so uncomfortable in my whole life," Carol's face looked stricken. "I'm so sorry, because of course I understand the position . . ."

"I don't think you do, you know," he cut in, and the edge of indulgent amusement had returned to his voice. "Come along, it's time we went back to change for our dinner date, or had you forgotten?"

"I hadn't forgotten, but I don't think that it's such a good idea, after all," she said quickly. "I feel horribly embarrassed for asking you, in the first place."

"Well, you needn't be. To put your mind at rest Maxine's car is somewhere up on the Berea by now. She's a nurse, by the way, and in conjunction with another nurse, is in charge of a wealthy invalid."

As Carol looked at him she wondered whether he was just being nonchalant about this whole business to save her further embarrassment.

"The understanding was that I take you to the hospital this evening—so why shouldn't we eat together first? After all, we've *got* to eat!"

It struck her that he was enjoying her discomfort. "You've got a lot to learn, Carol. If you take my advice, you'll wait before you form your final opinion about—things."

He saw her to her hotel, then went back to his own flat to change, and when she was back in the asylum of her suite Carol took a bath, soaking herself in the scented water and feeling its warmth and fragrance washing away the salt of the sea and the tiny grains of beach sand which still clung persistently to her skin.

She was not at all happy about her dinner date with Michael now, and when she had finished towelling herself she slipped into a short quilted gown and went outside to the balcony. Behind her, the suite was filled with air that was laced with the heavy smell of the sea and from the scent of the roses which were arranged in a white vase on the long dressing-table. She was reliving those moments on the beach when Maxine Mason had shown, in no uncertain manner, that she resented her. Carol's face felt hot and she began to toy with the idea of trying to telephone Michael Copeland to tell him that she would not be dining at the hotel after all and that she had made other arrangements about visiting the hospital.

However, at that moment her own telephone rang and when she answered it she was informed that Mr. Copeland was downstairs waiting on her. Thrown into an immediate state of confusion, Carol found herself stammering that she would be down presently and quickly decided to wear a white luxurious cotton lace dress, completely lined and encircled by a pointed minaret hemline. This seemed, to her, to be a suitable dress in which to have dinner at an hotel of this nature, and when she joined Michael downstairs he looked at her for a moment and then said, very softly, "*Wow:* No wonder you took so long. I wanted us to have a drink before dinner. Let's go out to the veranda and see the lights come on. I particularly want you to see the lights, Carol."

As the dusk thickened, whole strings of lights started their blinking and winking and people began to crowd the Marine Parades. The evening traffic became a roaring, hectic thing and cars swept to a halt beneath the hotel portico.

It was early and the waiters, in their scarlet jackets, stood around in groups. "Take my advice," Michael was saying, after he had given their order and looking very handsome in an immaculate dark suit, "and have a good look at the lights."

34

"Oh, I am," she replied lightly, "although not for the purpose of taking your advice. I'm looking because I want to."

"I wonder if it's bright lights you're after?" His voice was expressionless. "If it is, you're in for a disappointment. As they would probably say in Scotland—you're in for an awful disappointment!"

"Please put your mind at rest," there was a little sharp edge to her voice. "You see, I know just what to expect. Laine has described it all to me. I do *not* happen to be after bright lights and I know that we shall be in the country. Besides, there'll be the usual country lights. We're not going to be *that* cut off from civilisation."

"Oh no!" She noticed that he had begun to talk in that drawling, sarcastic manner again and she knew that it was done to annoy her. "You won't be *that* cut off! There will be lights—let's see if we can name a few at random. There will be the lights of the stars and the moon reflecting on the river, and let's see . . . oh yes, the dam glimmering away beneath them. And then there'll be the lights of the house shimmering on the swimming-pool, and of course you'll be able to see the curl of the flames around the African cooking-pots at the compound and the pinpoints of light scattered over the hills."

She laughed softly, as if this was both outrageous and untrue.

Their drinks came, and when he was finished with the waiter Michael met her eyes across the small table. "So many people imagine that people in England think of South Africa in that way," she said, dropping her lashes and then lifting them again. "I had a friend who came to South Africa. His name was Tony. Tony made his home in Johannesburg and he used to write to his friends in London telling them that he could hear the lions roaring half the night from his bed. He didn't add, not for ages, anyway, that he lived right near the Johannesburg Zoo. I thought that was *priceless!*"

"Ah, that's another thing," he started to say, "talking about zoos . . ." The dinner chimes could be heard coming from some secret place in the hotel, and she said quickly, "Oh, thank goodness! I'm starving. Aren't you?" The lights, the sea and the iced drink were beginning to have their giddy effect on her now.

"Famished." He gave her a slow, easy grin. "Well, finish your drink. There's plenty more where that came from. We'll have something with our dinner."

In the dining-room silent, soft-footed Indians in scarlet jackets and white turbans waited on them, and from their position at their table they could see through lofty glass doors, across the foyer, into the ballroom where there would no doubt be dancing later. The cutlery handles glittered on white damask-clothed tables and these were highlighted by beautifully folded scarlet linen dinner napkins. Above the muted strains of a small orchestra and the babble of well-bred voices champagne bottles were being opened, at odd intervals, with strongly audible pop-noises. On one side of the dining-room a range of windows looked out across the lights and the blackness of the sea beyond where, occasionally, the lights on some ship would transmit signals from its satiny bed.

As she sat listening to Michael's light conversation Carol was aware of her skin which felt caressed by the sun and she could still feel the strong movement of the waves as they had been when they swirled about her body in the surf.

After dinner he waited for her while she went up to her suite for a coat, which matched her frock, and then once again they were in the car weaving in and out of the traffic on their way back to the hospital. After the luxuriously furnished dining-room at the hotel, with its thick carpeting, gilt-framed paintings, soft lights, flowers and rich colour, the chill of the hospital corridors, with their smell of antiseptic and anaesthetic, seemed to bite into Carol's youth, and as they went up in the lift she caught her lower lip between her teeth, and her hazel eyes, shadowed by the amazingly long lashes, were serious.

Laine was in bed, but he was wearing an elaborate black dressing-gown, intricately embroidered with burgundy, Gothic-purple and antique-green dragons.

Once again the visit demanded a certain amount of exertion to meet the demand resulting from tension, and Carol was only too aware that her voice was high and forced with the brightness she did not feel. Several times she caught herself glancing towards Michael Copeland as though pleading with him to help ease the strain.

He, however, seemed set on letting her work out her own troubles and during some embarrassingly dragging moments he left the room to smoke in the corridor, leaving her with Laine, and she wondered then whether he was, perhaps, trying to do something to lighten the atmosphere after all.

"All dressed up—and nowhere to go," Laine was saying, taking Carol's hand in his own. "I'm dreadfully sorry about all this, you know."

As he spoke she glanced down at the slim-fitting white dress. "I had to change for dinner," she told him. Her perfume pervaded the ward.

"Of course," he replied briefly, "how very stupid of me."

"And to come here, of course," she added lamely, although she knew now that this was hardly the type of dress to wear to a hospital—unless the wearer had intended going on to a show, or to dance, maybe.

"You'll be going to Mother's tomorrow. Mike, as you probably know, has to go back. By the way, Mike *is* looking after you all right?"

"Yes. Yes, of course." Her reply came on a stifled breath because, suddenly, the thought of Michael Copeland going back—leaving her—filled her with a mental anguish so strong that it became almost a physical agony. She wondered where he was going back to, and then, exasperated with herself, she said, "Laine, I'm simply longing to meet your mother. I—I do hope she'll like me. I feel so nervous."

"That's probably just because you're feeling strange—and tired. You poor child!"

"I'm not tired, actually, but you're probably right—I do feel strange. I suppose the feeling will go when you're out of hospital."

"I wanted to buy you a ring," he said, and something inside Carol took a plunging drop.

"This confounded turn of events has prevented all that, I'm afraid, Carol. For the moment, at any rate. I wanted us to go shopping and for you to choose a ring—an opal, maybe, or a big pearl."

She gave a faint smile. "Oh, but they're unlucky stones, Laine. My grandmother wouldn't have an opal in the house." No sooner had she spoken than she felt herself

37

flying into a tempest of fright. What on earth had made her say such a thing? Her heart became wedged against her ribs, or so it seemed to her, and she drew a long breath. "I'm only joking, of course," she added quickly. "*I'm* not superstitious."

"Well, you would be a fool if you were." He seemed to be watching her with a new kind of apprehension.

Michael came back into the ward again and she immediately stood up, reaching for the lovely white coat which she had taken off and slipped over the back of her chair. "Is it time to go?" she asked him, and their eyes slowly veered around to meet and the look they exchanged was as personal as if they had been alone.

"If you're ready." His hand reached for the door-knob.

"There's no need to rush off, you know." Laine's dark eyes swept over them. "In a private ward it doesn't make any difference."

The ordeal lasted an hour and a half, but at last, however, it was over and they were outside making their way to where Michael's car was parked and he was opening the door for her. He got in, placed a cigarette between his lips and snapped his lighter, raising his head at the same time to turn and look directly at her. "I was going to say something," he said, "but I won't!"

"I know perfectly well what you were going to say. But don't. You see, I'm just not interested in any men you might know who have these wonderful connections you were talking about."

"This is a different chap, actually, from the first one. How would you like to travel back to London by air? *En route* you can enjoy all the comfort of one of the world's most popular jet liners."

"Oh, *please!*" Carol's voice was pleading. "Do you know, I'm beginning to wish that I had never met you!"

"For your record, I'm beginning to wish that too, Carol." He turned to her, shedding his gloom like an old skin. "Well, what shall we do? What would you like? A show? Would you like to dance?"

"No, thank you. At least, I—I don't think so. I'd better go straight back to the hotel, if you don't mind."

"What makes you think that?"

"Well, it hardly seems fair, does it? I mean, with Laine lying there in hospital."

He reached for her hand and her heart turned right over and stopped before it went thudding on again. "I think it's fair enough. You're still a free agent, aren't you? Besides, I want to give you something to remember—something you'll look back upon, perhaps with a certain amount of regret." He lifted her hand from the seat and turning it over he placed her palm against his lips.

She did not answer him but sat, hardly breathing. He had allowed their still-linked hands to drop back to the seat and she glanced down in the faintly illuminated darkness at their fingers. He disengaged his own first and took his hand away. "We'll go for a drive," he said, "and then I'll take you to see a fabulous sight."

They drove right next to the sea-front and above them the lights sprinkled the moving procession of cars beneath with colour. Except for the luminous line of the surf the sea and sky looked very black. As Michael turned off and headed the car in the direction of the town Carol felt some of the strain of the evening falling away from her, and because he did not seem inclined to talk, she sat quietly looking at the lights sparkling and trembling in an unruly confusion of reds, greens, blues and yellows.

The car began to climb and they left the intermittent chains of lights until they reached a point where they would be able to park and look down on the city—a glittering collection of shops, business houses, flats, hotels and night-spots and, in the distance, the suburbs which were linked to it by the long, sparkling necklaces of street lights. The immediate foreground held the dock basin with its wharves, offices and dockyards, where giant cranes, beneath arc lights, swung and dipped over the holds of waiting ships and long, wavering bands of light broke the blackness of the water. Michael cut the ignition and the motor died, leaving them curiously alone in the sudden silence.

Carol was instantly aware of the tension and the suffocating closeness of being alone with Michael Copeland in the intimacy of the car, and to hide her confusion she tilted her head forward so that she could look up through the widely curved windscreen at the stars. Although the stars from the ship had thrilled her, the luminous celestial points she saw now appeared to her to be even more thrilling—more beautiful..

39

"It's marvellous up here," she said, and wished that she did not sound quite so breathless. "What a magnificent view! It seems odd seeing all the activity down there. One would expect everything to be quiet. Somehow one tends to associate crane work only with the hours of sunlight."

"It's a pity it couldn't have been Laine beside you," he said. He spoke in a casual way, and yet, she thought, it wasn't as casual as it sounded.

As he spoke he moved slightly to switch on the car radio, and when the music came to them, softly at first and then increasing gradually, she knew a wave of almost unbearable emotion; then to add to these tumultuous feelings Michael closed his hand over hers, which was on the seat between them. She dared not look at him and knew that the music was having the power to quicken their senses and their awareness of each other.

They sat like this for several moments, not speaking, then Michael said, "Shall we go, then?" She noticed the strangeness in his voice and had the feeling that he was testing her to an unbearable tension. Because she did not want to sound like a prude and so appear insulting by creating a situation which perhaps existed only in her own mind she experienced a sense of inadequacy and said, "If—you like."

"I want it to be if *you* like." She was conscious of the faint pressure of his fingers upon her own.

"So be it." He released her hand and turned the key and when the engine started he switched on the lights, flooding the road with yellow light and immediately forming a barrier between them and the myriads of stars above. Before he set the car in motion they looked at each other, suspended for a brief moment in trembling balance, then the moment was over and he set about turning the car.

On the way back to town he began to whistle softly to the music and she found herself listening to him, struck by the soft pure notes and wondering whether he was bored with having her on his hands. "It will be perfectly all right if you drop me at my hotel," she said finally. "What I mean is, you don't have to feel that I need amusing."

"Carol," he said, and she could see a star speeding across the sky to lose itself in the blackness beyond the basin of lights, "*don't!*"

"Don't *what?*" Her voice was not quite under control.

"Don't throttle these moments together. I told you, we're going to make hay while the sun shines. Play while the cat is out of sight. You like dancing, don't you. Or don't English girls dance?"

"I do like dancing—and English girls dance very well!"

"Well, I like dancing too."

"But——"

"No buts, please. You're going to have all the tomorrows for the 'buts' and the 'ifs'."

"You frighten me when you say things like that." Her voice was tight.

"Good. I'm pleased to hear that. It means I'm getting somewhere."

"Oh!" When she spoke now her exclamation came on a note of breathless and angry disappointment. "It didn't take you long to resume hostilities again, did it?"

"You're so right—and I apologise." She knew that he was smiling, and she turned away from him in a quick restless movement.

He took her to dance at a place right at the top of a building which was separated from the stars by a hemisphere of glass, and when he ordered champagne she looked at him in surprise; he raised his brows and she saw the old familiar tantalising look in his green eyes. "Let's forget about hostilities," he said, "just for tonight—for tomorrow we must part. Tonight, at least, belongs to us!" Although she smiled when she raised her glass to her lips she heard it make a tiny rattling sound against her teeth and realised that her hand was shaking nervously.

Michael danced well and his movements were relaxed and easy, although perhaps a little formal. "I'm scared to hold you too tightly," he said, but when the music came to an end he held her close to him for a moment before they separated gravely and went back to their table.

Later, when they were dancing again, he said softly. "Your face looks childish and undefended in this light. Did you know that? Especially when you smile that slow, little-girl smile of yours. But then you *are* just a little girl. Do you want me to tell you something?"

"No. Not if it's about a man you know!"

"It's not. It's about this girl. The girl I was talking about. The one with the slow, little-girl smile. It's one of

41

the things about her that I've entered in my mental note-book."

She felt herself stricken into silence and her face was a vague pallor beneath her shining hair.

During each dance now he was holding her just a little bit closer, and once she even imagined that he had brushed his lips across the top of her forehead and she struggled to get her thoughts into some sort of order by thinking of Laine.

"I was thinking about Laine," she began, but Michael cut her short.

"I don't want to think about Laine right now." he said, "so don't tell me about it." He spoke with a sort of irritable affection, and she did not know what to make of him.

When it was time to go he helped her into her coat, and after she had slipped her arms into the sleeves he folded the coat about her, pinning her to him as he did so, and for one mad moment, she stood motionless in his arms before he turned her slowly to face him. "It is a temptation, isn't it?" he asked softly, looking at her mouth.

Her senses staggered beneath his look and she swallowed just a little noisily. "I—I'd like to—thank you for—tonight. It's really been very nice and it was good of you to take the trouble."

"You've got this wrong, Carol. It was no trouble, believe me. You might say that I was just throwing all caution to the winds."

She saw that the smile had gone out of his eyes and to steady herself she said, "Half the time I don't know what to make of you." She laughed lightly as though dismissing his night-spot nonsense.

"Half the time I don't know what to make of myself." Their gazes linked.

A fast lift send them whizzing down to reality, then they ran laughing in the direction of the car park, his arm about her waist. By the time they reached the car they were laughing and breathless, like children. When they were settled he said, "Do you want to go straight back?" Although his voice was carelessly off-hand her heart missed a beat. "Yes," she said with a queer kind of feeling that she could not breathe quick enough. "It's really very late now, and besides——"

42

"And besides, you were just thinking. Thinking of Laine—is that it?"

"Frankly, yes. I was thinking along those lines, in a way."

She could see his face in the light from the street and from the light of the beach-front illuminations and she was struck again by the sheer good looks of him. Somehow there was a vitality in him that gave rise to instant excitement, she thought with a desperate desire.

"Aha, you're turning that one over in your mind, aren't you?" he said. "Well, you'll have to get used to early nights soon enough—so I'll take you back to your hotel now and we'll call it a night."

In the hotel foyer he said, "Well, Carol, this is it. For tomorrow we must part. I have work to do."

"Yes." Her voice was scarcely audible. "I've—been meaning to ask you, actually—what kind of work do you do?"

"I'm a consultant engineer."

"Oh, I see."

"No, you don't." He was smiling. "You don't see at all, Carol."

She looked up at him, puzzled. "Don't I? Well, anyway, good night, and—thank you again."

"I'll see you up in the lift. Somebody might kidnap you. They do, you know."

"They do *what*?" She laughed softly, but when she saw the look in his eyes she felt her laughter drain away and the muscles of her throat tighten suddenly.

"Kidnap babies."

At the door of her suite he said, "And now it really is good night. I'll make a bargain with you—I'll have breakfast with you, if you're up in time. How's that?" He gave her a smile which made her feel giddy.

"I don't think I'll make it," she told him, yawning a little and laughing at the same time.

After he had gone, she stood with her back against the silver-grey door. She saw that a maid had been in to remove the heavy, quilted bedspread and to turn down the sheets. She had also switched on twin lamps and closed the French doors to the balcony. Carol crossed the room and opened the doors, and when she was on the balcony she could smell the sea which was heavy and damp. She pressed her forehead against a cool pillar and thought about Michael Copeland—who would be on his way to his flat now.

After a few moments she went back inside and closed the doors while she took a bath and changed into pale blue pyjamas. She felt young and excited and was conscious of the soft feel of the material against her body. Later she opened the doors again and slid between the cool sheets and lay listening to the sound of the sea above the late night traffic. She watched the lights of the headlights on the Marine Parade as they shone upwards and seemed to trail across the ceiling. Once she heard the deep throbbing note of a ship's siren.

When the telephone at her bedside rang she jumped and then looked at the white instrument with alarm. Who on earth could be calling her? It had probably been put through to the wrong room, she thought, then when the ringing went on she lifted a receiver. "Hello?"

"Carol?" It was Michael's voice—soft, lazy, amused—and she knew that he was smiling.

Her answer came after a slight pause, veiled with caution. "Yes?"

"Are you in bed?"

"Yes."

"So am I." She felt ridiculously shy, discovering this about him.

"I phoned to say good night."

Raising herself on one elbow, she looked at her small travelling clock. "You've already said that. You must have forgotten."

"I haven't forgotten. In fact, I was thinking that I hadn't said it properly."

She pushed back her hair which had fallen across her eyes. "In any case," she said, "it's morning."

"Well, good morning, then. What's the difference, so long as we say it together?"

"Good morning, then."

There was a pause and she could visualise his smile, that quirk of his mouth, and she knew that his coppery brows would be slightly raised above his green eyes.

"Good morning—*who*?"

Her own lips curled and she smiled. "You are persistent, aren't you? Good night—Michael."

44

It might have been a sigh—or it might have been that he whispered something; then the line went dead and she moved the white instrument from her ear and lay looking at it as though it was something wonderful before replacing it back gently on its cradle.

As she settled back on her pillows she was suddenly aware that she had added more fuel to the furnace which she had promised herself to quench.

CHAPTER THREE

The sun was up and the tray which the maid had brought in still untouched when the telephone shrilled again.

It was Michael. "What about our breakfast date?"

She looked at the tray with its thick geranium-red tray-cloth, lime-green cup and saucer and stainless steel coffee-pot, milk-jug and sugar basin, and then her eyes flew to the small clock. It was just after seven.

"I've had a swim and now I'm downstairs and starving," he went on.

She jerked herself up into a higher position. "You're here, did you say? *Downstairs?*"

"Uh-huh." She knew that he was smiling.

"I'll be down presently," she told him, getting out of bed and putting the receiver back in one easy movement. She quickly opened the French doors to the balcony and could hear the slow, endless beat of the surf above the traffic noises. Then, with a feeling of confusion, she opened a suitcase to see what she could wear that was not creased, wondering why she had not thought of this before, instead of leaving it to the very last minute. Finally she chose a white wrinkle-free, slim-fitting dress which was topped by a short-sleeved candy-pink jacket.

Michael was waiting on her in the foyer when she got downstairs and he was smoking, but when he saw her he went to find an ash-tray and stubbed out the cigarette. As he came towards her she saw that his dark hair was damp from his swim.

"I—I didn't think you meant it—about breakfast, I mean," she stammered and, despite herself, she felt a thrill.

"Of course I meant it." His eyes flickered over her and then dwelt amusedly on her mouth and, flustered, she turned away.

During breakfast he said, "When we have finished I must take you to Laine's mother," and across the table their eyes met. Carol's were the first to fall. "She is expecting you," he went on. "That was the arrangement. In any case, I have to get back."

"Yes, I know that." She glanced away, frowning a little. "I feel I must thank you again. I—well, I don't

46

quite know what I should have done without you." Her eyes widened and there was a look of intense seriousness in their expression.

He regarded the fruit knife he was holding. "Don't thank me, Carol. I feel as though I'm taking a sheep to be slaughtered. No, let's revise that. I feel as though I'm taking a lamb to be slaughtered."

She made a confused gesture. "Honestly," she said, "you can be *maddening!*"

"Tell me," he said, and there seemed to be a new hardness about the lines of his mouth. "Was it—love at first sight with Laine?"

When she met his eyes she decided to lie to him. "Yes. Yes, it was." She dropped her lashes.

"Do you mind if I smoke?"

"Please do," she said quietly, and did not look up. When she raised her eyes again she noticed how golden his lashes were against the tan across his cheekbones as he placed the cigarette between his lips.

He held a lighter to the cigarette. "While you're getting your glad-rags packed," he said, glancing at her over the tiny flame, "I'll be arranging for your luggage to be brought down—say in about half an hour's time. I'm going back to the flat. I also have to pack and I want to change."

"I wish you would stop calling them my glad-rags!" she flamed at him. "I'm getting a little sick of that one!"

"Personally," he shot back, "I'm getting just a little sick of this whole business." They both seemed to be caught in a snare they could not understand. "It's a bit thick for you," he went on, "to be saddled with a mother-in-law before you're even married to the guy, isn't it?" There was malice in his voice.

"Oh, stop it. Please!" Her hazel eyes were furious, yet beseeching. "You're making me so unhappy, Michael. On and off, you've been doing that ever since we met."

"You'll be a lot more unhappy by the time Laine Mulholland and his old lady have finished with you." He rose. "Well, are you ready? Or are we going to sit here all morning arguing about something which doesn't concern me?"

"You seem to be making it your business to have it concern you. *I* certainly didn't ask you to interest yourself in my affairs."

Carol went upstairs to complete her packing, and when she was finished she went on to the balcony and stood in the sea-smelling breeze looking over the sea which was sprinkled with the dazzle of the morning sun. Already the beaches were topped by umbrellas of every colour imaginable and she sighed, remembering how it had been with Michael out there in the sun. She turned and went back into the lovely but impersonal room, and allowed her eyes to travel round it so that they could scoop everything up—like the lens of a camera almost—and then, in the manner of a small girl, she whispered, "Goodbye!" She was ready now to go downstairs to find her luggage which had already been taken down in the lift by a page.

Michael had changed into a light-weight suit and his handsome face was set, his eyes brooding. He was ready to leave her, and Carol fought back the panic inside her.

"Well," she decided to make her voice light, "are you ready to deliver the—lamb—to the slaughterhouse?"

"Your luggage has been taken to the car," he said, and his own voice was entirely impersonal. He stood aside for her to move.

In the car she lapsed into silence, thinking that this was a chance meeting which would end as unexpectedly as it had begun, and she told herself that she was *glad*. Soon she would be with Laine in his home in the sun.

"What are you thinking about?" Michael asked suddenly, but he kept his eyes on the road, and in a queer little voice she said, "Nothing really."

"It couldn't have been nothing. You must have been thinking about something!"

"Well, if anything, it was about the sun, mainly."

"I see. About the sun. Well, I suppose, in a way, the sun must have played its part in luring you out to this country, in the first place. Quite apart from everything else." He turned to look at her.

"What do you mean by—quite apart from everything else?" Her voice was taut. "I suppose I'm to take that to mean 'quite apart from the Mulholland money'?"

"Did *I* say that?" He was smiling faintly. "Sometimes," he said, "that sun can stare down at you with an eye nothing short of a madman."

A little while later he spoke again. "I should have asked, I suppose, but did you want to cable your people in London?"

"It wasn't necessary. I cabled my grandmother from Cape Town and followed the cable with a letter. My father, as I told you, is in Peru."

"What's he doing in Peru?"

"Well, it's hard to explain. He has been a—a kind of free-lance wanderer, if you know what I mean. At the moment, it's a diamond field, with a large potential (or so *he* says) on the lower slopes of an extinct volcano—Quinsachata, if I remember correctly. It lies between San Pedro and San Padlo. That's where he is now, anyway, as I've just explained. My grandmother has given up the house now," she went on. "Do you know, I never realised until just recently that she had a great yearning to do this! I suppose she was only keeping it on because of me—to give me a home, I mean. She wanted to go and live in a comfortable home for elderly folk—people more of her own age. I—suppose—she was tired." Her voice dragged a little and then faltered. "I just found out by chance, actually. It all came out after—Laine and I became—serious."

"Is this why you decided to come to South Africa and to marry Laine?" He watched the road ahead and she saw that his hand was shaking. "Take me out a cigarette, will you?"

While she was taking the cigarette from the case he went on, "Wasn't there anybody in London? I mean a man, of course!"

"If there *had* been a man do you think I would be here now? It's not uncommon for pen-friends to fall in love, surely? I find this terribly embarrassing, you know. If there's any doubt in my mind about what I have done, it's only because *you've* put it there."

"You admit, then, that there is a certain amount of doubt?"

"I admit nothing." The words seemed to stick in her throat. "You keep trying to confuse me, don't you? This is so unfair of you. Everything has been so confused as it is—Laine being in hospital and—and the fact that I had to be met by a—perfect stranger."

"You don't look upon Laine as a stranger, then?"

She turned her head away and looked out of the window. "I refuse to be cross-examined like this. What entitles you to ask such personal questions? It has absolutely nothing to do with you, and the sooner you realise that, the better!"

"How right you are!" His voice was hard—so hard that she barely recognised it. "As you say, it has absolutely nothing to do with me, and frankly, I couldn't care less!"

They were travelling along a superb dual-highway now and the countryside was lush. It was difficult to believe that winter was just around the corner. Large houses were set back in tremendous grounds and in many of the gardens a swimming-pool reflected the colour of the sky. A fly-over bridge hoisted them right over the highway and it was apparent that they were in the centre of this flourishing suburb. In the distance the horizon was rimmed by the sea and, from certain points, the skyscrapers of the city could be clearly seen.

Eventually Michael turned into a drive and Carol was instantly aware that the garden had been professionally landscaped. The approach to the house was noteworthy for its long park-like drive ending in the dramatic architecture of a guest car-port and a covered entrance porch with rock-faced plant troughs and a hanging ormolu lantern. It was here that visitors could step from their cars to stand in front of the heavy double doors to the first entrance hall to the house.

He parked his car in this area, then got out and came round to open the door for her, and she discovered that her legs were shaking.

"Well?" he snapped. "How about getting out? There'll be no need to worry about the luggage. Mrs. Mulholland will send somebody for it."

The great doors to the hall were open and Carol found herself moving automatically towards them, with Michael just behind her.

"Go right in," he said. "I told you, we're expected." And so she went to stand just inside the entrance and knew that her hands were cold and clammy.

So designed, the white-walled L-shaped hall was a viewpoint from where the various vistas offered by the second hall, lounge dining-room and magnificent staircase, with its immense crystal chandelier, could be appreciated. A white alcove housed a truly magnificent marble and alabaster statuette. The marble floor was unmarred by the use of too many rugs, but its breathtaking whiteness was contrasted by one "stand-out" royal blue circular rug with luxurious white fringing. Two occasional chairs, near a white telephone fitment, taking up one wall, repeated the colour. Impressive white-panelled doors led to the lounge on one side and to the dining-room at the far end and they were both open to permit exciting glimpses of these rooms.

"I feel so nervous," whispered Carol. "I wonder what Laine's mother will think of me?"

"Oh, she'll *love* you, darling. She just won't be able to help herself," Michael replied, and she could detect the stiff sarcasm in his voice. He looked down at her, his mouth mocking her. "Isn't that supposed to be the correct answer to a question of this nature? It's a pity, isn't it, that it has to come from the 'stand-in'. Still, cheer up. There'll be other compensations."

A sedate black poodle, bejewelled with a rock-crystal-encrusted collar, came clicking across the marble floor of the lounge towards them.

"Well, Marcus," Michael stooped to pat the poodle's head, "how's it, old boy?"

At that moment a woman came down the staircase. The general impression she gave was one of sensational smartness.

Mrs. Mulholland, although she must have been in her middle sixties, was smart, as though she was in the habit of mixing with women much younger than herself and had adapted herself accordingly. Carol guessed that she was costumed with precious care and that she had sat for a long time in front of her dressing-table in the act of making up her face.

"Oh, and so you've arrived, Mickey?" The voice was slightly strident and, somehow, in keeping with the type of woman she was. At the moment it was also slightly complaining. "You're a little on the early side, aren't you? I wasn't expecting you till later." Mrs. Mulholland descended the last few steps with a little flourish to acknowledge Carol's presence she laid her fingers on the girl's wrist while her large grey eyes expressed the wish that she must get her little moan over first.

"I'm in a flat spin, Mickey. A *flat spin*. In the first place, I made arrangements to leave Marcus here with the servants. Of course, you know what *they* are, but what else could I *do*? I ask you? Then that struck me as absolutely impossible! So," she gave a long-suffering sigh, "I tried some kennels—these people have a *magnificent name* . . ."

"Why can't he go with you?" One eyebrow went up as Michael cut in. "Surely that would simplify matters?"

"Oh, for goodness' sake! Can you imagine Marcus fitting in down there? Well, as it so happens, he will just have to fit in there, after all. I'm not leaving him here and I'm certainly not going to leave him at those wretched kennels. They've changed hands. The new people drink like fishes, I believe, and there's no supervision at all. So here I am—desperate. You'll never know just how desperate." She gave Michael a pleading look and pressed her fingers to her temples. "I'll have to watch Marcus the whole time we're there. Really, it is so *trying*! On top of everything my head has come back and my taste buds are playing up."

"Cheer up," said Michael. "By the way, let me introduce you—this is——"

Before he could finish speaking, however, Mrs. Mulholland turned to Carol and gazed at her between hands pressed to her cheeks. "I'm so sorry," she said, "but you can imagine. The upheaval! Of course, I should never have taken this little trip—knowing full well what was in front of me. It's so trying of Laine to go and get hurt just at this time." She turned to Michael. "And this is— Cecily?"

"Not Cecily—Carol," said Michael and Carol together, and they all smiled thinly at each other and finally laughed, sounding rather ridiculous.

Michael glanced in Carol's direction and said, "Carol Tracey, Mrs. Mulholland."

Dallas Mulholland made a light gesture of dismissal. "Oh, *ot course*! How silly of me!"

Carol saw Michael run one finger inside his collar and then he tried to ease it away from his neck as Mrs. Mulholland went on complaining. "I'll have to take as little luggage as possible, of course. That's just about the final straw. But of course, what would I need down there, anyway? I got France to drive me down to the Valley last week—with some stuff. I knew Laine wouldn't have enough room in the car with all *your* cases to cope with."

Here she looked at Carol and then back again at Michael. "Another thing, I just don't know what I'm going to do without my own car—but in any case, what would I do with a car at Imihlaba?"

"I could take something for you—in my car," suggested Michael. "It would be no trouble."

"That's charming of you, Mickey, but I don't know what I want yet—that's the whole trouble. How to plan for this crazy excursion. Anyway, what are we standing here for? Come through to the drawing-room. I'll have to leave you to go and hustle up things in the kitchen. I expected you later."

"Don't worry," Michael started to say, but Mrs. Mulholland cut in, "Do go and sit down and amuse yourselves. I'll go and see what Salvina has done about tea."

Feeling quite helpless, Carol stood looking at Laine's mother—the woman who was to be her future mother-in-law. There was a look on Mrs. Mulholland's face which she could not quite fathom out.

"Well, come along, then," said Michael, after Mrs. Mulholland had left them, and somehow she followed him into the second entrance hall and was amazed a little later to find herself in the drawing-room and sitting on one of the Italian-designed chairs, which went so well with the room —for she had not remembered walking there.

"What the devil are you looking so glum about?" Michael's voice was sneering. "Or isn't it what you expected?"

Tears sparkled in her eyes. "Would you mind—shutting up?" she asked, and her voice broke.

"Frankly, I can't make you out," he went on, "all this *lover-ly* money in the family!"

"How dare you insult me!" she gasped. "You seem to delight in it." She turned away and tried to concentrate on the room to stop herself from breaking into a flood of disappointed tears. "It's strange," she thought, "a girl always expects the mother to fall in love with her—and yet why should it always have to be that way?" Looking

53

back, she could see now that she only had herself to blame for the hurt she felt now because all her dreams had revolved around Mrs. Mulholland liking her. "And so this is Carol? Carol, my dear child, you are *just* as I imagined you to be. I do hope we're going to be great pals, Carol? But of course we will be. You're going to take the place of the daughter I never had."

It hadn't turned out that way, though. She took a shuddering breath. Cecily! *Cecily:* Oh, Laine's mother, how *could* you? She tried to blink back the tears.

It was really a very elegant room, she thought, as she made an effort to get a grip of herself. A beautiful buttoned-back sofa, oyster brocaded and patterned with turquoise, was set against a backdrop of glass where sheer drapes filtered the daylight. The curtain fabric, obviously Italian, had an oyster-shaded background and was smudged with green, plum, and turquoise—all the colours of the occasional chairs. The exciting marble floor was a perfect complement for the sofa and for the fragile delicate lines, set off by the gilded ornamentation, of the chairs. Two more marble statuettes stood in specially designed niches and there was an area for cocktails. This area was carpeted in wine, which in turn gave way to the marble floor, and a white centre-beam at the ceiling accentuated this breakaway from carpet to marble beneath. There were several exciting lamps in the room and a fantastically large arrangement of flowers—obviously the work of some florist.

"Of course," Michael said, "there'll be things you don't like and many things you *will* like, but no girl in her right senses should be looking so dejected."

With a great effort Carol calmed herself. "Leave me alone," she said, "just leave me alone, will you?"

Mrs. Mulholland came into the room at that moment, followed by a plump and elderly African maid in a pink-and-white starched uniform. The maid was pushing a stainless steel trolley which seemed to be laden with gleaming silver and exquisite china.

"Salvina," Laine's mother said in her high harsh voice, "this is the young lady who has come from England—to marry my son."

After she had greeted Carol and Michael Copeland, Salvina studied Carol with complete candour. "Auow! Very nice, madam. Very nice." Then, in her own language, she said something to Mrs. Mulholland, and Michael, who apparently also understood the language, flushed slightly. Laughing heartily, the African woman left the room.

"She says you are too young to marry my son," Mrs. Mulholland said, "and that you should marry Mr. Copeland instead," and Carol felt that her face had turned to stone.

During tea Michael's face was cold and aloof, but Laine's mother kept up a constant stream of chatter— mostly concerning her own affairs and herself. When Salvina returned to clear away the tea-things she said, almost with impatience, "Salvina, for goodness' sake show this child to her room. She looks tired." Her eyes raked Carol's face. "*Are* you tired?" she asked, but there seemed to be no sympathy behind the words.

"A—little." Carol's mouth trembled slightly.

"Well, in any case, you'd better get settled in. Really, this business of Laine landing himself in trouble just when I need him is so trying!"

Feeling very much like a small girl, Carol stood up and, across the room, her eyes met Michael's and he gave her one of his long looks before getting to his own feet. Carol felt the need to breathe suddenly. "Goodbye," she said, "and thank you—for—everything."

"Not at all," his voice was polite. "I was glad to be on hand—it was the one great role of my life."

"Well, Im *so* glad you enjoyed it," she managed to get out, and the words seemed to come on a little gasp. She noticed the expression in his eyes changing and turned away quickly.

Upstairs she looked around the bedroom, which was nothing short of magnificent and which was to be hers until Laine came and took her away.

Practically everything in the room was ivory white, except for the sweeping expanse of royal blue carpeting and the frilled satin bedspread with its ivory background, patterned with blue flowers. There was a large painting on one wall of scarlet poinsettia and the only chair in the room was luxuriously upholstered in scarlet satin—quilted and elaborately buttoned.

A dressing-room led off the bedroom, also carpeted in royal blue, and the bathroom, with its fabulous touches of rose-tinted marble, led off the dressing-room. Everything had a lacquered, luxurious look, but Carol was conscious only of a deep feeling of loneliness. She turned to the African maid and smiled. "Thank you," she said and then, shyly, "Salvina. What a lovely name. I like it."

Salvina laughed and pointed to the dressing-room where the blue cases stood in a forlorn muddle on the fitted carpet. "France put all the cases in there," she said.

"Thank you very much."

"Auow, you are *very young*!" Salvina laughed, just as she laughed at everything, but there was no offence in the way she did it. "You are very pretty. Nice face."

Carol cleared her throat and tried to smile. "It's very kind of you to say that, Salvina."

When Salvina had left she stood in the centre of the room and then, with a small strangled sound, she went out through the glass doors to a long, terrazzo-tiled veranda which was equipped with cane lounging furniture with scarlet-and-blue cushions. In the distance the sea looked very blue and she knew that, at night, the view of the city must be like Fairyland.

While she stood there she discovered that Mrs. Mulholland and Michael were saying goodbye in the garden below, and then she heard his car start and it came into sight as he drove away from the portico. A short way down the drive the car stopped and he opened the door and got out. Carol watched him take off his jacket and toss it into the back seat, then he loosened his tie. Before he got back into the car he turned and looked up at the veranda, but gave no indication that he had seen her.

After the car had disappeared Carol was conscious of a shaft of loneliness and a feeling of such sheer despair that it was almost like a physical pain and she heard her own voice, "Michael! Oh, Michael!"

Somwhere in the house a clock gave eleven leisurely and fragile strokes.

It was during a strained lunch with Mrs. Mulholland that Laine arrived in a taxi, and Carol's heart gave a wild leap and she felt a nervous and excited fear at his unexpected turn of events.

"Dear boy, why didn't you *ring*?" There was impatience in Mrs. Mulholland's voice. "Good gracious, there was no need to come home in a stuffy old taxi. How silly can you get?"

Laine's eyes were resting on Carol, who stood tense and breathless next to the dining-table. "Actually, Mother, I couldn't stand it another day," he said, "I really couldn't. I talked the doctor into discharging me a day early. There seemed to be no earthly reason why I should stay on. He agreed on that point." He could have taken two steps to touch Carol, and she could smell the hospital smell which still clung to his clothes and realised, with horror, that her eyes were wet. Too much was happening to her, she thought wildly. She had no sooner tried to adapt herself to one situation than another had cropped up.

"Carol, *my dear.*" He brushed a hand through his distinguished greying hair, and then she felt his fingers beneath her chin. When his lips touched hers her shocked nerve centres immediately began to clamour for deliverance. "I'm sorry about everything," he whispered. "That it had to be the way it was. We'll make up for lost time, don't worry."

"You must have some lunch, Laine," Mrs. Mulholland's voice was almost shattering in its harshness. "I'l-have a place set for you."

Over Carol's head he said, "No need, Mother. I've had lunch—at the hospital."

"Well, coffee then. You must have coffee."

"Very well, then—if you insist. Coffee." He sounded a little exasperated. "But I'd like to change first. I reek unpleasantly of hospital, I'm afraid."

After he had gone upstairs Carol sat down again and struggled to finish her lunch. She was experiencing a feeling of unreality, as though the girl involved with the Mulhollands was somebody else.

Later, Salvina brought coffee to the long veranda, just off the elegant marble-floored drawing-room. Here colourful tile from Italy, framed in black wrought-iron, hung at intervals on the walls and a pale mauve creeper clung to the stone pillars.

Dallas Mulholland had her coffee at the long white telephone unit in the hall where, for some unknown reason, she was putting through one telephone call after another. When she had finished she came through to the veranda.

"I've just been speaking to Maxine," she said, looking at Laine. "Poor girl!"

Carol, who had dreamed incoherently and romantically all through the past year of her arrival in South Africa and her meeting with Laine Mulholland, felt her mind staggering beneath a weight of unaccountable emotions.

"Your description of her has absolutely nothing to do with me!" He seemed to be waiting for the moment when his mother would say something else, but she turned as the telephone shrilled inside.

Laine adjusted his cravat with a quick, nervous movement. "I've decided that we must celebrate tonight, Carol. You'd like that, wouldn't you? Just the two of us?"

She looked earnestly into his dark eyes. "Oh, I hadn't thought about that. You've only just been discharged from the hospital—and a day early at that! I don't expect to be taken out, Laine."

"It's what I want us to do," he said, smiling. "In fact, I got busy organising things at the hospital. I made telephone reservations for dinner and a play. Tomorrow, of course, whether Mother likes it or not, we'll leave for—home."

She dropped her eyes to his tanned hands which were long, sensitive and expressive in movement. Several scars still loooked red and a little raw in patches—the skin cracked and peeling a little—as though both hands had been very inflamed at some time.

"*Don't:* Please don't." He spoke on a sharp breath and, startled, her wide eyes flew up to meet his. "Don't stare like that," his voice was gentle now. "I'm so *tussy* about my hands."

"Of course. I'm so sorry. I didn't mean to stare—only they still look sore and I was wondering about the dinner and the play."

As she spoke she was wondering whether Laine would tell her now about the accident to his hands—but he didn't. Instead he said, "Mike very kindly arranged to have my car brought here because, of course, after this lot," he raised his hands, "I was brought to Durban in my doctor's car."

"Talking about—Michael," said Carol, "he—er—introduced me to—Maxine."

58

Laine's eyes were curious. "He did? This would be in Durban, of course?"

"Yes. I—it—I think that she was—upset, at meeting me."

"I see. It's like that, is it?"

"But surely she understands, Laine, *why* Michael had to meet me?"

He gave her a long look. "I'm not certain that we're talking about the same thing," he said quietly, "but suppose we drop the subject? After all, we are the people who count right now."

Later, as she prepared for their date and lay in the rose-pink marble bath which was filled with expensive bath cubes and bath champagne, set out by Salvina, Carol kept telling herself that it would take time to recapture some of the magic she had felt for Laine during their courtship by pen. If only things had not gone wrong for them. If only Michael Copeland had not been sent to meet her, everything would have been very different. The uncertainty and unrest, which she now felt, would never have sprung to life in the first place—would never have been allowed to flourish like a rank growth. She was suddenly determined not to show her disappointment in anything, so eager was she to get settled.

Laine took her to dinner at a place where the décor was subdued and highly expensive. A wall bracket, in the form of Bacchus, indicated the direction of the cocktail bar and they had a drink there first before going in to dinner. Carol was not unaware of the amount of bowing and scraping which Laine seemed to attract. It seemed as though those in authority would go out of their way to attend to his dinstinctive good looks.

The *maître d'hotel* found his name and table on the floor plan, and Carol thought that Laine was the type that *maître d'hotels* would always escort to his table and head waiters hover around suggesting special dishes and wines.

During dinner, while waiters moved about quietly, she found herself concentrating more and more on Laine while she struggled to put Michael Copeland right out of her mind.

They saw *I Shouldn't Care to Fall* at the Lexington Theatre, and when it was over they went to an adjoining

59

hotel for something to drink before going back to Laines' mother's house.

"Well," Laine swirled the last amber drops around in his glass, "have you enjoyed yourself?"

"Oh, immensely!" She gave him a quick look of gratitude. "This is how it was supposed to have been, isn't it? Right from the—beginning."

"Do you know, when you look at me with those wide eyes of yours," he told her, smiling faintly, "I'm really very much aware that you exist for me, Carol." She turned her face slightly, uneasy because of his remark.

Mrs. Mulholland had left several gorgeous lamps burning in the drawing-room. "For once," said Laine, turning off the chandelier in the hall, "Mother has had an early night."

Carol followed him into the drawing-room, then her eyes widened in dismay when she saw him beginning to turn the lamps off, one by one, until the room was suddenly in darkness, except for the light which filtered in from outside. Her nerves tensed when she saw him coming towards her. "Oh God," she whispered, and it was a prayer.

"Well, I suppose we'd better say good night." Laine's voice was soft and she was aware of the hair oil he used and of the expensive after-shaving lotion. He placed his arms lightly about her and as he drew her towards him she quickly stepped out of his embrace.

"Good night, Laine," she stammered, "and—and thank you so much for a lovely evening. I loved it." Then, without waiting on an answer, she found herself running up the marble staircase and knew that she was crying.

In the morning they left for the Valley, and Mrs. Mulholland fussed so much before the journey that Carol felt sure she would be on the point of a nervous collapse by the time they reached Laine's home. This arrangement seemed to be uprooting her in no uncertain manner and it appeared doubtful if the plan was going to be a success. As the cases were being stacked in the car, in front of the entrance hall, her voice could be heard, high and petulant, as she spoke on the telephone.

"What a woman! What a woman!" Laine made no attempt to conceal his irritation, and he spoke as though he and his mother were strangers.

When Dallas Mulholland eventually emerged from the house, holding a nerve-racked Marcus by his leash, she was followed by France, the African manservant, and Salvina, their faces impassive, as though they were quite used to the way in which she went on.

"And don't forget," she was saying, "to let the sun awnings down, first thing in the morning. It has got to be the *first thing*—just the way it has to be when I'm here. I don't want to arrive back here and find everything bleached white. You must tell France, every morning, to let them down for you." She wagged her finger at the maid. "Now don't forget, Salvina. I'll be very cross with you if I come back and find that you haven't listened to me. And don't keep using the telephone. I don't mind a call now and again, but I remember once before when I was away the account for *that* month was sky-high, and I know *I* wasn't the culprit."

At this particular moment a light delivery van, with the name of a florist printed in purple across its back, came up the drive. An African got out and went round to the back of the van where he unloaded a large white vase which was already filled with a fan-shaped arrangement of flowers.

Mrs. Mulholland stopped talking, her mouth slightly open, then she gasped, "Oh *no*! This is the last straw!" She crossed over to the van with short quick steps. "I *thought* I told you people not to deliver anything until further notice? Really, this is *too* bad. Why won't these firms listen? I particularly phoned through myself and the stupid girl took the message. 'Yes, Mrs. Mulholland, no, Mrs. Mulholland, that will be quite in order, Mrs. Mulholland.' Really, it's enough to drive you round the bend! They just don't listen. No, no—don't unload any more. Just you take them right back! Wait a moment, on second thoughts, you'd better bring them all inside. They're my blessed vases! Now, listen to me. Don't come back here until I phone the shop. Salvina, just you put all the arrangements where they usually go, and if these florist people come back send them packing. The cheek of it! The nerve! What's the use of phoning them if they're not even going to listen?"

Carol and Laine stood looking on helplessly, then finally they were in the car, but not before Carol had received another exhibition of Dallas Mulholland's deficiency in consideration for others. Certainly she had not known what to expect, but she was nevertheless unprepared for the ungracious way in which the older woman had brushed her to one side so that she and Marcus could sit in the front seat next to Laine. Carol had, in fact, made up her mind to stand back and suggest that Laine's mother sit in front, but she had not even had the chance to do this. She looked ruefully down at her ankle where the leash had coiled around it as Marcus danced around in a frenzy, worked up by Mrs. Mulholland, until he did not know whether he was coming or going.

At last, however, they were on their way, and once the hurt had spent itself Carol was able to smile as she watched the back of Marcus' woolly head. "Here comes the bride," she thought, her sense of humour coming to her rescue, then she bit her lips as she wondered what Michael would have to say if he could see them.

"Marcus senses it," Laine's mother was saying—for the umpteenth time. "He knows where we're going. I'll have to watch him like a hawk. You realise that, of course? There'll be no peace for me. It's all very trying, and if you only knew how I suffer with these heads—the least little exertion sends it thumping and throbbing."

The drive was beautiful and despite everything Carol relaxed and began to enjoy it. At least, she thought, she was on her way now. On either side of the National Highway stately homes were set back in exotic gardens and the higher they climbed, winding round the hills, the bigger were the gardens and the more impressive the country mansions. Eventually they were in more rugged-looking country and the mansions made way for small farm holdings. Several times Mrs. Mulholland got Laine to stop at one of the fresh produce stalls just outside the gates of these farms because she said she wanted to buy something to take to the Valley. Each time Laine parked the car beneath one of the colourful awnings he would sit drumming his fingers on the steering wheel while his mother fussed about outside the car, with Marcus tripping in and out between her ankles.

After numerous such stops she said, "Here is another of those farm stalls. Stop and see if they have any young lettuce, Laine."

For the first time he began to protest. "Really, Mother, this is quite ridiculous, you know." She cut him short.

"It is nothing of the sort! I don't suppose you have any decent lettuce growing. I'll buy enough for Ramesh to stack the deep-freeze, and while we're about it we might as well buy a couple of chickens. They look fat and firm."

Exasperated, he said, "But confound it, Mother, we have poultry at my place. All I have to do is have one of the boys kill a bird when we need it."

However, Mrs. Mulholland had her own way and bought whatever appealed to her in the line of marmalade, home-made jam, fresh cream. "I believe in a good table," she said, "and that's *that!*"

"Well," he snapped, "at my place you get it. I have an excellent cook. A darned sight better than your own cook. I might go so far as to add."

"I *wonder*." Mrs. Mulholland made sure that she had the last word.

Several times Laine stopped the car to point out the view to Carol and each time they were approached by African women and girls who appeared, like magic, out of the long grass to offer bead necklaces, woven grass mats and primitive black pottery for sale. The girls were strong and well-curved as African girls should be, and looking at them Carol was made to realise that she was in a strange land with incomprehensible tongues. The countryside was green and luscious while colour seemed to run riot as scarlet, pink and yellow ponsettias moved with sinuous sweeping motions in the breeze. A variety of exciting shades of bougainvillea clung to gate-posts and pergolas while mimosa trees spread carpets of yellow upon the ground. Gernaiums grew like weeds on either side of the road next to clusters of wild flowers which looked like huge rust-red tarantulas.

The car appeared to be climbing steadily, and for this reason they were able to look down on smaller hills which looked as if they were in motion. This, explained Laine, was because of the sugar cane moving in the breeze. Sugar cane was a fairly new venture by farmers in these parts. In the distance, cupping it all, were mountains which looked almost purple, and he explained that these mountains were casually referred to as "the berg".

They stopped for tea and scones with strawberries and whipped cream at an hotel which had an incredible view, from its tea garden and windows, of the hills—hazy now and blue-mauve, slashed with dark-shadowed crevices.

Mrs. Mulholland took Marcus to stretch his legs and to sniff around in general, and Laine and Carol were left alone. He looked enquiringly at her. "Well, what do you think of it all?" He turned his head in the direction of the hills. The hotel seemed to be on top of the world, and she said, "It's wonderful!"—and meant it. She was thrilled with the scenery and the wonderful air, but she was beginning to wonder where they were going—and when they would reach there. "Your—home seems to be a long way from town," she ventured. "We've been travelling flat out for hours." She smiled sweetly. "In between stops, I mean!"

"I told you that I was in the country. I think I made that quite clear."

She tilted her head over the pattern she was tracing on the table-cloth with the tip of one oval-shaped finger-nail, then she looked up, shaking her hair back from her cheeks.

"Yes, I know you did, but I—well I just didn't visualise it this way, if you know what I mean."

"I'm afraid I *don't* know what you mean!" he said quietly, looking away.

Finally they were on their way again and soon afterwards left the National Highway to begin a long, twisting descent into the Valley. Everywhere there was a slow-changing pattern of the sun's rays and Marcus' scarlet leather collar, with its semi-precious stones, caught the light and sent out a shower of colour against the upholstery of the car.

Laine seemed wrapped in his own brooding thoughts now, and Carol, sensing that his mood had changed, left him alone but his mother kept up a senseless, never-ending chatter about nothing—and everything—under the sun.

The hills, richly studded with green bush and trees, closed in on the car as the road turned and writhed around them like a smokey blue ribbon. Carol thought it was like a pass and her idea about Laine's home became more and more confused every moment. Nervously she looked towards the side of the road, which fell away in a never-ending drop to the river below. It was much hotter here than it had been in town and she knew that she was having a sample of the heat that was lying in wait for the summer.

Foliage and wild blooms seemed to rise harshly from the hills, far in the distance and from the very floor of the

Valley spreading themselves up and over them, and Laine explained that the orange candelabrum-type flowers were aloes and that they were just coming into flower. "You'll see a lot of them," he said, his voice sounding taut. "They come in a variety of shades, from this orange shade to almost scarlet, I should say. The juice of the aloe is very bitter. Isn't that so, Mother?" As he turned to speak to his mother Carol noticed his sensitive mouth. He looked as though he might be constantly hurt about something, she thought.

"How the dickens should *I* know about the juice of the aloe, for goodness' sake?" Mrs. Mulholland's voice was petulant. "*You* know how I feel about this place. The only time I enjoy it is when I'm rushing through it on the way back home. I wish you would sell out, Laine."

At the roadside African children performed weird, un-inhibited dances for them, and as Carol met their eyes and the expression about their mouths, she felt that she was only just beginning to find out what these children already knew about life and expected from it. There was about them an eternity of living, although they were barely out of the blankets which had strapped them to the swaying backs of their mothers.

She found herself shuddering a little while an immense dread of the hills, boulders, bush and even of the river, glittering below with its silver cascades of water pouring over rocks, took hold of her.

"We're nearly there." Laine destroyed the painful silence in the car. "You'll get used to these little blighters, by the way."

Carol had turned her head to look out of the rear window at a group of children who were shouting abuse and sticking out their tongues because Laine had not stopped to give them anything.

"You'll have to get used to the bare-breasted girls too," chipped in Dallas Mulholland, and Carol laughed a little, feeling strangely embarrassed. "I've—I've seen pictures, of course," she said, but quite suddenly her teeth came down on her lip and she found herself wondering whether the outcome of her pen-friendship with Laine Mulholland had advanced beyond the limit of all reasoning.

CHAPTER FOUR

THE place which was to be Carol's home, when she married Laine, was all scents and dust and set back a little from the river bank. To get to it the car crossed a bridge, the metal of which wavered and danced in the sun. The main building overlooked a point where the water could be seen cascading over some slippery black-ribboned rocks and, in the distance, there was a glimpse of the huge dam—a blinding dash of water now as the sun beat upon it. Laine's home was a sprawling affair of thatch, stone and black scroll-work wrought-iron.

Carol's heart was thumping slowly beneath the vivid pecan-pink shirt she was wearing with tan linen slacks and her neck felt tight, as though the most important arteries supplying her heart were ready to burst.

"Well?" Laine's mouth twisted slightly, almost as though something was hurting him. "This is it, Carol."

She did not know what to say, so she said, in a whisper, her eyes hidden behind dark sunglasses, "Yes."

Perhaps it was fortunate that Mrs. Mulholland took over at this stage, fussing and becoming agitated about Marcus. "Do hurry up and open the door for me," she snapped. "I must get Marcus inside as quickly as possible. Down, Marcus. Down, I say! Really, this is too much. Too much!"

Carol remained in the car, watching with a numb kind of apathy, while Laine got out and opened the door for his mother. "Look at him sniffing," Mrs. Mulholland said. "He knows. He knows!"

A handsome Indian came to Mrs. Mulholland's assistance and Carol followed them with her eyes as they made their way towards the house. "Mother *fusses* so," Laine remarked, in the tight voice she was beginning to know by now. "Fuss, fuss—and all over that dog, too!"

They were standing in the drive and he took her arm. "Come, Ramesh will see to everything when he comes back."

Ramesh was, in fact, already back on his way down several shallow steps. "I have attended to Mrs. Mulholland, sir," he said to Laine. "She has gone to her room. Everything is ready. I hope you are better, sir?"

"Quite better, thank you. This is Miss Tracey, Ramesh, from England." Ramesh inclined his turbaned head very slightly. "Good afternoon, miss."

"Good afternoon." Carol removed her dark glasses, frowning a little against the glare. She was trying not to meet Laine's eyes. Instead, she shot a quick trapped glance round, taking in the rough untamed beauty of everything. For it was indeed a place of beauty, but in a remote and rugged kind of way.

When the Indian had gone back to the house she turned to Laine, "What do *I* call him?" she said.

"You will call him Ramesh."

She was noticing the footpaths, as they wriggled down the succession of hills which, to her, were so awesome because of their size and because they seemed to close right in on Laine's home, concealing it from civilisation. They looked hostile, somehow, in their tendency to dwarf the buildings which were cupped in their unsoftened and irregular outlines.

The main building, with its tropical jalousies and overhanging eaves, appeared to be in two parts—the tea room and the curio shop next to it, on the one side, and the house on the other. A long veranda, pillared in rough stone and railed off by means of black wrought-iron, stretched from one end of the building to the other but, in the centre, a pair of magnificent black wrought-iron gates separated the tourist section of the building from the actual dwelling place. A few mid-week tourists were having refreshments, and although several cars were parked in the grounds they did nothing to dispel the fear of loneliness which had gripped Carol's heart.

The blue-watered swimming-pool lay immediately in front of Laine's private section of the building, and she knew that she would have to turn to it to enable her to bear the intolerable weight of the hills pressing down upon her—making her a prisoner.

It was all just exactly as Laine had described it to her in his letters. Everything was there—the sun, the blue skies, the hills, the dam, the pool and the curio shop with its peculiar smell of woods, hides and straw—just as he had described it—all except for all the loneliness. *Laine had not mentioned the vast loneliness.*

He led the way, through the wide glass doors which were open to reveal the living-room and Carol stood, like the stranger she was, waiting on him to make the first move.

"In a moment, I'll show you to your room," he said. "I've had everything changed, as a matter of fact, and I hope you'll like it. After lunch, I'll show you all there is to be seen—when it cools off." He lifted a cuff to glance at his watch. "It's going to be a very late lunch, I'm afraid—however . . ."

She tried to smile at him. "It *is* hot," she agreed. "I can hardly believe that your winter has started. It seems to be hotter here than it was in town, don't you think? It must be terribly hot in the summer, Laine."

He looked at her narrowly. "Not really," he said and his voice was cool. "Not really."

All the time she was thinking of the vastness outside, the loneliness waiting to engulf her when those sleek cars and station wagons took the tourists away. And later, after she and Laine were married, even Mrs. Mulholland and the poodle Marcus would be gone. She could see now what Michael had been trying to tell her.

"What the devil is Ramesh doing?" With an impatient movement Laine left her and she could hear him shouting to the Indian to "step on it".

Carol took this opportunity to look around. The personality of the room, to a great extent, reflected the personality of the owner and one was, somehow, immediately aware of Laine. She stood, shock still, listening to Laine and the Indian Ramesh, but all the time her eyes were taking in the strong colours of the Persian rugs, the simple form and scale of various pieces of furniture and the fine oil paintings.

For the rest, her bewildered inspection took in the crossed sabres on the wall, the pieces of pewter, copper and brass and the huge African drum which obviously acted as a bar and was, at this moment, topped by an array of bottles and a collection of red glass.

A massive stone fireplace extended across the whole of one wall and in front of it there was a lion's pelt, its yellow-green eyes glaring back at her from the floor. Over all was the pungent fragrance of wood which was, in some peculiar way, mentally stimulating.

She swung round at the sound of Laine's voice, half expecting to find him changed, but he was just the same, with that peculiar and deceiving look of youth which she had noticed about him from a distance and in certain lights.

It was strange, she thought swiftly and with some bitterness, but she had never imagined Laine to be the type to live in a self-imposed prison—away from people. Away from neighbours. Somehow, through his letters, she had been given the impression that he would attend art exhibitions, symphony concerts and premieres.

"Well?" He was beside her, his voice cool, abrupt.

"Well?" she replied, in a small contained voice she did not know. Then she smiled. "I'm waiting. You said you would show me to—my room."

"Oh yes, I'd quite forgotten. By the way, Carol, you'll find that I keep fantastic hours here. So, even after we're married, it will always be *your* room."

"Fantastic hours? Here? She tried to make her voice light, but her eyes were suddenly afraid.

"Yes, *here*. And why not? In my own way, I lead a very full life."

"Oh, I see."

"I—wonder if you do?" His voice was quiet, but before she could answer there was a shrill, almost maniacal screaming and then, from somewhere in the house, came the whining of a dog followed by the voice of Dallas Mulholland, wheedling and pleading.

Carol caught her breath, all her muscles clamped together. "What was that?"

"Oh?" He gave a small embarrassed laugh. "Actually, I—don't think I mentioned it, Carol, but I have quite a zoo here."

"A zoo?" Her voice was incredulous. "But I didn't see a zoo when we arrived. Did I?"

"Quite possibly you missed it, because, you see, it's at the back, or rather, slightly to one side of the curio shop. But you must have noticed the bird-cages as we came up the steps, surely?"

"Oh—yes, I recollect now, but it didn't register." Suddenly she remembered having seen one or two aviaries.

"That was a baboon you heard just now, by the way."

"A baboon?"

"Don't, for pity sake, keep repeating everything after me. I find it a most exasperating habit. Yes, Carol, a baboon."

"Oh no!" She raised her head in quick dismayed fear and then ran the tip of her tongue over her lips. "You didn't mention the zoo, Laine."

He turned away from her and went towards the sliding glass doors, where he stood looking out.

"Perhaps not, but now that you see it all for yourself, it falls into pattern, doesn't it? About the zoo, I mean! It would have been difficult to explain in a letter." He swung round. "You must see that, surely?"

"I—I suppose so," she said miserably. "I can see *now* why your mother was so fearful about Marcus."

"So she didn't tell you about the zoo? Not even casually?"

"No, she didn't—not even casually."

"I take it, then, that Mike didn't mention it, either?"

She remembered, then, a certain remark passed by Michael Copeland just before they had gone in to have dinner at her hotel. "Talking about a zoo . . ." he had said.

Laine came towards her. "You've got nothing against it, surely?"

"Of course not." Her reply came quickly and she forced herself to smile. "I—Laine, it's all right. I'll get used to it. We seem to be so *tense* over this."

"You are the only one who is tense," he said curtly.

"Well, forgive me. It's just that I—well I'm a little strange, that's all. I've—I've never lived this close to a— lot of wild animals before."

However, tension was still hanging in the humid air, as he made to show her to her room and she knew at once that he had become touchy and withdrawn.

"As I mentioned," he said, "I've had to make one or two changes, moving rooms around, and so on. There was Mother to accommodate, in the meantime, and then there was—us. You are to have the big room, which used to be mine. I've moved into my den. Mother will have the guest-room, and when she goes I'll move into it."

"Oh." She was caught by a paralysing embarrassment. "You shouldn't have, Laine. I mean—you shouldn't have given me the big room. I could quite easily . . ."

He cut her short. "These arrangements were all part of a plan. You must see that. It was something which had to follow the turn of events brought about by your accepting my proposal."

"Yes." Her eyes contained sheer misery. "Of course, I'm sorry, Laine. Please be patient with me. I feel so nervous, now that I'm actually here. I seem to be saying the wrong thing all the time."

"I quite understand," he answered, but she had the uncomfortable and unhappy feeling that he did not understand at all.

The big room had quite obviously been changed around to suit a new and feminine taste and it was quite beautiful. Avocado-green slipper satin was used for the bedcover and the curtains, which had apparently been made to order. Walls, paintwork and the Mirzapore Indian carpet on the black slate floor of the room, were all white, while twin lamps on the long dressing-table had pale geranium-pink satin shades.

The windows were open, but the pale pink venetian blinds had been only slightly drawn against the glate which, nevertheless, struggled easily through the long narrow openings. The slats rattle dryly in a tiny movement of air.

She allowed her beautiful bone-coloured leather handbag to slip from her fingers to the satin bedcover, trailing her rose-tinted nails over its quilted surface. "It's a beautiful room, Laine. Thank you so much. You've gone to such trouble. You must have had expert advice."

He turned to face her, leaning against the wall, with his arms folded in front of him, and she was amazed that he should be so full of grace, so lean—at *his* age. Then she pulled herself up sharply. All during the time of their pen-friendship she had never once thought about Laine's age. So why start now? Was it because of Michael Copeland? She felt unsettled and nervous.

"Well, of course I had expert advice," Laine was saying, and she could detect the irritation in his voice, "is there any earthly reason why I shouldn't have? We're not that cut off from civilisation, you know."

"Oh no," she thought with some bitterness. "Perhaps it's just an optical illusion—on my part." However, she did not say these things—she merely smiled carefully and listened to him.

"You'll see delivery vans here every day. They have to supply my requirements here, and not only the requirements of this place but of the village and the people at the dam. There is also an adjoining nature reserve and the Ranger has to have things. We're between two big towns, but in between there is a small dorp. To get to this dorp one continues straight on instead of taking the turning to the Valley. And now you know," he said.

"Oh. Then we're quite in the swing of things, aren't we?" She was amazed at this new hardness in her voice. Laine had deceived her. Certainly she had not come out to South Africa as a gold-digger hoping for bright lights and all that money could buy, but, on the other hand, neither had she come out to lead the life of a recluse.

"Oh," she thought, in despair, "I could bear all this if I loved Laine, but I don't. I *don't!*" She fought for better thoughts. "You—mention a village?" Her voice was more hopeful.

"Well, by a village I mean the four houses, occupied by the water scheme people, a trading store and, of course, the hills are just teeming with African people. Your idea of a village, no doubt, revolves around country lanes, a local post office complete with post-mistress, the local pub and tree-lined cobbled streets flanked by the baker, the grocer and so on. I'm sorry if you're disappointed."

He crossed to the dressing-table and turned on the lamps, and she stood uselessly by, not knowing what to say. "We have electric light. You'll be pleased to hear that, no doubt. However, to be quite honest, when I'm here alone I hardly ever use it. I prefer ordinary tall tallow candles, massed about the place. The electricity only goes as far as Imihlaba, the village. The nature reserve people rely on their own generator system. Look, Carol, settle in, will you, and then join me in a drink on the veranda before lunch."

Later, she joined him on the veranda and, from the expression on his face, it looked as though he was enjoying an exaggerated sense of reprieve from the two women who were complicating his way of life here in the Valley. For a moment Carol watched him rattling the ice-cubes in his glass and in the background she could hear Mrs. Mulholland moaning and complaining about something to the patient Ramesh.

Lunch, also taken on the veranda, was a colourful affair with bottle-green linen place-mats on the yellow-wood table and a pile of exotic-looking fruit spilling out from a wicker basket in the centre. The cutlery had bamboo handles and as Carol looked at everything she was amazed that she would be mistress here soon—for whatever way she looked at it, she had to go on with this thing she had started so carelessly with the scrape of a pen.

Beyond the veranda there was a monotonous drumming of insects in the lazy heat and the hills, with their prickly covering of bush clinging to them, arched their rounded breasts against the sky.

"What about your mother?" Carol raised perplexed eyes. "Ramesh doesn't appear to have set a place for her."

"Mother wishes to eat with Marcus in her room," Laine replied, and she was aware of the sarcasm in his voice.

She bowed her head as Ramesh set soup before her. "I see. It's not going to be very pleasant for her here, is it? She'll be living under constant tension."

"Well, it won't be for long," he said, "will it?"

She kept her eyes down. "No, of course not."

After lunch Laine took her to see the animals and the intensely delightful and colourful birds. The cages were all large and well equipped, and Carol found, in spite of herself, that she was becoming interested in Laine's private zoo.

In the moments of pleasure the depression she had felt earlier lifted a little and she was amused to see several girls scrutinising Laine with frank appraisal. He had placed an arm lightly around her waist and was leading her past the aviaries to some cages where a number of small monkeys sat staring at them with impertinent curiosity. However, it was when he guided her to one large cage, which accommodated two very thick-set baboons, that Carol's expression changed. These animals were by no means attractive and looked back at them with curiously human eyes, tinged with a terrible kind of hidden madness—or so it seemed to her.

"Well?" Laine was smiling faintly. He looked down. "You don't like them, do you?"

She shook her head. "No. I must be honest and confess that I don't. In a way—a terrible way—they're almost human." When he threw back his head and laughed lightly she looked up at him, perplexed.

"It's nothing really," he said. "Your remark just brought to mind a joke I heard recently concerning two Irishmen who were doing very much the same as we are right now. They were looking at some baboons. 'They're almost human,' said the one fellow. 'Wouldn't you say so, Pat?' However, Pat replied, 'Nonsense. They're no more human than what you or I are.' "

Carol laughed politely and then Laine gesticulated in the direction of the larger of the two animals. "Actually, this fellow here was responsible for the din you heard earlier on. His tantrums are a byword through the whole Valley."

"No wonder your mother fears for Marcus. If he *did* get hauled into this cage . . ." Her voice trailed away.

"Oh, what utter rubbish you talk!" Laine's voice was suddenly caustic. "*It he did get hauled into the cage:* Frankly, Carol, I've spent a fortune housing these animals."

She lifted her shoulders and shuddered. The idea of being in this Valley with all these creatures frightened her. Then she swallowed, pointing to the next cage. "What are those? Would they be—leopards?"

Laine laughed. "Not leopards—cheetahs! Magnificent beasts, aren't they? The male, Dorcas, is an unfriendly young devil. I hope to break his pride in the not-too-distant future." As he spoke Carol was aware of a sudden uneasiness, like a shiver, filling the cheetahs, then the animal concerned got up in one smooth cat motion, its superb muscles rippling beneath its skin. He seemed to look right past Laine and Carol, through them almost, as though he enjoyed doing this on purpose. Then his expression changed, but it was so slight that Carol wondered afterwards whether she had imagined it. The animal had seemed to look at Laine with a tense immobility which was almost like the prelude to a planned attack.

"Yes, you young devil." Laine looked down at his scarred hands. "You might as well admire your handiwork."

Carol felt her eyes widen and heard the catch of her own breath before her eyes flew to Laine's hands and then upwards to meet his dark eyes which were slightly mocking.

"Don't tell me you *really* didn't know," he said, very quietly.

"I didn't know." Her voice was tight, disbelieving.

"Mike—Mother? They said nothing? I can hardly credit this."

"They said nothing—nothing at all." Suddenly she felt her depression coming back. "I've been wondering about your accident, but nobody said a word about it. Michael said *you'd* tell me. Your mother—hasn't said anything much to me at all." Her voice dragged and she looked back at the cage. "I thought you said they couldn't get out?"

"Well, they can't. But that doesn't stop *me* from going in, does it? The female, by the way, is called Selika."

"You went in? Oh, Laine! Whatever for? What were you doing in there?"

His laugh was soft. "I was being careless mostly!" he said, and because he seemed set on keeping her from knowing just how he was bitten she turned away, feeling childish and offended.

"I don't think I'll sleep tonight," she whispered finally.

"Oh, rubbish. You'll sleep like a log—and you know it." He compelled her to look at him and stood gazing down at her with his dark, sardonic eyes, lifting his shoulders in the slightest of contemptuous shrugs.

"It's all perfectly safe and a great attraction to tourists. You've got to know what makes the tourist tick, Carol, and this is one of the little tricks." His smile had such an avuncular quality that she could see he was sick and tired of the conversation. "Another trick is the dancing," he added.

"I know I sound terribly childish and stupid, even," she made a confused gesture with her hands, "but you didn't mention any of this in your letters. The zoo—the dancing. *What* dancing? I'm completely at sea." While she was speaking she noticed that he flushed very slightly and she saw also that his mouth had become a little ugly.

"I think I told you *why* I didn't mention it. It would have sounded a complicated business all round. A little ridiculous, maybe. To you, that is."

"Well," her voice was barely audible, "it *is* complicated, isn't it?"

"Only because you seem set on making it so. When I referred to the dancing I was referring to a form of tribal dancing which I arrange for tourists. It's colourful and exciting, certainly to people from overseas—perfect foil, in fact, for colour-slides. Over there you will see the path leading to the huts where this dancing takes place, but the huts are out of sight from here. We'll go up another time."

She turned her head and could see the wide path which was flanked by mimosa trees, vivid now with yellow puffs. This would, she could see, create an element of excitement —the walk up the slope, between the trees and bush towards the sound of beating drums and urgent tom-toms.

With a terrible kind of despair she knew that she could begin to understand all this with a man she loved, but she did not love Laine Mulholland. She had known it at the hospital, at his bedside. She could be happy *anywhere* with the man she loved, sharing his way of life, but to be trapped here by these hills in the Valley of the bitter aloes with Laine Mulholland was going to be more than she could bear.

"Come." He began to lead the way across a strip of hard-baked ground, and it was almost as if a magnet was pulling him. "I want you to meet Leo and Lisa." The tension which was having its way with him communicated itself to her.

A separate cage held another shock. At the sound of Laine's voice a lioness got to her feet and padded towards the thick-meshed wire. In the corner her mate slept on, his nostrils twitching as the flies worried him.

"Hello, Lisa, old girl. I'd go in," said Laine, "if there weren't so many confounded people about."

"Go in?" Carol's eyes flew open in shocked surprise. "Oh *no*, Laine! Do you mean—to feed them?" Of course, she thought. How stupid of her—the animals had to be fed; but Laine replied, "Don't look so alarmed. It isn't to feed them, actually. Lisa knows me. Don't you, girl? She expects me to go in."

The lioness stood gazing at them with her grape-green eyes and the only indication she gave at recognising Laine was an intense stare—a kind of widening of the eyes. That was all. It was a green, penetrating look and yet, even in

76

its intensity, a strangely indifferent look. Then she began to pace the length of the cage on her tremendous silent pads, crossing her husband in the middle as he got up and immediately took up pacing with her, in the opposite direction.

"I didn't expect to become—part keeper of a private zoo." Carol tried to force some lightness into the tone of her voice, but knew that she was failing miserably.

"I get tremendous satisfaction from these two beasts," Laine told her. "I tease the old girl, but it's all in good part, of course, and she knows it. Don't you, Lisa?" He raised his voice and it had the sound of the quick lash of a whip.

"You must be joking! You wouldn't tease them, Laine? I can't believe this."

"These animals—all animals, for that matter—will attack merely as self-protection."

"But you said you *tease* her! How do you make that one out? Were you teasing—Dorcas—when he attacked you, then?" Carol felt quite sickened suddenly.

"Actually, for your information, Carol, Dorcas and Selika are as well-behaved as a couple of trained dogs. This was just unfortunate." He lit a cigarette and his hands were not quite steady and Carol watched him—marvelling at him.

"I can't—understand all this." The words were dragged from her.

"It's all perfectly simple really. My skill against theirs."

"Perfectly simple to you, maybe, but to me it's frightening. You honestly frighten me. I don't quite know how I'm going to stand all this."

Suddenly the pent-up emotion had its way with her and the tears came and she turned away from him. "Poor animals! Poor, sad, captive animals."

That seemed to anger him. "Poor animals? Poor animals, you say? They're perfectly content, I can assure you."

"They're only content because there's nothing else for them, can't you see that?" she stormed at him.

"You must try to understand about the zoo, Carol, if you are to understand *me*, because you see it's just one of the things I'm silly about."

"I'm sorry," her voice was muffled. "But I feel all strung up."

The late sun gilded her beautiful face. Laine was a stranger to her. His letters had conveyed nothing after all. They had been suggestive of people—sophisticated, wealthy people, but this was only because of the tourists who visited the Valley and left again within a few hours. His letters had not given much indication to his elected solitude.

All sorts of emotions were tearing at her now. She reproached herself. Had Michael been right, then? Was she nothing but a little gold-digger?

The house seemed cool after the yellowness outside as Laine walked with her to her room, and she felt touched when he removed the satin bedcover, folding it fastidiously and neatly and then placing it upon the long stool in front of the dressing-table. When he had done that he turned back the blankets to reveal apricot-pink sheets. "Have a rest. I'm a fool," he was saying. "I should have realised that the heat and the strangeness were all playing their part with you."

She tried to smile. "Thank you, Laine. I'm terribly sorry. I've made such an idiot of myself. As you say, I must be tired."

When he was gone, there was nothing for her to do but to set about thinking about the passing of time which would help her to clear her mind of all this utter confusion and bewilderment, because of course she couldn't go back on her word.

It was too late for that. She felt unutterably lonely and her slim, almost childish body felt lost between the apricot sheets.

Outside, the animals, made irritable by the heat and the flies, snarled between naps.

CHAPTER FIVE

THEY had dinner, by candlelight, in the dining alcove which led immediately off the living-room, and Ramesh, silent in his faultless white uniform, served them.

The setting was romantic, right from the thatched roof to the spangled white flowers set upon gleaming wood and the light of the candles which flickered with every breath. The windows were open to the night which was smelling of cooling earth, animals and wood smoke from the cooking-fires in the compound.

Carol ate in silence and listened to Laine's repetitious small talk and to the endless chatter of Mrs. Mulholland, who had decided to dine with them, the poodle Marcus safely secured beside her.

Before dinner Carol had gone to stand on the veranda by herself, and was instantly aware of the drums in the hills as they pounded in rhythmic cadence. In the distance, the dam looked silent and forbidding and, surrounding it, the hills were moon-shadowed and mysterious. The hopelessness of her position here at the Valley stunned her, and she had felt that she just wanted to stand there quietly, not even thinking, just standing and waiting for enough time to pass—so that she could begin to get over feeling tired, hopeless and depressed.

After dinner Dallas Mulholland complained of a headache and retired to her room, so Laine suggested that they go out to the veranda again, and Carol followed him aimlessly, weary and appalled at what she had done.

Bats veered against the black, star-studded sky and she cringed back. "Oh, come on, you silly little thing," he said with amusement. "Come and sit down."

"It's all right," she replied shakily. "I'll get used to them."

"Yes, I suppose so. Anyway, come and sit down." His voice now was poised somewhere between tenderness and irritation.

Ramesh had brought drinks and left them set out on one of the tables, and she watched Laine pour himself something after having refused a drink for herself. Conversation was strained and slow, so she asked him to tell her something about the shouting which she had heard in the hills, from time to time, and patiently he explained that this was the African way of exchanging news.

She laughed a little at this and he watched her, swirling the liquid round in his glass, before tipping back his head and swallowing the contents. She had a feeling that his moodiness seemed to have increased. She studied him as he put his glass down and began to look at his hands, flexing his fingers, and she could feel his nervous fear about them.

"I'm going inside to play the piano," he said eventually. "What will you do? Stay here? Come in—and listen?"

Because she felt that perhaps he wished this she said, "I'm longing to hear you play—so I'll come in, I think. That is if you don't *mind*?" Her voice was light and girlish and she stood up, looking at him anxiously.

"Not at all," he replied, but his voice seemed cool.

As she listened to him play she could feel every nerve trembling beneath her skin as though reacting to the haunting music. He played spasmodically and uncertainly at first, as though testing the endurance of his fingers, and she closed her eyes and listened to the running of sombre chords, which seemed to travel from one end of the piano to the other.

Listening to his kind of music she was aware that Laine was an over-sensitive, withdrawn person; she was going to be alone with him here in the Valley and there was nothing she could do about it. It was too late, she kept telling herself, over and over again. Her grandmother was now happily placed and her father was praying that this was not just a venture on her part, fated to end in disaster, causing him to feel that he had failed her. He had suffered too much for that. Then there was Laine's mother who had been uprooted from her own home and her way of life, and finally, of course, there was Laine who had changed his whole home about for her sake.

Oblivious to everything but his music, Carol became immaterial and soon ceased to exist, so when she left the room Laine did not notice and continued playing.

There seemed to be nothing for her to do but to stand, or sit, on the veranda, and her tense expression stretched across her cheekbones as she stood now at the railing just looking out at the shadows and the tiny pinpointed and controlled fires on the night-blackened hills. The thought struck her that these tiny points of flame could almost be likened to roses on the robes of a nun.

She turned so that she might see into the living-room. Behind his grand piano Laine's face looked haunted by some wild melancholy and she had a sudden feeling of intense self-pity. He appeared to have completely forgotten her presence in his home.

Ramesh had placed an arrangement of azaleas on the piano, and from where she stood she was able to see one of the wilted blooms falling.

Laine stopped right in the middle of a passage and stood up, an irritable expression about his mouth, then he removed the offending bowl of flowers to a small table before picking the faded petals up between his fingers and flinging them into an oriental-style waste-paper basket. Before he sat down to play again he used his handkerchief to wipe clean the surface of the piano.

As the little drama spent itself Carol sighed and turned back to face the hills. In the direction of the dam, to the one side, the lights of some vehicle moved with a kind of calculated slowness, as though this was an indication of a rough or winding road, then the motor seemed to gather speed. When the vehicle drew nearer and crossed the bridge she was able to make out that it was a Land Rover. It turned into Laine's drive, the headlights picking out the flowers of various shrubs before it stopped and they went out.

A man got out, slamming the door behind him, and began to walk past the swimming-pool, which was just a pale glimmer. When he came up the shallow steps leading to the veranda Carol caught her breath when she saw that she was looking at Michael Copeland in khaki gaberdine slacks and an open-necked shirt.

Reacting with shocked amazement, she let her breath, which was a tight spring, escape through her teeth.

Michael stood for a moment before mounting the last shallow step to the veranda and in the illusive light of the moon their eyes, without a will of their own, met and clung together. At last he said, "So? We're settled in, I see?" At the same moment he was beside her.

Unexpectedly, he tilted her chin with the tip of his forefinger. "Well? Have you lost your tongue? Why don't you say something?"

"What on earth are you doing here?" Now that she had found her voice she had difficulty in using it. "I—I thought town was *that* way?" She made a confused gesture. "Over there, somewhere."

"So it is." He was smiling in his usual handsome and sarcastic manner. "However, I come that-a-way. From my bungalow."

Her heart diverged from its regular tempo and came to a complete standstill. When it started beating again she said, "Your—*bungalow*?" Her eyes were wide.

"Well, yes—at least until I'm finished my work here.''

She ransacked the corridors of her memory. "Your work? But I thought you said that you were an engineer or something?"

"So I am. I've come from the dam. Translated, that means the Department of Water Affairs."

A pulse jumped in her throat. "Why didn't you tell me that you'd be here?"

"That's a very good question, as Laine would say," he mocked her. "Why didn't *he* tell you?" He turned suddenly, so that he was facing the living-room. "Back to the old routine, I see." When he looked back at her a tawny blade of moonlight slanted across his cheek. "Tell me, how is the lion-tamer? Because by now, of course, you must have seen the big act? Am I right?"

"Please keep your sarcastic remarks to yourself," she said, on a quick note of temper. "You're speaking about the man I'm going to marry. Call yourself a friend of Laine's?" She looked up at him with, what she hoped was undisguised contempt. "Some friend!"

He lit a cigarette and tossed the burnt match into the darkness. He seemed to be looking at her with mildly amused speculation, she thought with resentment.

"Carol," his voice was soft, "the man you're going to marry happens to know what I think of him, in case you're under a special illusion that he doesn't."

It was then that the piano stopped and there was the sound of the lid being closed. A short while later Laine came out to the veranda.

"Well, Mike? I didn't hear you arrive! How's it? Back on the old job, I see?"

"Back on the old job, as you say. How are the hands?" Michael asked, and Laine's tenseness at this remark communicated itself to them.

"Oh, so-so. Fingers feel a bit stiff, and all that. It will take time, I expect. One has just got to be patient. What can I offer you to drink, Mike? Do sit down, old chap." Laine went towards the table with the bottles and glasses.

When they were seated and sipping at their drinks Carol listened to the two men talking, and from the conversation she gathered that Michael Copeland would be leaving the Valley in about two months' time.

Apparently another dam was being built, in addition to the existing dam which could be seen from Laine's property. Michael spoke about what appeared to be a lengthy series of negotiations, including a submission of a report by him, in his capacity as consultant engineer.

She sat back in her chair listening to them, but taking no part in the conversation. This, she told herself, was man's territory. A discussion was taking place about the siltation problem which had plagued other dams and which had been virtually eliminated by a weir for diverting heavily silted water before it entered the reservoir.

As Michael went into detail about a new aqueduct, with an ultimate capacity of millions of gallons a day, to carry additional water, Carol listened and recognised the signals of fear. She cast her eyes in the direction of the dam and found herself wondering what they would do if those walls ever cracked.

Eventually Michael stood up. "I must be off," he said. "By the way, how is your mother?"

"Oh, so-so. You know Mother, Mike. Anyway, she won't be here for long." He looked at Carol. "Will she?"

"Oh?" Michael's voice sounded curiously taut.

"Well, we'll be getting married quite soon now. I'm only keeping my promise to Carol's father in waiting." Laine smiled down at Carol, who was standing next to him now. He lifted his arm so that he could place his fingers, on her neck, just beneath her hair. "By the way, Mike, what do you think of my new lioness?" Carol felt herself stiffening beneath his fingers.

For a moment Michael made no reply, then he said, "You're doing all rightee, Laine. Quite a menagerie you have here, old boy." He turned to Carol. "What do you think of the big beat, by the way?" He shrugged towards the hills. "Have you told her, Laine, that half the evil spirits and devils of Africa hang about on those hills out there?"

"Mike's only kidding, of course," Laine cut in quickly. "The evil spirits and devils he refers to are completely imaginary, something cooked up by the black man. He'd be lost without them. Just as wild animals would be lost without the smell of the bush. And talking about the big beat, Mike old chap, that same beat you hear out there can be heard in the most exclusive ballrooms and night-clubs around the world. Basically, there's no difference at all."

Michael gave one of his wry grins. "You'll find, Carol," he used her name with ease in front of Laine, "after you've been here a while, that we're all very much at the mercy of one another. You'll notice it after your world has shrunk to the trading store, the pool out there and the beat of the drums and tom-toms." She knew that he was amusing himself at her expense.

"That's piling it on, isn't it?" Laine's voice was stiff. "Let's walk with Mike to the Land-Rover, shall we?" He looked at Carol.

The house threw its lights across the swimming-pool, especially as Laine had switched on the lanterns suspended at each end of the veranda. As they walked towards the vehicle there was a cool silence between them broken only by the minute clinking noises made by Carol's bracelets.

"I'll be seeing you," said Mike, getting into the Land-Rover. To Carol, he said, "You're one up on Tony, aren't you?"

When the tail-lights of the Land-Rover had disappeared from sight Laine said, "Mike might have been more civil. Might I ask what he meant about being one up on Tony? Or is that a secret between the two of you?"

"It's not a secret," she replied. "Michael Copeland is just trying to be funny, at my expense. I happened to tell him that a friend of mine, Tony, came to South Africa from London. His home is in Johannesburg now, right near the zoo, and he kidded his friends back in London that from his bed at night he could hear the lions roaring. He made it sound as though there were wild animals roaming the streets."

"I see." His voice remained cool. "I thought you didn't discuss—animal life—with Michael? By that I mean—the zoo."

"I didn't. We didn't. We merely spoke about the way in which people imagine this country to be."

They were on the veranda now. "Have a nightcap, Carol?"

"No, thank you." Her voice was cold. She was thinking that perhaps Laine drank too much and she had been quick to notice that Michael's drinking was purely social. This could be easily deduced from the way in which he constantly forgot about his glass.

"Would you mind terribly if I went to bed?"

"Must you?" he asked quietly and, unobtrusively, her shoulders moved from his hands.

"Yes, please. If you don't mind." She tilted her head so that she could look up at him, trying to bribe him not to be disappointed in her and hoping that he would turn to her with his oddly sweet smile, but he was frowning a little in his controlled, nervous way.

"Has that young devil Michael upset you?"

"No, it's not that. I'm just tired and I have a headache."

A muscle twitched in his cheek. "I see. Well, in that case you'd better turn in. Good night." Already he had turned from her and was pouring himself a drink.

As she prepared for bed she could feel the night's breath on her body and for a few brief moments she thrilled at being able to stand half-naked, like this, at the beginning of winter, without the cold biting into her bones.

Outside, an animal snarled, then she held her breath as she heard Laine's footsteps approaching her door.

"Carol?" Her mouth went utterly dry.

"Yes?"

"I just wanted you to know that was Lisa. You're not worried, are you? She was probably just warding off the advances of her husband."

"Oh, I see." She knew that his remark was aimed at her.

"Well, thank you for telling me. I'm—I'm not worried really."

"Good," he said, from behind the closed door. "Well, then—good night."

"Good night." There was undisguised relief in her voice.

As she got into bed she heard Laine at the piano again and remembered how he had told her that he kept late nights in his Valley.

She lay for a long time in the darkness—a slim girl with the frightening image of a bride in her mind, searching for the answer, and it seemed that every time she was dropping off to sleep she was aroused by the fierce staccato bark of a dog way back in the hills—the hills which according to Michael Copeland were supposed to be alive with half the devils and evil spirits of Africa.

A tom-tom started to thud near to the house, with that rapid urgency she was beginning to associate with the tom-tom, and she lay frightened and yet, at the same time, slightly elated.

Some time later there was a slight sighing sound as she allowed the pent-up breath to escape from her lungs and her body began to relax, very slowly, dubiously at first before she fell asleep with a complete suddenness—but not before she had turned her thoughts to Michael Copeland.

CHAPTER SIX

SHE woke in the morning to the fierce quarrelling of monkeys, then a tap on the door brought her fully to life. When the tap came again she lay feeling strange and embarrassed, wondering what to do, and then she decided. "Yes? Who is it?"

"Your tea. May I come in?" It was Laine.

She did not quite know how to handle this sutation and sat up quickly, reaching for a small quilted bedjacket which she had left on the satin-upholstered boudoir chair next to her bed. When she had slipped into it she called, "Yes, come in."

When the door opened Laine moved just inside the room. She had a glimpse of Ramesh behind him, in the corridor, before Laine turned to take the tray which the Indian was holding. Ramesh closed the door and her heart skipped a beat as Laine proceeded to carry the tray towards her.

"Well?" He was looking for somewhere to put the tray, so she moved some magazines away from the little side table. "And how did you sleep?"

Feeling somewhat embarrassed by this unexpected call, Carol put on the best front she could. "Very well, thank you. You were right—I fell asleep in next to no time."

"I told you so!" He smiled at her. "Didn't I?"

She smiled back. "Yes, you did. By the way, thank you for the tea. You're really spoiling me." Her eyes flickered over his slim-fitting mustard-coloured trousers and the honey-shaded shirt which he wore with the long sleeves down and a tangerine and honey cravat tucked into the open neck.

"It's quite early," he was saying, "you don't have to get up yet. I had Ramesh take Mother's tea in to her first. Very well, I'll leave you, then." She watched him going towards the large window, silent and graceful in his casual honey-coloured suede shoes.

"But first let me open the venetian blind." While he was adjusting the slats she sat against her pillows, unhappily fidgeting with the satin bow of her bedjacket. She'd have to get used to this, she supposed a little resentfully, but it was a bit unexpected—almost as though she and Laine were married already.

The sun cast golden spears across the floor and she could see that the morning was all blue skies and sunlight. When Laine turned to smile at her, her shoulders relaxed and her heart warmed towards him—his was such a sweet, tender smile. Perhaps, she thought swiftly, today would be different. Now that they were actually settled in the tension would surely slacken. From the open window came bird sounds and somewhere a rooster crowed. Suddenly she yearned to get up and see Laine's home again, after a good night's rest. Incredibly, she felt that things would work out for her—with Laine.

"After breakfast I'll show you around," he said. "I'll take you to the curio shop, and before morning tea you might like a swim. Would you like that?"

"Oh, that sounds wonderful! I'd like that very much."

His crooked smile revealed his insight into her thoughts. "Don't let the term *winter* mislead you, Carol. The weather is still very mild. Quite hot, in fact, as I think you, yourself, noticed yesterday."

"Does it ever get cold?" she asked. "I mean— *really cold?*"

He laughed. "Ask me that in a couple of months' time." He explored the fine shape of his fingers. "Actually, yes, Carol, it does. I'll take you up to the Berg when it snows."

When he went out, closing the door softly behind him, Carol lay back and heaved a sigh of thankfulness. She was so relieved that he had not tried to kiss her, not forced himself upon her, before she was ready.

Dallas Mulholland had breakfast with them on the veranda, Marcus secured by his leash to one of the curved scrolls of the wrought-iron gate which separated Laine's private section of the building from the tea room and the curio shop.

"Ramesh has got a couple of hefty umfaans digging holes for the posts for Marcus's pen," Laine told Carol.

"Thank goodness you still have a lot of that stout wire mesh about," his mother cut in. "I simply won't rest until Marcus has somewhere to walk about. It's ridiculous to go on like this! My nerves just won't stand it."

Carol turned her head in the direction of the swimming-pool, which was glittering beneath the sun, and saw two black youths busy digging. Their bursts of loud laughter caused her to smile. "They certainly seem to be enjoying themselves," she said. "They look as if they like digging." However, Dallas Mulholland ignored her remark and Carol had the sensation of being subtly snubbed.

It was too early for tourists, and so they had the whole place to themselves. Somehow the hills did not seem quite so overpowering, Carol told herself, as she sat back in her chair gazing at them. Why did Michael Copeland have to spoil things by telling her stories about evil spirits?

"How would you like to have a driving lesson?" Laine asked suddenly. "I realise that you are a licence holder, but it wouldn't do any harm to acquaint yourself with my car. You will then be in a position to take yourself off to the village or up to Aloeberg, if you want to."

Carol raised her brows. "Where is Aloeberg?"

"We turned off to get to the Valley before we reached it, actually. If we had continued straight on, for a couple of miles, we should have even passed right through it."

"And never even have known that we had done so," Dallas Mulholland chipped in. "It's a one-horse dorp if ever there was one; a hotel, butchery, school and a couple of garages."

"You forgot to mention the cemetery!" Laine's voice was sarcastic.

When breakfast was over they left Mrs. Mulholland supervising the pen and crossed the lawn to get to the garages. The morning dew-drenched grass was alive with jumping insects and on either side of the drive there were red crotons and frangipane trees with apricot and pink waxy-like flowers attached to their gnarled elephant-grey branches.

"It's a heavenly day," Carol said, tilting her face to the sun. "It's wonderful to be kissed by the sun, like this." The remark came out thoughtlessly and there was an instant uneasiness between them, ill-defined and yet verging upon embarrassment. Laine's face remained impassive, but she could not help noticing that he had flushed slightly.

On the whole, the driving lesson went well, but Carol was amazed to find that, although Laine was so patient with her one moment, he could become very impatient in the very next instant—so much so that he took her breath away.

"For pity's sake, Carol, do be careful, will you? You aren't handling a four-ton truck, you know. If there's one sound I can't stand it's the grating of gears. It's nothing short of vandalism, and nowadays, with cars the way they are, there's absolutely no need for it."

"I'm sorry," she murmured. "I'm just nervous, that's all."

He directed her to take a circular drive which took them over the viaduct on top of the massive wall, behind which stretched the dam—some five miles long.

The scenery, from this point, was quite breathtaking; the rugged hills reflecting their majesty in the blue depths of the still water. Laine told her to stop the car in the centre of the bridge and they got out to look down at the water. "Mike will know all about this, of course," he was saying, and Carol's heart contracted at the sound of that name, "but I think I'm right when I say that there's something like six thousand million gallons impounded by this wall, covering over five hundred acres. The lake stretches back for five or six miles from it. I think the wall is about one thousand three hundred feet long."

As he spoke he turned her gently by the shoulders so that they could look back down the length of the bridge.

"It's a marvellous structure," she said. "Somehow, even the hills can't intimidate it, can they? It makes me quite nervous—all this water. What if it bursts?"

"You're a fanciful child!" He drew her closer and for a moment she allowed her back to rest against him and then very gently freed herself. She started to walk back to the side of the bridge so that she could look over the wall, which reached just short of her chin. In the distance, she could see half a dozen dazzling white, thatched-roofed bungalows. Laine followed casually and placed an arm about her shoulders. "I—I suppose," she was aware that her breath was a little uneven, "Michael Copeland lives down there?"

"He'll be moving on soon, as you probably know. It just so happened that there was this vacant bungalow, furnished of course, and he was given the opportunity of living in it while the people are overseas on their long leave."

"Is that what you call the Village, then?"

"Part of the Village, yes. I might have mentioned this, but the name given to the Village is Imihlaba. Farther back, around that curve over there," he turned her gently, "is a trading store and a house owned by the owner of the store. We'll drive past there presently."

"What does Imihlaba mean?" They laughed together at her pronunciation of the word.

"I believe it's a Zulu word for candelabrum-type aloe growing throughout the Valley."

As she stood looking in the direction of the bungalows Carol thought what a twist of fate it was that Michael Copeland should be in the Valley too. He was so capable of filling her with unrest and uncertainty.

"Come along," said Laine, "we'll take a look at the trading store and then home for tea. We'll make our swim a quick one, if you don't mind, because I have work to do later, but I'll show you the curio shop, and after lunch, if you're very good, you can have the car—if you promise not to wreck it."

"But where would I go?" she smiled.

Instead of replying he turned her round to look up at him and she forced her eyes to meet his. "Carol, do you think you're beginning to"—he paused—"know me?"

When she answered him her voice was so low she could hardly hear it herself. "Yes, I—think so."

She stepped quickly out of his light embrace. "The trading store sounds—exciting." She wished she could control her breathing. "Are you going to take me to see it?"

His dark eyes held hers. "Just as you like," he answered precisely.

A blast of music exploded through the door of the Imihlaba trading store and Laine, who was driving now, slackened speed so that she could see the promiscuous assemblage of swaying, twisting African shoppers inside it. Outside, the lean-to veranda was swarming with more people, half-starved looking dogs, scraggy fowls and even a couple of tied-up goats.

Here, at the trading store, everybody seemed happily indifferent to time. Near by, the local goats champed, standing on their hind-legs to get at the leaves of some

91

scrubby bush. An old man, his nails the colour of old bones, crossed the road in front of the car and the shifting breezes gently tugged at the strips of furs and monkey tails which he wore in front to cover his manhood.

"I'd like to paint the old boy, wouldn't you?" Laine gave one of his twisted, gentle smiles.

"Yes, if I could paint," she replied. His eyes held hers. "You're very sweet, did you know that?" he asked softly. "Very sweet!" He set the car in motion, and with the thought of love growing stronger in her mind she answered: "It's very sweet of you to say so."

They had their swim before tea. Carol, her hair swept up under a flowery bathing-cap, was the first to dive into the water, and her young body had all the obliviousness and confidence of young bodies. She came up gasping. "Ooh!" she shrieked like a child. "It's jolly cold! Why didn't you *warn* me, Laine?" She looked up at him, the water dripping from her long eyelashes and running down her cheeks, and he laughed delightedly, looking down into her eyes.

"We can expect the water to be colder now. It cools down a lot in the hills at night and the water takes time to warm up. In the hot summer months the water is practically luke-warm at times, but I think I prefer it this way." She watched him dive in and he came up near her and then swam towards her. "You look like a child in that funny little cap," he told her, "innocent and impossible. But then you *are* just a child. Especially when you scream like that!"

Suddenly his presence excited her and she laughed shyly. Looking at him, she thought that there was always this elegance about Laine, even in the swimming-pool.

One of the straps of her bathing costume had slipped off her slender shoulder and he lifted it into place. This time she did not move away from him and accepted the caress of his fingers upon her skin.

As she pulled herself out of the pool and stood dripping water she told herself that falling in love with Laine would take time. "I *must* fall in love with him. After all, I came to this country because I thought I was in love with him—because I *was* in love with him."

It was after lunch that he said, "Look, Carol, I must leave you to yourself for a while now. Take the car out on your own and see how it goes, but for goodness' sake watch what you're doing. Don't land up in the dam," he grinned down at her. "Go back and visit the trading store. Go inside this time."

"Will it be quite safe?"

"For pity's sake, child, of course it will be quite safe."

"Shall I ask your mother to come too? Or do you think she would be nervous because I'd be driving the car? Perhaps *she* would like to drive?"

"Can you imagine Mother at the trading store? However, I'll ask her. Come along with me."

Mrs. Mulholland's door was closed and he knocked lightly on it. "Mother? Carol is going to the trading store in the car. Would you care to join her? You might find it interesting."

"Oh, go away. Nothing interests me here." The voice behind the door sounded irritable.

"There you have it!" Laine smiled faintly. "Frankly, I think Mother is a bit put out because Marcus refused to stay in his pen. Anyway, dearest, do be careful—don't drive too fast and—don't forget to come back to me!"

"I won't." She looked slim and almost boyish in her slacks and bright pumpkin-yellow shirt.

As she drove back to the store Carol thought of the man she was going to marry. It was strange how his mouth still seemed to bear the uncertainty of youth.

She parked the car outside the store, which was considerably quieter now, and went inside where the air was thick with the mingled smells of leather, cloth, soap, food, liquorice strips and human sweat. An African man was languidly sweeping the floor and she stepped over the brush, her eyes becoming excited at the sight of so many rolls of cheap and gaudy cottons upon the shelves. "Why is it," she thought, "that the sight of a vivid fabric will always excite a woman?"

"You must be Laine Mulholland's girl," the man behind the counter said, and she swung round.

"Oh," she stammered shyly, "I didn't notice you standing there." She went towards him. "My name is Carol Tracey. You must be Bert James because, of course, Laine told me about you. As a matter of fact, we drove slowly past here this morning. Laine was showing me around."

"Not much to show, hey? No Big Ben chiming here. I suppose you could say it's a bit like Piccadilly Circus though, at times." He laughed, and then moved a curtain of belts which dangled from the ceiling. "You're very young," he said. "The wife and I were beginning to wonder when Laine Mulholland would make up his mind about taking a wife."

"I suppose, then, he would have told you that we were pen-friends?" She felt at ease with Bert James, who was big and tanned and looked as if nothing worried him.

"Well, we heard rumours, of course. The folks about here don't know Laine Mulholland all that well. He can be pretty deep, you know, but we knew there was something in the wind, anyway. He hinted at it."

"His mother is staying—with us," she said, seized by a spasm of embarrassment, "until we're married."

"I've met his old lady, as it so happens. She's a card, if ever there was one. She only comes here when Maxine Mason brings her which, admittedly, isn't often."

Carol's blue eyes were curious. "Oh? I didn't know."

"What can I do to oblige?" Bert asked, turning to look back at the shelves.

"Well, actually, I just came to try the car out on my own and—to look around. I've often wondered what a trading store was like because, of course, I've read about them. In fact, I tried to read as much about South Africa as I could after I had started corresponding with Laine."

"Go right ahead and enjoy yourself, then. There's everything here from a pot of vaseline to an axe handle."

Carol laughed. "What would I want with an axe handle? Or a pot of vaseline, for that matter?"

"Aah, you never know, you know. Vasline might come in handy for a nappy rash on the baby one day."

Carol felt the blood rush to her face. "May—may I go behind the counter?" she asked quickly.

"Sure."

Some time later, Bert James laughingly passed her a small shabby case containing an assortment of cheap jewellery—bangles of every colour beneath the sun, brooches and rings all set with huge glittering pieces of coloured glass.

When she had made her choice from the cardboard case he wrapped her purchases up in a sheet of newspaper while she stood looking at the buckets, lamps, axe handles, tin luggage, eating utensils and cheap clothing.

There was the suggestion of a shadow across the counter and, turning quickly, she found herself looking into the cool and amused green eyes of Michael Copeland. "Oh!" She knew she had failed in an attempt to keep her voice adequate. "Hello, there."

"Well, well, well—out doing the family shopping?" As soon as he spoke she knew that Michael was taking a pleasure in his own power over her. "Laine isn't wasting any time in training you, is he? But then he never does waste time, so far as his training activities are concerned."

"He is not training me," Carol did not try to conceal her annoyance, "and it's none of your business, but in any case, I'm out shopping for *myself*!"

His long-drawn out and highly amused "*Oh?*" infuriated her. She had come to think of this as his "secret agent" kind of voice.

"Well, thank you, Mr. James," she said, and when she turned again she saw that Michael's eyes were resting with amusement on the newspaper parcel on the counter.

"Tell me," his voice was soft, "this is just a matter of interest, of course—don't answer if you'd rather not," he hunched his shoulders, "but how does shopping in this part of the world compare with shopping in London?" And then, when his laughter ended, they regarded each other soberly.

"Mr. Copeland," Carol's voice was choked, "please keep away from me!" She wondered what had changed him and suddenly her voice seemed to disintegrate. She put out one slim, trousered leg to get past him, but he made no attempt to move to one side.

"Would you mind allowing me to pass?"

"Not at all," he answered maliciously. "You'll be wanting to get back to the menagerie, won't you? By the way, I dropped the post there on my way to the Village from Aloeberg." He followed her in his loose-kneed, easy stride.

"Is that so?" She spoke over her shoulder, shaking her hair back. "And by the way, haven't you forgotten the purpose of your visit here? I take it that you *did* come to shop—and not just to annoy me?"

"I've changed my mind," he said, his smile breaking out again.

From the veranda she could see the Land-Rover which he seemed to make a habit of riding about in.

"Come and say hello to Maxine," he said. "I collected her at the Station in Aloeberg. She'll be my neighbour while she's on leave," and for some unknown reason Carol was aware of a deeply embedded pain.

Maxine Mason got out of the vehicle. She looked tall and there seemed to be a kind of untiring quality about her. "So we meet again," she said. "Is the Valley going to take both of us, do you think?" She was wearing a Ming-yellow shift, cut like a toga, and quite casually wore an incredible jade necklace and bracelet with this cotton garment. Her feet were thrust into Italian-style sandals encrusted with rhinestones and her toenails were painted scarlet.

"Well, I don't see why it shouldn't," Carol replied, and next to Maxine Mason, who was so poised, so easy and so sublimely certain of every movement and gesture, she felt like a child.

"If it isn't, we'll just have to make a plan, won't we?" Maxine said, and Carol's eyes darkened with some deep and confused concern.

"And *if* I didn't know you were—joking," she said, in a stiff little voice, "I'd wonder what all this was about—Maxine."

"Apparently the only person who thinks I'm not is me!" Maxine widened her wide green eyes and smiled, and she spoke with an insolent assurance that left Carol guessing whether or not her words had any ulterior motive. The two girls stood face to face, less than six feet apart.

"Keep going," Michael looked first at Maxine and then at Carol. "I'm waiting to hear more of this."

"And why is this, do you suppose?" Maxine gave him a full look and he grinned and turned to Carol.

"I must warn you, Carol, Maxine is something like Laine's cats—she attacks merely as a form of self-protection." He put his fingers beneath her chin and she drew back quickly as if to prepare herself for sudden flight. He dropped his arm and stood back. "Well, we'll be seeing you around."

Carol watched them going towards the Land-Rover feeling a curious kind of relief—and a more obscure pain. She stood in the glare of the sky, thatch and mimosa, and above her a hawk sailed with dark outstretched wings. She put a hand across her eyes to watch it and knew that her cheeks were wet.

"You forgot your parcel," Bert James said at her side, and she dropped her hand.

"Oh—thank you." She looked at him vaguely. "I—must have forgotten about it."

"You'll have to watch her." Bert's voice was quiet, and she knew that to show concern would be a mistake, so she said, "I honestly don't see why. Miss Mason is welcome to Michael Copeland, Mr. James."

A curious flicker, almost of sympathy, passed over his face. "I can see you're misunderstood my remark."

"I'll have to go now." Her eyes reflected her unhappiness as the hurt caused by Maxine Mason was filed away along with that other hurt she'd received on the beach. "Goodbye, Mr. James—and thank you very much."

She got into the car and sat for a moment, her mind a muddle. Somewhere in the distance, she could hear African music, faint, wailing and full of unrest. Life, she thought, was going to be quite unbearable if she was going to keep bumping into Maxine Mason and Michael Copeland. When she got back Mrs. Mulholland was having tea on the veranda, with Marcus at her feet, his leash firmly secured to her chair.

"Mike brought the post," said Laine, coming to the steps to meet her. "There are a couple of letters for you, Carol."

"I met Michael and Maxine at the trading store," Carol said, trying to keep the grievance she felt out of her voice as she thought about the bitterness Maxine carried around—the bitterness that kept her always poised to strike, as though the fact that Michael having met her at the Marine Terminal was a personal thrust. "*He* told me."

"You simply must ask Maxine to dinner," Dallas Mulholland cut in, and somehow her expression seemed outraged and accusing. "Mickey too, of course."

Laine gave his mother a sharp hard store. "Why *must* I? I'll ask them *when*—and *if*—it suits me, Mother." He turned to Carol again. "Your letters, by the way, are on the hall table. I recognised your father's writing, of course."

There were two letters. As she thought—one from her father and one from her grandmother. She went to the bathroom to wash her hands first before reading them, then went out to the veranda, where Ramesh had placed a small tray of tea-things for her.

Her heart began to beat heavily and sickeningly as she read her father's letter first. "It is nice to be able to write to you, knowing Laine's address as I do," he wrote. "I am more than anxious, of course, to hear all about your views on your possible new home and possible husband. I find myself constantly praying about you, Carol, and I have not prayed for a long time, I very much regret to say. I could never forgive myself if things went wrong for you . . ."

Her grandmother's letter started by stating how pleased she was to receive Carol's letter posted in Cape Town and how thrilling it was to hear that Carol loved Table Mountain and that everything seemed to be working out so beautifully.

Apparently her grandmother was under some vague impression that Cape Town and Table Mountain were just a stone's throw away from Laine's home in the Valley and if Carol loved them—well, everything was running smoothly and according to plan. "Write soon," continued the scratchy writing, "and tell me all about your exciting meeting with your future husband and about your lovely new home. I suppose that by now you will have made new friends. I can't tell you how happy I am here. We have all sorts of entertainment . . ."

"Well?" Carol lifted her eyes from the writing paper as Laine spoke. "Are you satisfied with your letters?"

"They're both well," she replied. "The other one is from my grandmother, of course. They are—happy—for me." Her voice faltered.

"Good. Then you'll be able to write back soon and tell them you're quite settled in." His closed face told her nothing.

"Yes." She bit the inside of her lower lip so that it would not tremble and swallowed hard. She poured her tea and stood up, the cup and saucer in her hand, and carried them to the edge of the veranda where she stood leaning against the wrought-iron scroll-work. "Standing again," she thought, "on the veranda—just looking out."

"All the visitors appear to have gone," she said, before she began to sip her tea.

Laine made a gesture of dismissal. "Yes, thank heaven."

She turned. "But why thank heaven? I thought you liked it when the curio shop and the tea-room are both full?"

"So I do. Make no mistake about that." He got to his feet and came to stand next to her. "There are those times, however, when I prefer to have the place to myself, for a change." As he spoke, she was aware of the strange quality of his voice.

"When you've finished your tea," he said, "come for a walk with me. Just to do the rounds. Mother has gone off to write letters, I understand." Carol stood perfectly still, staring at his shadow, immobile on the floor. She looked up and they both, from that moment, knew what was bound to happen.

"Must we?" she said, and her voice was tight. "It's— it's so hot."

"Finish your tea," he said, and then, when she set the empty cup in the saucer, he took them from her and went over to the tray. When he came back he placed an arm lightly on her shoulders. "Let's go and visit Lisa, then, shall we?"

Her shoulders stiffened and she had a feeling that she was going to fall apart. "You've gone very pale," he said, "so I don't have to mince matters. I'm going in, of course." It was a statement.

"Oh *no!*" She faltered and stopped. "Oh no, Laine. No!"

He grinned down at her. "Oh yes. Oh yes, Carol. Yes!"

"Must you do this crazy thing?" Her voice contained dismay. "It all seems so silly, somehow."

"Does it? Well, I suppose it would—to *you.* I'm afraid, Carol, that it's something you'll have to get used to. I've been doing this for an age—long before I knew you existed —and I'm certainly not going to stop now."

"I don't want to see it, then," she told him. "Please don't make me, Laine."

He cursed mildly. "I'm not *making* you, for pity's sake. I'm merely *asking* you to come and watch. Don't you trust me, Carol?"

"Oh, how stupid can you get?" She looked at him with mutinous, frightened eyes. "What on earth has trusting *you* got to do with it? I don't trust the animals."

Their glances clashed. "One of these days," he said, "I'm going to go in when the place is full of tourists. That's how much I trust them."

"Just as much as you trusted Dorcas?" Carol's voice went up and her eyes went to his hands.

He did not reply but began to walk on and, reluctantly, she followed him, wondering all the time whether she should appeal to Mrs. Mulholland.

Vaguely, she took in the plan of the lions' den and it seemed to her to be in three parts, although it was in fact one large cage separated in the centre by a thick mesh wire where an iron trapdoor was slipped into grooved cement posts. This trapdoor could, apparently, be worked by a short pulley from a cement construction next to the cage, on the outside, and to do this one stood on the roof of this construction.

Laine had an African youth go up on the cement roof and drop the trapdoor between both cages and then, at the sound of Laine's voice, Lisa got up and began to pace restlessly to and fro on her silent padded feet, her geen eyes staring past him. It seemed as if she was determined not to look Laine in the eye, but one was acutely aware of the fact that she was only too aware of his presence.

The outside gate to the cage was unlocked, then Laine moved quickly into it and, still with his back to the gate, closed it. The African slipped the bolt on the outside, and as Carol watched Laine alone in the cage she picked up a nervous and excited fear, like a wavelength, and she stood rooted to the spot, tense and breathless—just watching and waiting. When she drew her tongue across her lip she discovered that there was no saliva in her mouth.

For one mad moment she wondered whether she should run screaming to the house for Dallas Mulholland to come and reason with her son, but then Laine's voice rang out, halting her before she even had time to begin to will her legs to move.

"Lisa!" The beautiful voice was commanding. Laine stood flicking his narrow trouser leg with a thin stick. "Come on, girl. *Look* at me, I say. Lisa!" It was a voice of great seductiveness now.

The lioness stopped her pacing to turn her head slightly in Laine's direction, but still with that peculiar green gaze which seemed to go right behind his shoulder somewhere.

In the adjoining cage Leo moved in his sleep, lifting one massive paw to his nose and then telaxing the muscles beneath his wonderful tawny coat and beneath the warmth of the sun. The tip of his tail moved very slightly.

Lisa commenced her pacing again and Laine advanced towards her slowly. When she stopped he flicked the stick lightly across her nose. "Look at me, Lisa!" Nothing in the unblinking expression seemed to change, but Carol was aware of the slight hardening in the green gaze—a sort of puzzled hardening—but she was too terrified to utter a sound, and when Ramesh came to stand beside her she jumped violently. The Indian's face was impassive. In fact, he looked just a little bored, as though the whole exhibition had lost its flavour for him, but when he heard Carol's sharp intake of breath as Lisa lifted a paw to ward off Laine's stick he said quickly, beneath his breath almost, "Don't move, miss. Don't worry. Mr. Mulholland doesn't know it, miss, but I always carry a firearm with me. Whenever I know he is going inside the cage I go into the house for the firearm. I happen to know where he keeps it."

"Aah . . . aah!" Laine's voice was like the clear resonant sound of vibrating metal. It was an exulted sound that was frightening to Carol's ears. "You're beginning to take notice, Lisa." He lifted the stock and Lisa advanced towards him on three legs, the fourth raised, paw ready to strike at the whiplike stick. Her hostile green eyes were coldly calculating, and Carol's own blue eyes widened as she saw Leo slowly coming to life in the next cage. The wire mesh which separated him from Laine and the lioness seemed to be very frail.

The animal got up, in one powerful ripple of tawny hair, muscle and bone, and lifted his head questioningly, gazing through the wire, then he deliberately walked over to the trapdoor and flung himself against it. Carol automatically reached out for Ramesh.

"Tell Mr. Mulholland to come out, *please*, Ramesh!"

"This is nothing," Ramesh told her, not moving. "Mr. Mulholland is nearly finished."

"Oh, please, *please*, Ramesh!" She tugged at his arm. "You must listen to me. He'll get killed. I can't stand it!" She made to run and the Indian stretched out and caught her by the arm. "No, please, miss. You must wait!" Something in the tone of his voice caused her to stop.

When Laine spoke again Carol realised that she was hiding her eyes with her fingers.

"That will be all for today, Lisa." Fascinated, and still rooted to the spot, but with a feeling of utter thankfulness, she uncovered her eyes and watched Laine as he backed towards the external gate. "Tell your old man to relax, Lisa girl," he was saying, then in one swift and graceful movement he opened the gate, which had already been unbolted, and eased himself quickly out of the cage. The whole affair had taken place with the precision of a ballet.

Laine bolted and locked the gate himself and then, as though this was expected of her, Lisa thudded her brownish-yellow body against it and he laughed, throwing back his head boyishly. Then he started to walk towards Carol, fastidiously wiping his face with a handkerchief.

"Well?" As he spoke she stepped back from him, feeling his elated expression like a blow. He gave the impression of latent physical power and there was a hint of ruthlessness about him. "And how did you like it?"

Without a word, she turned and left him, running like a wild thing towards the house, where she sagged down into a chair on the veranda. Her limbs were trembling and she could not control them. She felt suddenly dehydrated.

And then Laine was mounting the steps—slim, agile and looking much, much younger than he was. An exotic green bird with a scarlet beak was perched on his shoulder and impertinently pecking at his ear.

With his dark wavy hair, longish and sprinkled and winged with silver, his touchy lean dark face and the unusual clothes he wore, he looked very theatrical—as though he was taking part in some film.

He took absolutely no notice of Carol. Instead he shouted, "Ramesh? Ramesh? Where the devil are you, man?"

Ramesh, however, was well trained to these rituals and he appeared, quite unperturbed carrying a tray of drinks and clinking, melting ice.

"Coming, Mr. Mulholland, sir."

Laine gesticulated towards a small table. "Put it down, man. Put it down. I'm just going to wash my hands."

Ramesh set the tray down and Carol looked up at him, a hopeless and bewildered look in her eyes.

"It is all over now, miss. Don't worry." Ramesh smiled, giving a brilliant display of white teeth. "Tonight Mr. Mulholland will play the piano. I know him well. Perhaps he will play all night."

When Laine returned he seemed to be a little pale, beneath his tan, although relaxed—and they did not talk. In fact, Carol was determined not to talk to him at all—unless she had to.

Laine sat down, with the soundless control of a cat, and threw one elegant mustard-coloured-trousered leg over the other. He still took no notice of her and finally, because she couldn't help it, she said, "Oh, Laine, you're so hard. Why do you do these things?"

"Hard? Do you really think so? Aah, if only you knew, Carol. If only you knew," he said, and she had the strange feeling that he was crying inside and that the episode with Lisa had, for him, a profound—almost spiritual significance.

"Yes. Yes, you are. And you frighten me. No wonder your mother keeps out of this." She watched him dribbling a handful of salted peanuts into his upturned mouth, then he picked up his glass and came over to her, going on his knees before her. "You're being utterly unreasonable, you know." His voice was gentle and she drew a deep, quivering breath. He looked round for somewhere to put his glass. "Don't cringe from me, Carol. I can't bear it!"

"I don't know how *I'm* going to bear it!" she cried. Her handkerchief was a tiny crumpled thing in her hand.

He stood up and his face changed as he looked at her, becoming leaner, more disdainful. "Is there any more?" he asked angrily.

"No," she whispered, "it's just that I don't know how I'm going to bear all this."

"Well," he said coldly, "that's your problem, isn't it?" Miserably, she watched him as he stooped to recover his

103

glass from the floor of the veranda, then her eyes followed him as he took it with him into the living-room.

It would appear that the routine was always to be the same; a drink again before dinner—on the veranda. Ramesh seemed to be the one to decide whether they should dine indoors or outside and when dusk fell Carol stood watching him with some impatience as he prepared to set the table. She wondered childishly how he would accept her as Laine's wife, and what his reaction would be if she made it clear to him that he was no longer at liberty to run Laine's household in the way *he* thought best.

Later, Laine joined her again. "Mother will be eating in her room—with her dog," he said shortly. "She likes to make herself unhappy just for the sake of it."

Because the moon was already up, the long veranda was patterned with twisting shadows caused by the wrought-iron work and the trees and flowering shrubs which made black mysterious outlines on the white walls.

"Mother has chosen to make things as hellish as she possibly can," Laine said. "You've noticed that, of course?"

Suddenly Carol felt hopeless. "Now that we're on the subject," she told him, "I—I just can't seem to make any headway with your mother."

"If you are unhappy about this, on my account, don't be." His dark face was moody. "Sometimes Mother miscalculates herself." He looked at her directly. "I think you will agree with me that the sooner we are married the better? I realise that your father expressed the wish that we allowed a certain period to elapse, but under the circumstances, I feel that the time has come when you must write to him—putting his mind at rest. You do see that, don't you?"

She bent her head and moved her bracelet up and down her slender wrist. "Yes." Her heart was beating thickly. She looked up and Laine's shadow on the wall became immense and then dwindled to its proper size as the candles flickered. "I'll write and tell him."

After dinner Laine excused himself and went through to the softly lit living-room to play his beloved piano, and she was left alone with her thoughts on the veranda.

Ramesh always seemed to hover around long after Laine was finished with him, and Carol turned now, as he came to the veranda with a fresh drinks tray, ready for Laine when he needed it again.

"Mr. Mulholland loves his piano better than anything," he said, and his voice was almost gentle, as though he wanted to soothe the wild staccato of the heart of the young girl in front of him.

From where they stood they could see Laine playing, his face tense and dedicated.

"Even—better than his animals?" she could not resist asking, but she tried to make it sound like a joke.

Ramesh set the tray down carefully and straightened himself. "Not better than the animals, miss. Good night."

"Good night, Ramesh."

She stood listening for a while and then when Laine stopped playing abruptly she knew, without even turning to look into the room beyond, that he was flexing his fingers—examining them.

Fear gripped her by the heart. Soon she was going to be just another caged thing, just another Lisa—a plaything for Laine, when the time came.

CHAPTER SEVEN

CAROL'S mood lifted a little in the days to come, but this was only because she was still determined to settle down. She went out of her way to be with Laine as much as possible in her effort to get to know him better and with the idea of falling in love with him growing stronger in her mind. Constantly she had to remind herself that she had come to South Africa to marry him and that she had always looked forward to his letters in England. The fact that she had suddenly found herself bewildered and disappointed in him and his Valley was only the result of feeling strange and no doubt a little homesick—but this disappointment had to be shoved to one side. To really get to know Laine and to try to recapture some of the emotion she had felt towards him, before actually meeting him, she had to make up her mind to savour each moment as it came.

Laine had not gone near Lisa again. There seemed to be plenty for him to do—checking books, ordering or unpacking curios and giving personal attention to various matters concerning the clerical side of the tea-room.

At night, after dinner, he played the piano, and Carol, after a humiliating experience, had learned not to disturb him.

Ramesh always left the drinks on the table on the veranda, and although she had noticed that drinking only seemed to make Laine morose, never sociable or relaxed, this did not seem to interfere with his music. Mostly he seemed to be busy trying to compose, and he would break off in the middle of a succession of running chords to make entries into a theory book.

On the particular night concerned, Carol decided to go into the living-room to listen to him.

Laine did not look up as she walked past the piano to sit on a chair, her legs tucked up beneath her, but she knew that he was aware of her by the nervous twist to his mouth. Closing her eyes, she listened to the sombre chords and could feel every nerve reacting to the music. However, when he started working on his own fumbling composition again she stretched an arm across to a small table for a magazine and then, careful not to disturb him, turned the pages over as quietly as she could. She had looked through several pages before she realised that she had no idea what any of the pages were about.

In the middle of a passage he stopped playing and flung up his hands, then dropped them to the keys again in a harsh discordant jangle. "Carol," his voice was raised in quick anger, "do you have to sit there rustling the pages of that confounded magazine? I do wish you would shut up. You're getting on my nerves!"

Her face showed blank surprise for a moment and then she said, "I'm sorry. I thought I was being very quiet."

"You sound like a mouse in a stationery cupboard," he told her unpleasantly. "What the devil do you come in here for, if not to listen?" He swung round to look at her and she noticed again that misleading look of youth about him which was always bestowed to him in certain lights.

"I was listening," she said, trying to hold back the hurt that had welled up within her. "When you stopped playing from a music sheet I could see that you were working on something of your own, so, quite naturally, *I* think, I stopped giving you my full attention—but I was listening, for all that."

She stood up and placed the magazine back on the table. "Has it ever struck you, Laine, that I don't know what else to do? I just don't seem to be fitting in. Your mother keeps to her room now. You—you keep to your keyboard and your —drinks."

She watched him rub a hand wearily across his face. "You're so right," he said, "but you knew how it was with me. I think I explained it all very clearly about my music —and what it was that I was trying to achieve here."

A faint flush had crept up under her new tan. "Yes, I know you did, and I'm sorry. I should have realised that you're longing to get your composition finished."

He smiled humourlessly. "You talk as though I have an endless length of knitting, or something, dangling from a couple of needles. I don't think you understand what it's all about, do you? Of course, I realise that I should make certain allowances for you."

"Make—certain allowances for me?" She looked at him curiously. "Whatever for?"

"Well, let's put it this way. I had no idea how—well, I had almost forgotten, shall we say, how maddeningly young twenty is."

"Oh." In the droop of her slim young shoulders there was dejection. "I see."

She left him then, and went back to the veranda, and after a short silence the cold moonlight of Laine's sonata flowed out into the darkness and she felt herself shivering.

The days were hot and sunny, not like the beginning of winter at all, and she swam a lot and secretly delighted in her deep tan—if nothing else. Over sundowners one evening Laine said, "By the way, I've invited Mike to dinner tonight," and as he spoke Carol wondered desperately whether he could see her tighten at the sound of that name.

"You quite appear to have overlooked the fact that *Maxine* is in the Valley," Dallas Mulholland said, and Carol noticed how she isolated that name, as though it was something very special.

Laine interrupted her with one of his nervous, impatient gestures. "I haven't forgotten," he snapped.

"And will she be coming? I expected to see more of her before she goes back to town, but I suppose you can't blame the poor girl for staying away."

Carol was quick to notice the way in which mother and son held each other with their eyes, and there seemed to be an unpleasant constraint between them.

"Maxine will be coming to dinner," he said.

"Oh, that's nice. It will at least be something to look forward to, instead of this perpetual eating in my room."

Laine put his glass down on the table with some violence. "Well, nobody, so far as I am aware, has asked you to perpetually eat in your room, Mother. If you choose to eat with your dog, that's entirely your affair."

He poured himself another drink and sat down again, turning the chilled glass between his long, brown fingers. Then he looked at Carol. "You will wear white tonight, Carol, and some of that perfume I've noticed about you."

She lifted eyes which had a bewildered expression in them. "I—well, all right, if you want me to. Is there anything I should see to for you?" she stammered. "I mean, is there anything I should do to supervise the dinner?"

"There's nothing for you to do—except to look madly beautiful. There's no need for you to go into the kitchen.

I do have people to dinner, you know. Occasionally, it's true, but I haven't lost the art of entertaining all together."

Before dinner Carol took a shower, then when she was back in her room she opened the slats of the venetian blinds and stared through them at the hills, towering around the house and outbuildings. The hills were gathering the mist which rose up from the river and the dam so that they looked as though they were wearing flimsy veils. "Like brides," she thought, and a shudder went through her.

She turned and went towards the cupboards and prepared to dress to please Laine, choosing a white shift which hung straight from breast to knees and which emphasised her slenderness and her youth. Then she decided to wear an old-fashioned chunky bracelet ,strung with jade and set in heavy silver, as her only piece of jewellery. This had been another gift from her grandmother.

Laine looked up when she joined him on the veranda where Ramesh had set the table for dinner. For a moment they gazed at each other and then he drew a long breath. "You're quite, quite lovely," he said softly.

"Thank you," she replied, but she felt no joy and her heart seemed so heavy that it was a wonder that it could still beat.

Now that the time was practically here for her to come face to face with Michael and Maxine Mason she began to feel nervous and apprehensive.

"It looks as though they've arrived," Laine said, at the sound of an engine. "Let's go and meet them, shall we?" He slipped an arm about her waist and they went down the steps of the veranda, past the swimming-pool with its silver surface, towards the drive.

Michael and Maxine had driven from the village in his car and he got out, slamming the door behind him, and went round to the other side to open the door for Maxine. As Carol stood there, next to the man she was going to marry, she wondered why it was that she felt so wretchedly unhappy at the sight of Michael's hand reaching out for Maxine's fingers. Fascinated, and yet still with a tight feeling in the region of her chest, she watched them link those fingers.

It was light enough to see that Maxine was looking very glamorous in a green linen dress, banded over each side to display an under-skirt of bright printed silk. Her red hair had been drawn back and she wore a loose chignon, but this was probably not her own.

Not only did Maxine look ravishing but also she looked composed and entirely sophisticated, and she had the power to make Carol feel young and naive in her simple white dress.

"This is what I've been waiting for, I might tell you." Maxine's voice was deep and throaty. "I feel that it's only fair to warn you, Carol, that I'm a fighter. I never give up, which means that we should all get together more often."

Carol felt a rush of fury. Why did Maxine keep on talking as though she was interested in Michael? She glanced at Michael and turned away. "If Maxine only knew," she thought, panting inwardly, "I *hate* him!"

Maxine disentangled her fingers from Michael's and then, with a feeling of cool astonishment, Carol watched her link an arm through the arms of both men, so that she was in the middle.

She had the sensation that she would have to match Maxine's coolness, but nevertheless she remained standing slightly in the background, listening to Laine making his greetings to his guests, and she had the miserable feeling that Maxine Mason could have her choice of both men—if she set her heart on it. As though she could sense these thoughts, Maxine turned her head. "Darling," there was spite in her voice, "you look so *young*, so appealing, standing there in that little white shift! Tell me, did you rustle it up yourself, on your grandmother's treadle machine, you clever little thing?"

Although this remark was designed to annoy, Carol's hazel eyes veiled themselves. "Thank you," she replied softly, "but no, I can't take the credit, Maxine. After my grandmother sold her house—and her treadle sewing machine, incidentally—she took me on a short holiday to Paris. I bought it there." For a moment she was almost overcome by a terrible giddiness and this, she knew, was because she was so furious. To end the round she could not help adding in a cold little voice, "It's just a little rag I picked up in Paris."

Michael disengaged himself from Maxine and permitted himself to look directly at Carol. "How's tricks?" he asked. "Been in with the lions yet, or are you too scared?" Their eyes met in pure antagonism.

"No, but Laine has been in, if that's what you mean."

"He knows about it," she thought, "so why pretend?"

"Has Laine told you that *I've* been in?" Maxine asked, and she seemed to be impatient for Carol's answer.

"No, he didn't tell me." Carol felt weak, lost and helpless. She could quite easily imagine Maxine in with Lisa, moving back from the lioness with a rangy rhythm in all her movements, her red hair flaming beneath the sun. "I— I hope he doesn't expect *me* to go in," she added with a smile which she hoped was normal. "Because, you see, I *am* scared!"

"You don't know what you're missing," there was an undertone of excitement in Maxine's voice. It's a *thrilling* experience—especially when Lisa comes for you in one swift and famished movement." She laughed delightedly.

Dallas Mulholland was already on the veranda and she and Maxine made a great show of greeting each other. "Poor, poor Dallas!" Maxine kissed Laine's mother for the third time.

"Poor Dallas. *I* say it all the time." Mrs. Mulholland's face was set in that I-have-every-reason-to-complain expression.

Carol stood by herself, trembling and fascinated, listening to Mrs. Mulholland's being called Dallas and painfully aware that Laine's mother was giving Maxine Mason all the love and affection she had never given her. She dropped her eyes as Maxine turned to smile at everybody, her triumph secure behind her.

Carol was bitterly disappointed, but certainly in no way surprised, because it had not taken her long to discover that Dallas Mulholland, who still vaguely referred to her as Cecily, had not accepted her as the future wife of her son.

It was difficult to determine what Maxine's game was and just what it was that she was constantly trying to prove—and why? *Why?*

Carol's eyes automatically went towards Michael; it was too late to save herself from meeting his intent gaze, and then when this gaze had spent itself he said, very softly, and for her ears alone, "You're so quiet tonight."

"I'm—not really," she answered on a false light tone. "I'm enjoying listening to everybody."

"I thought you'd forgotten to smile."

"Well, I haven't," she tried to match his mood.

During drinks Carol was fully aware of the fact that Laine was having a difficult time steering them through those moments before dinner in his controlled and nervous manner.

"This is hardly the setting for a London girl." Maxine said, looking up. "You're so *tense*, Carol. Don't you like Laine's Valley?"

"I'm not tense, Maxine. In any case, I more or less knew what to expect. Don't forget we corresponded for a year, and in that year Laine described everything to me in his letters."

"But you don't like it? Do you?" Maxine's beauty had a queer harshness, and Carol felt that they were both suddenly aware of a moment of suspense which took control of them.

How could she tell Maxine that she shuddered away from the Valley because she was not in love with Laine Mulholland? Perhaps her lips were set a little more firmly than usual, when she answered, but there was no other sign of emotion.

"You're quite wrong, Maxine. I *do* like it."

Beyond the lit circle of the table, with its dazzling white damask cloth, the hills were black and forbidding, and Dallas Mulholland made a loud sound of shivering. "Well, I don't like it. I don't know how Laine stands it and how he can be bothered with all this farce—all this formality—in a place like this." She waved an arm over the table.

"What do you expect me to do? Would you have me eat over the kitchen sink?" Laine's voice revealed his temper. "What a stupid woman you are, Mother!"

"I'm not the one who is stupid. If you weren't so stupid yourself you would sell out here and come and live a civilised life near town, and if anybody could make *him* see sense," she said to all at random, "Maxine could."

Laine dropped his napkin to the table and stood up. "Let's relax over coffee, shall we?"

They went into the living-room, where Ramesh served coffee with globes of whipped cream and huge goblets with minute quantities of brandy, and for a while the drinks, conversation and the small jokes pulled them together in continuous murmuring of voices.

All during this time Carol had been trying to make up her mind about Maxine. Her presence seemed to insinuate itself into Laine's life with all the assurance which acted as a full testament to her ability to be in tune with the kind of life he led—or the kind of life his mother would have him lead. She seemed to be going out of her way to show Carol that *she* belonged here—or at any rate, by Laine's side, whereas she, Carol, did not belong.

Why was this? It all seemed so senseless and so cruel. Perhaps this red-haired girl felt a pity in her heart because she could see that things were not as they should be between Laine and herself, but, looking at Maxine's cool arrogant face, however, Carol knew that this was not the reason. There was no pity there. Was she the type of girl, then, who was never satisfied unless she knew that she had the power to hurt the man who loved her? Carol cast a glance at Michael. Despite everything, she thrilled at his good looks and found it hard to believe that he had held her while they danced and brushed his lips across her forehead. If this was the way Maxine treated him it was no wonder that Michael indulged in a little lighthearted flirtation when the opportunity presented itself.

When Laine went towards the piano his mother yawned behind her ringed fingers. "His playing bores me to madness," she said loudly, and then got to her feet, freeing Marcus's leash from beneath the leg of her chair. "Really, one would have thought that Laine would have suggested something for tonight, a drive up to the hotel at Aloeberg or something, but instead it's the same old routine, visitors or no visitors. A late night wouldn't have mattered for once. As it is, *he* keeps late hours," she added in a voice that sounded childish and querulous. "I'm going to my room, as usual. Maxine, my pet child, would you drop in on me later on? I want a little chat. I have something I want to discuss with you."

Carol felt as though she had been hurt deep down somewhere and dropped her lashes to hide the sparkle of tears. When she thought of the number of times that Laine's mother had snubbed her in her attempt to show that she wanted to love and to be loved she felt as though her legs had been knocked from under her.

Laine completely ignored his mother and started to play, while Maxine had almost draped herself across the piano, giving her whole attention to his playing—absorbed and deliberate—and once again Carol wondered what it was that this girl was trying to prove. Whatever it was, she thought bitterly, Maxine was overdoing the demonstration.

As she looked at them she could not help thinking of the night when Laine had shown such impatience as she sat quietly and harmlessly, in another part of the room, looking at a magazine.

"Come out to the veranda?" invited Michael, shattering her thoughts, and then, before she could protest, he had taken her by the hand and pulled her up to him.

When they were outside he lit a cigarette and she watched the tiny flame momentarily show up the dim outline of his face. They stood slightly apart and an embarassment came over them. Then beside her, in the dark, he said, "And now tell me about *you*." When she made no reply he said, "I'd like to revise what I said earlier on."

"What did you say?"

"I said I thought you had forgotten to smile. Well, I don't think. I know!" He flipped the spent match out into the darkness and all she could see of him in the shadows was his face where the light from the room beyond just caught it.

She moved away, turning her face from him. "For your information," she began, before she tripped over a cushion which had been left lying on the floor and nearly fell. He reached for her hand and then slid it into his palm, and instinctively she held her breath.

"I almost expected to see a ring here." He lifted her hand and smoothed her finger with his own. "Why isn't there?"

"For the simple reason that we haven't been to town yet." She allowed her hand to rest in his, feeling the warmth and hardness of him, and then she freed herself.

They stood for a moment with the shrilling of crickets all about them, then he said, "I should have thought one of the rings in stock would have done, in the meantime." His voice was hard. "I noticed one myself, recently. You might have seen it yourself. It's a large moonstone—quite exquisitely set. Perhaps, however, this isn't good enough for you. Perhaps you have something better in mind—a diamond—the size of a knuckleduster, maybe?"

"It gives you pleasure to insult me, doesn't it?" she said, and then added, "If this ring—this moonstone—appeals to you so much why don't you buy it for Maxine? Or is she too, waiting for something better?"

There was a short silence and then he said, very quietly, "Just don't try to trap me, Carol!"

A little later he said, "Your innonence startles me. Maxine is nearly thirty." He turned to her. "She gives you nine whole years, did you know that?" She watched him walk away, then he stood looking into the living-room beyond its expanse of glass. He came back to stand next to her again. "When Maxine is with Mulholland she's like somebody with a high temperature. To my way of thinking, they're both eccentric."

"Well, if she's eccentric I have no doubt that you'll be able to tame her," Carol said childishly.

"You say the most ridiculous things. Anyway, Laine's the great tamer, not me! By the way, that music is getting on my nerves. Let's go for a walk."

"No, I don't think so. Why not just stay here?"

"Because I want to go for a walk," he said shortly, "and I want you to come with me."

"Don't you have your own affairs to worry about?" she asked in a sharp voice. "There's absolutely nothing we have to talk about that we can't discuss right here on the veranda. Every time you see me you do your best to—to—unsettle me!"

"There are some things that can't be said on the veranda." There was light mockery in his voice. "Come." She raised her shoulders and then let them drop and went with him towards the steps.

When they were in the garden he said, "Are you still going to try and convince me that you're happy?"

"Yes. I'm *madly* happy!"

"And—*madly* in love with Laine?"

"Yes. You took the words right out of my mouth."

"I don't believe it." His voice was full of the irony of disbelief.

"I don't care what you believe. It's the truth." She was afraid she was going to cry, and she did not want Michael to see her cry.

"The trouble with you," he said, "is that you're going to care when it's too late, Carol."

115

"Well, that's my problem," she replied, using the very words Laine had spoken to her.

They began to walk on again. The grass was wet with dew and she could feel the dampness penetrating the soles of her shoes. The air was filled with scents and, overhead, the stars looked almost terrifying because they were so low. Behind them, Laine's house appeared low and mysterious.

"Have you heard from your father? Laine writes to him, doesn't he?"

Clutching at this ordinary, conventional remark, Carol said, "Yes. I have had two letters—one from my father and one from my grandmother."

"Have you written to tell them how things are with you?"

She stopped walking to answer him and her voice contained resentment. "No. No, I haven't, but this has absolutely nothing to do with—with not being happy here here or a ring not being *here*," she lifted her left hand. "It's just that I haven't had the time to write. I've been too busy—settling in." She seemed to be reassuring herself.

"I can't stand by and see you throw your life away on Laine Mulholland," his voice was harsh.

"You always run him down, don't you?" she replied bitterly. "Every time. You never fail." The darkness held the sound of her long quivering breath.

He threw his cigarette away and trod on it savagely, then to her shocked surprise he took her by the shoulders, his hands dropped to her arms and she could hear his quickened breathing. "Look, Carol, I'm not running him down. He is what he is, and it has nothing to do with me. It's you I'm concerned about. Can't you see this? You don't fit in with the Mulhollands. Laine is cut out for this place, regardless of what his mother says. In a way this whole Valley was made for him. He seems to go with the solitude—the hills, his animals, but *you*, if you marry him, you're going to have to live here, day in and day out, listening to him strumming away at that piano, seeking some elusive lost chord or other and then, when he can't find it, he'll go into the lions' den to terrify you and to perfect his big act. You're going to be trapped here, alone with him, and there'll be nothing you can do about it— after you're married to the man. Even Mrs. Mulholland will have gone. For that matter, not that it counts for

116

much, so will I. Laine is a man of moods. To my mind, it's something much more serious than just moodiness. For this reason, my dear girl, he has no close friends. I suppose one could say that Laine is essentially a lonely man—but he enjoys his loneliness."

"You might be a qualified engineer," she said angrily, "but don't try to arrange my life, or Laine's. This is something you are *not* qualified to do."

His arms fell away and he walked away from her, then, turning abruptly, he came back to where she stood. "Look," he said again, and she hardly recognised the tone of his voice, "just because you happened to write a lot of girlish, infatuated letters to Mulholland it doesn't necessarily follow that you have to marry him. Can't you get this into your head?"

"I'm marrying him because I love him," she said wildly. "*Love him*. Can't you understand this? Isn't that reason enough?"

"It's not true," something shrieked inside her, because of course she knew. She had known it at the Marine Terminal when she had heard a voice saying, "Miss—Tracey?"

Between them now there was a silence which was becoming unbearable. He was the first to recover. "All right," he said, "all right," but he did not say it in his voice. It was just as though he had allowed the words to escape on a long breath. "In that case, there's nothing more to be said, is there?" His voice was normal now, but it was like ice.

"It's taken you a long time to find that out." She struggled to keep the tears from coming. "That's what I've been trying to tell you all evening. There's nothing more to be said."

"Then let's go back, shall we?"

When they went back into the living-room Laine went on playing.

"I have an invitation to convey to you," said Michael, looking down at Maxine who was stretched out on the floor with her wonderful red head in the centre of the tawny ears of the lion skin.

Laine lowered his playing a little but did not stop.

"And that is?" Maxine lifted eyes which were the colour of those glaring up at them from the pelt.

117

"An invitation to get in the car and come home."

She got to her feet, deliberately taking her time. "And what if I'm not ready?"

"Then I'll leave you to walk."

Laine stopped playing and closed the lid and then sat looking at the small scars on the back of his hands. He looked up, "Have one for the road first," he said, "before you go." He got up and went to the great African drum which served as a bar top and a kind of cellaret.

With his usual graceful movements he began pouring drinks, taking his time to ensure that no drop was spilled. Then he picked up two glasses and walked towards Carol and Maxine while Michael went for the other two which were still on the drum.

"Well," he said, after he had given one to Laine and kept one for himself, "here's mud in your eye!" Looking at him, Carol saw that there was a new hard look in his green eyes and in the expression of his mouth she felt a hopeless pang of love. Maybe, she thought, he was jealous of Laine and Maxine. And in a way he had every reason to be, so far as Maxine was concerned. Laine was concentrating on spinning an ice cube in his drink with a finger.

"Don't look at Michael like that, Carol darling," Maxine shocked her by saying. "One would honestly think you were in love with him!"

Carol felt the colour drain from her face and she had to adjust herself quickly.

"That's surely the joke of the week," she said, and knew that her effort to sound casually off-hand had fallen hopelessly short. ,

Laine looked at Michael. "Have another one for the road," he said, going towards the cellaret, but Michael stopped him. "No, thank you. My quota was reached some time ago." Laine, however, poured himself one and he tilted his head and poured the neat drink down his throat.

When Maxine and Michael were ready to leave, Laine's hand moved as though to circle Carol's waist, but with a small movement she avoided him. When she darted a quick look in Michael's direction he met her eyes briefly in a private look, then he took the final long swallow which drained his glass and placed it back on the drum.

They went out to the veranda and Laine led the way to the steps towards the garden where the scene of shifting shadows produced a feeling of intense loneliness for Carol.

"Oh, Laine, don't forget about tomorrow, will you? Let me know at the crack of dawn itself whether we're going or not," said Maxine, then she turned and placed her fingers on Michael's arm. "By the way, my sweet, you might well be losing your neighbour tomorrow. Dallas wants Laine to take her home tomorrow so that her doctor can prescribe some more pills for her, and she wants me to go with them."

"I see." Michael gave her a sharp look. "Well, dear girl, my role is a very simple one. I'll just carry on without my neighbour." His voice conveyed nothing. "I know you well enough to realise that you always finish what you begin, and for that reason you'll be back. Right?"

"I'll let you know as soon as I've discussed the position with Mother myself." Laine sounded slightly irritated. "Personally, I can't see the reason for it. Why can't she wait until the end of the week?"

"Because she can't sleep. I told you what she said. Don't be unreasonable. After all, Dallas has been absolutely uprooted, you know, and she's desperately unhappy about things." Maxine went towards the door which Michael was holding open for her, and when she was seated he went round to the driver's side and got in beside her and started the engine immediately. The car revved aggressively before he set it in motion and Carol and Laine had to step back quickly.

"Good night," Maxine called, from her open window.

The red tail-lights headed in the direction of the bridge and Laine said, "He might have been more civil, I think."

"What is this I hear about—your mother?" Carol asked, and heard him mutter a curse beneath his breath. He took her hand at the steps and when they were at the top he said, "Mother had a chat with Maxine tonight. It appears that she's not sleeping at night and her pills have run out. She wants to go home tomorrow so that she can see her doctor."

"And she wants Maxine to go with her?"

He shrugged. "Certain things ought to be explained, Carol. Underneath, Mother is often scheming and unfeeling. As you say, she wants Maxine to go with her." His tone was gentle. "I'm sorry about this. You won't

119

mind terribly much, will you, should we decide to go? We'll only be away a day." He held her with one arm, while with his free arm he stroked her wrist. "I suppose it's only fair to make allowances for Mother, at this stage. This is simply a—personal thing, Carol. She had known Maxine for a long time." Carol knew that he was weighing his words carefully.

"What is the position, then? Does your mother mean to come back here after the consultation?"

"Yes, of course. As I explained, we'd be away for the day, that's all. We'd be back in time for dinner. In any case, I don't think you'd enjoy the trip very much, under the circumstances. It simply means, Carol, that you'll be left here for the day by yourself."

"That will be quite all right." For his sake, she tried to make it sound all right—as if she meant it. "I quite understand the position, Laine."

"I'm glad of that," he said softly. "It will be our turn next week. I have to be in town on business—and we'll combine business with pleasure. Mother will be asked to stay here while you choose your ring. In fact, we will choose the two rings at the same time. I don't see any reason for postponing our marriage, do you?"

He turned her round to face him. "It's not working out with Mother here—the sooner she is free to go home, the better. Presently I'll go to her room and tell her it will be all right about the trip tomorrow. If she's unable to sleep at night, well then she must still be awake. You agree with me about—not waiting, don't you?"

"Yes." Her heart was pounding slowly.

"In that case, you'll write to your father and tell him that we're to be married? Perhaps if you're not too tired you can write it tonight and I'll post it in town tomorrow."

"Yes," she whispered again. "I'll write—before I go to bed."

As his lips sought hers she closed her eyes against the tears.

CHAPTER EIGHT

SHE watched them the next morning as the car drove away —Maxine Mason in front with Laine, which was more than she, Carol Tracey, had been able to do on her way to the Valley.

For some time afterwards she remained standing just where she was, staring at the hills, her mind a dull blank. Somewhere encased by those hills was Laine's car bearing away the letter which she had written to her father the night before. In the letter she had told him that she and Laine would be married as soon as they were able to make the necessary arrangements.

As she thought about it she gave way to the awful depression which had been waiting to take command of all her senses and she wondered frantically how she was going to fill in the hours with nothing to do but *think* while Laine was away.

It was only after she had finished her morning tea that the idea of sunbathing at the river came to her, so she changed into the brief bikini which she had brought with her but had not dared to wear and probably never would wear again, even after she was married. Then she slipped into a pair of slacks and a tangerine shirt and nudged her feet into some Indian sandals. Draping a towel over her arm, she started to walk to an inviting point of the river, walking along the grassy bank where she could look down into the water which was very clear and did not hide the smooth, rounded boulders beneath it.

Once she had reached her intended spot, a flat smooth rock, she stripped down to her bikini, folded her slacks and shirt and placed them to one side of the large rock, then she lay on her back, squinting through her fingers at the sky and feeling the warmth of the stone on her back until the beating sun caused her to turn over on her stomach. She allowed one arm to dangle idly in the water, splaying her fingers so that they caught the water and caused it to build up and gush through them in a little silvery wake.

She put her hands behind her back and undid the straps of her bra so that she would tan evenly, and for a while was oblivious to everything but the sun biting into the skin of her back and upon her arms and the backs of her legs. Then, like a sudden thunderbolt, the impact of her position here at the Valley hit her and her eyes closed. Very softly she began to weep as all the hurt, disappointment and bewilderment had its brutal way with her. It was almost impossible for her to believe that she had landed herself in this situation—so young and with all her hopes dashed to the ground.

She suffered agonisingly over what a change of decision on her part would do to three people—her father, her grandmother and Laine Mulholland, because although he did not seem to need her here in this Valley he certainly showed no signs of regretting his proposal of marriage. It was only now that she realised that her courtship with Laine had only been something which bordered between reality and fantasy and a confused succession of letters where nothing conformed to the ordinary course of nature, and before she had realised quite what was happening to her it was too late to turn back—to go back on her word. Her grandmother had, by then, sold the house. It was taken for granted that Carol was deliriously happy and longing to get to her Laine Mulholland in South Africa.

"Carol?" The sound of Michael Copeland's voice caused her to jump and she caught her breath, stifling her weeping. "Ramesh told me where to find you," he said, but still she did not move, and then she was aware of him coming down the bank towards her, dislodging small boulders and shale beneath his feet on his way to the rock.

"Carol?" he said again, but still she did not move, hating him with a nerve-tearing intensity for coming upon her like this, and then he was beside her. Her eyes opened and in despair she could see the two fragile straps of her bra straggling near the surface of the water. She caught her breath when Michael, squatting next to her, took the straps and fastened them across the warm flesh of her back. "It's wrong to go about this," he said, "half-naked, down here at the river."

"Is it?" She mumbled the words in despair. "What difference can it possibly make? The African girls wear less."

"That doesn't come into it. They've been doing it for generations in this Valley and they certainly won't respect *you* for doing it."

122

Carol had the feeling that she just wanted to die there and then, with Michael next to her, because she no longer had the strength to go on with this thing.

"Turn over," he was saying gently. "I want to talk to you, and I can't talk to the back of your head."

"I don't want to talk," she told him, praying for her cheeks to dry.

"You're crying, aren't you?" There was a pause, and then she said, her voice stronger, "No."

"Well, look at me then, Carol," he repeated, and suddenly he gathered her body up and turned her over. The contact with him stunned her as though she had received a blow and all the strength that she had struggled to regain went out of her.

"I'm not crying," she whispered, and tried to open her eyes to prove her point, but the tears and the sun caused her to close them again. She knew that he was bending over her and that he was waiting for her lashes to uncover her eyes, and then, when they did, she watched him as he shadowed her face from the harsh glare with his hand.

His eyes were very slightly narrowed and she gazed at him with wonder as they opened widely, and he continued just to look at her while she lay back, breathing deeply and fully aware of the fact that his own breath was coming fast.

There was a strange look of purity on his face and in the expression of his green eyes—it was a kind of wholesome freedom from all physical and moral corruption, she thought. Her soul was wrapped in distress and she yearned to touch him as the desolation of her life, when he left, swept over her.

He began to trace his fingers beneath her eyes, along her cheekbones, and she knew with a sickening despair that her cheeks were still wet.

"Are you going to tell me that you're jealous because Maxine went with the Mulhollands?" His jaw was tight. "Are you, Carol? Are you jealous, after all?"

She reacted swiftly and sat up to stop him from saying such things. "You keep finding me, don't you?" she said, her voice coming on a long breath, "wherever I go. Are you jealous too? Because Maxine has left you?"

"You're not making sense," he said quickly, "and we'll delete her name from the conversation, so far as my name is concerned."

123

"Suit yourself," Carol's voice was a gasp, as though it hurt her to use it, "but I wish you would leave me alone!"

Mercifully, the breeze lifted her hair and blew skeins of it across her face, and in between the tangle the tears began to spill out from her half-closed eyes. Michael made no effort to comfort or to calm her and he remained apparently unmoved—except for a look in his eyes which she could not see.

Suddenly she swept her hair back from her face with her two hands, the palms flaring out past her cheekbones to the tips of her wet eyes in a wild effort to sweep clean the traces of her tears.

"Please let me go," she said, trying to move, and he stood up first, then when she was standing he closed the small distance between them and his hands closed about her waist. "Carol, once and for all, are you going to tell me you're in love with Laine?"

"Yes." Her face now was impassive and motionless. He continued to hold her and, feeling his arms around her, she could think of nothing else.

They could hear the gentle rise and fall of the small rapids in the river and above it there was the mingling of their breaths. For a moment his arms tightened and he held her as if he would never let her go, then he dropped his arms and she watched him leave her, making his way across the water-wedged boulders towards the waving grass and warm rubble of sharp-edged rocks and ant-hills on the bank.

Without turning, he continued up the bank to where his Land-Rover was parked on the side of the road. He opened the door and eased himself behind the wheel. When he had driven away she stood still and then, covering her face with her hands, she cried bitterly, like a child.

The rest of the day was a dragging, miserable affair. After she had tried to eat the lunch which Ramesh had placed before her she sat on the veranda watching the visitors as they strolled past the cages or came up to the veranda for refreshments. Later, she tried to read, but that too was hopeless and she could not concentrate on the words.

Eventually, Ramesh turned on the reading lamps. Outside the air was heavy and laden with the damp scents of flowers, leaves and undergrowth laced with wood smoke and cooking meat from the compound.

When the telephone shrilled its coarse, country-sounding ring Carol started up and listened, with indrawn breath, while Ramesh answered it, then she heard his footsteps as he came to call her to the instrument.

It was Laine, and somehow his tension seemed to communicate itself to her across the wires. "Carol? Carol, Mother has met with a slight accident." He must have heard her breath over the wire because he went on quickly, "Now, don't be alarmed. It's nothing serious. She slipped and fell on the marble floor in the hall. It happened just as we got back from seeing her doctor in town."

"Is she badly hurt? In pain?" she asked.

"She's in pain, yes. Naturally she's in pain and she's badly shaken. As you are aware, Mother is pretty highly strung. However, it's not serious. There are no bones broken, no internal injuries—but she came down a smacker."

"I'm sorry," she murmured, and then waited for him to say something over the line which had suddenly deteriorated.

"I can hardly hear you," he said. "The line is poor and I had a devil of a job trying to get through in the first place. However, the position is this—I can't leave here. Mother is rather upset," he went on reasonably, but a great fear caught at Carol's throat, like a dog shaking a small animal.

Was she to stay here alone, then? In this loneliness? This vast, dark loneliness—with not even the sun to keep her company and the drums throbbing in the night—all night?

But she whispered, "Of course."

"Lift your voice," he said. "I can't hear you, Carol."

"I don't expect you to leave her," she shouted.

"Listen carefully, then, before we get cut off. The position is this—Maxine, who as you know acts as a nurse to a wealthy invalid, is still on leave. There are two of them, by the way, who share these duties. Well, Maxine is going to help Mother. Maxine's been *marvellous*, by the way. Simply taken everything into her own hands. Are you there?"

Carol slumped over the mouthpiece with an exaggerated sigh. "Yes."

"Well then, Maxine has phoned her aunt and uncle—the Masons—and you're expected there. Old Man Mason will be calling for you at any time, in fact. I couldn't get a line earlier to let you know."

This remark sent Carol's mind reeling. "Oh *no*! Oh no, Laine! I couldn't go to the Masons. I'd much rather stay here." When she thought about being Michael Copeland's neighbour *anything* was preferable to going to the Masons.

"For pity's sake, why?" Laine sounded irritable. "For your information, the Masons are charming. Now do listen to reason, Carol. I have no time to stand here trying to make you see sense. Try not to act like an unreasonable child."

She bent over a little, looking down at her feet, and a great tiredness washed over her, making her feel giddy.

"Are you there, Carol?"

"Yes, I am here, but you sound so ruthless when you talk like that. Why do you try to force me to do something I don't want to do? Surely I have *some* say?" Closing her eyes, she tried to visualise her grandmother's tastefully preserved, flat-fronted terrace house in South-West London, but she couldn't, and when she looked up the Balinese Dancer mocked her from her place on the wall.

"Nonsense! Oh, what utter nonsense you talk." His voice sent her thoughts staggering in a plunging shock of despair. "You will go to the Masons, and that's that. Unless something very unforeseen crops up, I'll be home tomorrow some time. I can't say, off-hand, what time— we'll have to sort things out this end, but at any rate, I'll keep in touch with you."

She knew it was useless to protest, so she said, "All right. I hope everything will be all right with your mother." She could not say, "Give her my love." Dallas Mulholland did not want that.

"Thank you, and—good night, Carol."

"Goodbye," she said, and before she removed the instrument from her ear she could hear the sound of his receiver being hastily dashed to its cradle, over and above the crackle of the line.

Old Man Mason, as Laine had referred to him, was not as old as Carol expected him to be, and she judged that he must have been good-looking in a slim, exciting fair way when he was a young man. He had a neat moustache and

126

his eyes, beneath the jaunty black beret he wore, were very blue and emphasised his light tan on a face considerably free from lines.

He greeted Carol cheerfully. "I'm Old Man Mason. I suppose Mulholland has explained everything to you. Do you know, why the devil I've always been called Old Man Mason I'm blowed if I know. So you're the girl from London, eh? What part? I've been in this country for—oh, close on thirty years."

Carol stood shyly beneath the Balinese Dancer. "I'm from Selwood Place, actually. Do you know it?"

"Selwood Place. Selwood Place? Can't say I do."

"Well, it's south-west," she told him, "almost on the line where Kensington and Chelsea join."

"Aah, now you're talking. Now you've set me thinking." He snapped his fingers. "Course I know it!" He had the direct drive of a schoolboy, although the resemblance ended there, and as he spoke about London Carol swallowed and smiled her far-away smile and agreed excitedly with him. He stopped suddenly. "Well then, where is this bag of yours?" He cleared his throat. "We'd better get back before Mrs. Mason has the police out looking for us."

Alice Mason was plump and round-faced and spoke with a slow slurring drawl which was very different from her husband's rather precise English. In a way, she was a disappointment. She was not the type of wife one would expect Old Man Mason to have chosen for himself. "What is this I hear about Laine Mulholland's old lady?" she asked. "Had a fall, hey? I can just imagine the scenes that are taking place there right now. Laine won't know whether he's coming or going."

"Oh, I don't know!" chipped in her husband. "All you women are very much the same, you know. You just go to pieces."

"Since when are you an expert on women?" Alice lifted her eyebrows above her glasses at him. Then she turned to Carol. "Did he tell you he comes from London, too?"

Carol glanced shyly at Mr. Mason. "Yes. Yes, he did. But you—you don't?"

"*I* don't. Sometimes I wish he would get back to blooming London." She laughed, discarding the words as nonsense. "Anyway, Maxine tells us that you're to have her room? Come along then, and I'll show you where it is.

I want you just to take us as you find us and make yourself at home."

"Thank you," murmured Carol.

The room was in keeping with the kind of house that it was—white-walled with a thatched roof and beams—and everything in it was floral. On one side, windows opened out to the long veranda and to a side garden on the other and, from where she stood, Carol could see the lights of the bungalow next door.

"You've met Michael Copeland, of course?" Alice Mason's eyebrows lifted in the direction of the lights opposite. "That's where he's staying while he's down here. The Taits, who normally live there, are on long leave, so it was arranged that Mike move into their bungalow. Their cook boy stayed on to look after Mike, but I might tell you, more often than not he eats here with us. I told him to come around after dinner tonight, as a matter of fact, but I didn't tell him you were here. In fact, I didn't know myself that you would be here. By the way," she went towards a chest of drawers, "you can make use of these drawers, and there is some hanging space in Maxine's wardrobe. We call this her room. She always comes to the Valley when she gets a big of time off. She's not fully trained, you know. That's why she took on this job. She looks so sophisticated, but she seems to fit in when she's here. She always seems a bit untamed to me. You should just see her with those lions of Laine's. She needs her head read, if you ask me—and so does he!"

Michael arrived after dinner when they were sitting on the veranda trying to make light conversation—but without much success.

The veranda light had been switched on and Carol saw his eyes narrow in puzzlement when he saw her. Alice Mason explained the position and he raised one brow and smiled indulgently. Then he lifted his shoulders. "I'll bet you never got round this much in London? Every time I see you it's in a different place." Carol was saved the necessity of having to answer him by the servant bringing coffee.

The two men spoke about the dam, but Carol noticed that there was a definite change in Michael's attitude towards her. He seemed to be doing his best to avoid looking at her directly and his handsome face was quiet.

Eventually Alice Mason cut into the conversation. "You men never stop talking about work, do you? Mike, why don't you take Carol for a little walk round the garden? You young people must get bored stiff here with nothing to do but to look at the dam and the hills and nothing to listen to but those nerve-racking drums."

"The drums seem to be much louder around the other side," ventured Carol. "They're much louder at Laine's." The idea of being alone with Michael, in the garden, disturbed her.

Alice Mason stood up. "Well, after you've had your little walk come back, and by that time I'll have some snacks and a nightcap on the table to round things off. If you'll excuse me, I'll go inside and start buttering some wafer biscuits and so on."

Carol looked up at her from a haze of anxiety. "Mrs. Mason," she got to her feet, "do let me help you, please!"

"Ach, nonsense. I don't need help. You go with Mike. I'm only going to put out some biscuits and cheese. There's nothing for you to do."

"Well, won't *you* come for a walk?" Carol looked down at Alex Mason, who was filling his pipe. When he had pressed the tobacco well down and lighted it he lifted his head. "I want to put the car away," he said. "It's still outside." He took his pipe from his mouth and pointed with it towards the rim of the hills. "Might get a storm in the night."

Far away, lightning flickered in the sky, in what must have been the direction of the sea, and yet there were no clouds in this part of the world.

"Have you noticed," he looked at Michael, "that some of the worst storms we get are right at the end of the summer, when the weather is cool? Extraordinary, don't you think? One would think it would be quite the reverse. The winter seems to be ushered in by a succession of electric storms which often give way to a three-day downpour, and before you know where you are you're in the middle of winter."

After he had gone Carol and Michael looked at each other silently and gravely before he said, "Well, there seems to be nothing for it but for me to take you for a walk."

"You don't have to," she said, with resentment. "I haven't come here to be entertained by you."

"Oh, rubbish! Come and listen to the nocturnal noises." She watched him getting up, then he came towards her and reached for her hand. "It will not only please Alice but it will also help to ease the unpleasant constraint between us. After all, we have to put up a front."

His mouth mocked her, but she allowed him to lead her out to the garden. She was aware of the heavy scent of some kind of flower and there was a coolness in the air which was being carried across the Valley from the river and the huge expanse of water which formed the dam. Although it was not hot, there was a peculiar electric feeling in the air—a feeling of tension, almost, that seemed to wrap itself around a person's forehead.

"So the Mulhollands have dumped you a second time?" he said, breaking the silence. "Tut, tut!" They walked across the lawn which was damp with the heavy dew of the year.

"That remark is completely unjustified," her voice was irritable. "You know what happened. You heard what Mrs. Mason said."

"Fall or no fall, you'll always take second place." He sounded immensely confident, she thought bitterly. "When it's not to his mother it will be to the animals, and when it's not to the animals it will be to the piano." He knew that he had the upper hand, as usual, she thought bitterly, and her steps faltered and then stopped.

"You encourage me immensely. If you don't mind, I'll go back. I didn't come out here to discuss Laine—or his mother. I suppose I should make allowances for you for taking your own jealousy out on me because *you* took second place, this morning, didn't you? When Maxine went away and left *you*."

He laughed. "Birds in the wilderness, eh? Well, you're quite wrong. I've got nothing to worry about in that direction. Leave my emotions out of it, Carol."

"Emotions!" It was her turn to give a scoffing laugh. "Are you capable of any kind of emotion? All you are capable of is sneering and jeering and—humiliating people. I feel jolly sorry, deep down, for Maxine Mason ,as a matter of fact."

"You're making yourself ridiculous, not me," the scorn in his voice stung her. "If you really believe that about me it shows an uncommon lack of understanding, on your part, of the opposite sex."

There was a short silence and then he said, very softly, "As a matter of fact, I feel sorry for Maxine Mason too, although perhaps not for the same reason as you do."

They walked on again in the direction of the dam which they could see glimmering beneath the stars. Although the drums were not so noticeable from this part of the Valley they could still hear them; muffled—but as urgent as ever.

As they turned to go back she looked at the flickering sky behind the dim outline of the hills. "Do you think there *will* be a storm," she asked, "later on, like Mr. Mason said?"

"Maybe." She knew he was looking down at her and she was acutely aware of him. "Why? Are you nervous?"

"You'd like me to say yes, wouldn't you?"

"And you would like *me* to say yes, wouldn't you?" he remarked placidly.

"Oh," she expelled a breath, "I can get nowhere with you!"

"Oh come, that's a bit sweeping, after all. You really haven't a clue just how far you could go with me."

It was while they were having their drinks and snacks on the veranda that they could see the visible electric discharge between the clouds and the hills, uneasily changing position and working itself higher into the sky. Every time the sky was lit up by a flash of diffused brightness or a zigzag line it revealed a thick congestion of cloud which was parted by this blinding energy without audible thunder.

"Looks like one of those wretched affairs that hit you about midnight and keep coming back and back," remarked Old Man Mason.

When the storm did hit the Valley it was twelve-thirty by Carol's watch. Ahead of the rain came the wind, a great shrieking force, and then the rain struck with remorseless splintering fury.

She got up and rushed to the window to close it and looked out into the moving darkness which was being lit, from time to time, by fierce flashes of lightning and which was now full of the splashing and kettle-drum noises of rain.

After she got back into bed she lay terrified, but trying to keep calm, as salvo after salvo of thunderbolts seemed to be thrown violently back and forth across the electrostatic-charged heavens. It was soon after one particularly loud clap of thunder that she heard Michael's voice at the window overlooking the veranda, and springing out of bed, she quickly reached for her short dressing-gown and slipped into it, terrified to get to the window before he was struck by lightning there and then.

When she opened the window the flashes of lightning showed him to be dripping water. Now that the window was not shut the sound of the rain was an awesome thing, and it seemed to be something uninterrupted by drops—a formation of water of equal depth and length. It was the kind of rain that would leave the flowers and leaves beneath it bruised and smashed to the ground. All round, the earth shone whenever lightning opened the black sky.

"What are you doing here?" Carol cringed from the window. "What on earth did you come out in *this* for? Do you want to get killed?" She stood to one side as he proceeded to hoist himself over the sill, then before he drew the curtains they stood aghast as a filament of lightning lit up the garden where a large tree could be seen surging against its roots in a squall of wind. Michael closed the window and flicked the curtains across.

"It will give you great satisfaction," he told her between small pants, "to hear that I couldn't rest over there knowing that you were probably alone—and scared. You must be scared, are you?"

"No," she lied. "Besides, I'll have to get used to it, won't I, if I'm going to live here?"

There was an explosion of fierce electrical energy, accompanied by a cacophony of ear-splitting thunderclaps in fast succession, interspersed with what appeared to be sheet, ribbon and fork lightning all at once, and it sent her running into his arms.

"Michael! Oh, Michael! Hold me!"

He cleared his throat, "Have you any idea what you're saying, I wonder?" he said before his arms closed about her. Oblivious to the rain on his coat, Carol clung to him, but presently he disengaged himself, though only to remove his coat, which he flung across one of the small cane chairs in the room before he folded her to him again.

"Don't tremble like that," he said, against her hair. "Don't tremble, Carol. It's all right, I tell you."

At this moment Alex Mason tapped on the door. "Are you all right," he called, "or would you like to come into our room?" Carol broke free and her hand flew to her mouth. "I'm all right, Mr. Mason, thank you."

"The lights are down, of course," he called out. "Light a candle."

"I—I have," she told him.

"Well, in any case, if you can't sleep, just come along to our room."

"No. No, I'll be fine, Mr. Mason, thank you."

After he had gone Carol looked at Michael aghast. "Oh! what if he'd come in?" she kept repeating. "Michael, what if he'd come in?"

She watched him sit down on one of the cane chairs and stretch his legs on the chair opposite, loosening his collar.

"You curl up on the bed so you can bury your face in your pillows," he said, as he saw her cringing from the flashes which seemed to be performing for them alone in the room.

With sporadic rumblings and diminishing flashes the storm showed signs of abating eventually, while a gentleness eased itself into the rain.

After a long time, Michael stood up. "I'd better be going now," he said, but he had no sooner got into his coat than the storm showed signs of returning with equal fury, accompanied by more lashing rain, but this time the attack was short-lived. In the end, the fury gave way to the rain.

"Thank you for coming," she said. "I *was* nervous."

In the flickering light of one candle their eyes met and clung together, and with quickened breath she watched his own drop to her mouth. It seemed natural to go into his arms. When she felt his mouth upon her own her senses reeled as, unresisting, she allowed him to kiss her as she had never been kissed before.

"I'm sorry," he said, letting her go. His voice had changed. In one easy movement he had slipped into his coat and out of the window.

"You'd better close your window," he said from the veranda, and then he was gone.

When she turned her eyes fell on his cigarette box and matches which he had forgotten to take with him.

"Michael," she whispered. "Oh, Michael! What have you done to me? What have I done to myself?"

CHAPTER NINE

A WATERY dawn broke and all the following day the rain fell in a never-ending undertone and sudden lakes sprang up. Everywhere, plants and foliage had been dragged from the walls and from the earth by the wind at the height of the storm.

Carol did not see anything of Michael, and she wondered whether he was working in this weather and if so, where. There was nothing for her to do at the Masons' except to sit on the veranda watching the slanting rain, and when she grew tired of this she went indoors nd curled herself up in a big chair in the lounge.

Her thoughts kept turning to Michael and the way in which she had allowed him to kiss her the night before, and she wondered how she would be able to face him again and how she would ever be able to submit to Laine's caresses—when the time came.

During the course of the morning Old Man Mason went out, but returned for lunch, and after the meal he put a match to the firewood which had been placed ready in the fireplace. Carol watched the panting flames as they began their licking and devouring of the logs, with their dragon-like flame tongues with the blue veins running through them.

"What do you think of the South African climate?" Mr. Mason asked. "Hot one minute, storming the next and now a cold, three-day downpour!"

Hiding her depression, she smiled at him. "Do you think it will last for three days?"

"It looks very much like what we call a set-in," he replied.

"You're going to need that marvellous fireplace, then."

In her present frame of mind, however, she thought, "Even the flames are writhing and tormented in this Valley of the Aloes."

"Well, I must go out again." Alex Mason nodded in the direction of the bookcase. "Help yourself to some books or magazines over there. Might be something to suit you. I'm blessed if I know, though."

"Thank you," she answered. "I'm sure to find something."

Alice Mason sat with her in the lounge, in the afternoon, her knitting needles clicking this way and that, and Carol felt that the day would never end.

"Michael might as well join us in a sundowner before the fire," Alice said, before dinner. "I've sent a message over to tell him that he's expected."

"I don't see why he can't have dinner with us," Old Man Mason said. "I don't know what has prevented him from popping over today."

"As a matter of fact, I told Johannes to tell Mike that he *is* expected here for dinner," Alice told him.

Michael, however, sent word back to say that, although he would join them in a drink in a few moments, he would not be staying for dinner, and Carol felt a sudden sense of grievance. When he arrived he accepted the drink which Alex gave him, said hello to Alice and nodded curtly in Carol's direction, then he chose a chair right away from her.

"What's your case, Michael Copeland?" Alice complained. "I'm not going to take no for an answer. You're staying for dinner and that's that. Johannes has set a place for you, and besides, I sent him back over to tell your cook not to prepare you anything. I said you'd given him the evening off."

"Translated," Michael said, smiling faintly, "that means that you're a very bossy woman!" He swirled his drink around in the glass, keeping his green eyes on it.

"Now you can see what *I* go through," Old Man Mason said, getting up to refill his glass. "You haven't a leg to stand on, man. Say yes and be finished with it. It will save a lot of trouble in the long run."

"We all go through it, some way or other." Michael lifted his eyes in Carol's direction, and her heart contracted when she saw the expression in them and the new hardness about his mouth.

"He's disgusted with me," she thought in despair. "He is egotistically aware that he draws me towards him—he kisses me like that and then despises me for not resisting him."

Some time later Alice said, "I want you to come and carve some meat for me, Alex. I don't want to bring it to the table—we had a calamity in the kitchen this afternoon. It's slightly sizzled."

"A bit of a burnt-offering, eh?" Old Man Mason got to his feet.

"May I help you, Mrs. Mason?" Carol's eyes roamed for some sign of escape.

"You sit right here and talk to Mike."

Then they were alone. The silence grew bigger and bigger with only the locking, devouring noises of the aloe-red dragons' tongues in the fireplace to break it.

Michael cleared his throat. "When do you expect Laine back?" He seemed to be concentrating on the shape of his glass and did not look up.

"Tomorrow, I think." Her voice was small.

"You'll be counting the hours, won't you?" He looked up, one eyebrow raised slightly, one corner of his mouth lifted slightly. The ripple in his tanned cheek deepened— but not because he was smiling.

She dropped her lashes and noticed furiously that the glass between her fingers was shaking, then, because it was empty anyway, she set it down next to her. It hit the table with a loud click.

"Well, won't you?" There was the sound of glass upon wood as he put his own glass down and then he came over to her. "Let me take your glass away from here before you knock it over."

She watched him as he gathered both glasses and went towards the small trolley next to the fireplace.

He came back. "So you have one more night—free—to enjoy by yourself? It's a pity that there won't be another storm, and the side-effects, to keep you amused, isn't it? Just the rain. However, you will doubtless find something else to supply the deficiency."

"I can't say that I found the storm—or the side-effects —amusing." Their gazes were linked now. "I—don't know how you can *say* that!" Her eyes were full of bewildered unhappiness.

"Of course," he went on, "there'll be more storms," and she wondered at the sarcastic hostility about him. "More storms—and then there will be—*Laine*, to see them through."

"Why are you like this?" Her voice broke. "I suppose you kissed me last night so that you could jeer at me after-

137

wards? So that you could bring your point home again? I don't give kisses easily—no matter what you think." She brushed her fingers across her eyes. "You're always insulting me."

"You leave me with very little alternative," his voice was cold, "and in future I should save your kisses only for the man you came here to give them to—the man you claim you love. You could quite easily give some guy the wrong impression. Fortunately, *I* take you with a pinch of salt. You have, as you put it yourself, merely succeeded in proving my point."

"Thank you," she gasped bitterly. "Thank you!"

"For what it's worth, you're very welcome."

"If I were a man," she stormed, "I would—I would— answer your insults with the blow of my fist!"

The door opened and Alice Mason came to tell them that she was about to serve dinner.

As soon as she could after dinner, Carol excused herself on the pretext that she was feeling tired and, for the benefit of the Masons, she made some sort of display of saying good night to Michael, but they looked at each other coldly, like strangers, withdrawn and aloof, but with an awareness of an event shared.

In the morning it was still pouring, and Laine rang early explaining that as the weather was so bad, and owing to the fact that she, Carol, was being cared for by the Masons, he would postpone his homecoming for yet another day. "I've phoned Ramesh," he said, "telling him when to expect us, and I'll pick you up at the Masons' tomorrow, some time. How are you?" and when she did not answer he went on, "It's most tantalising hearing you, but not seeing you." There was an undertone of irritation in his voice, but she had the feeling that he was smiling at the other end.

"I'm fine." Guiltily she tried to shake off the depression she felt, remembering how it used to be when, excitedly, she had opened Laine's letters back home.

It was soon after the telephone conversation with him that she decided to go back. She told herself that she would rather be alone than face Michael Copeland again— to have him so suffocatingly near. Her eyes travelled to the window and she could see the bungalow streaked and dampened by rain.

Alice Mason, of course, tried to talk her out of it. "What a crazy idea, Carol. Don't you *like* being with us?" Her voice was teasing but sympathetic, the kind of voice an older woman uses to a young girl, but her face looked hurt.

"No, it's not that, Mrs. Mason. Please believe me." Carol floundered miserably. "You've both been so kind to me."

"Well, if it's not that, what is it?" Alice looked at her guardedly.

"It's just—I—just want to get back, that's all. As a matter of fact I have—things to do. We're to be married soon and I still have some sewing I want to finish."

"But another day, Carol. Another day, that's all. And another night. Laine will most certainly be back tomorrow. Come on, stay, there's a good girl! Don't let me down. This weather is depressing enough without being on your own at Laine's place, with just the servants there. There won't even be any visitors there in his weather, you know. Alex will take you over in the car, later on, for your sewing. Besides, Laine will be mad with us, if we allow you to do this."

Carol's hazel eyes gave up and drowned. "Mrs. Mason, please—I have to go!"

"What is it? What's on your mind, Carol?"

Carol bit her lip and then, on a sudden impulse, she said, "I—I want to get away from Michael."

"So it's like that, is it?" The look Alice gave her was long and leisurely.

"He does his best to upset me. To—I find him very insulting. It's not what you think. I'll be glad when his work is finished at this place. I want to get settled, and with him about I'll never—I'll never be able to. I'll be perfectly all right at Laine's place. There's Ramesh—and the waiters and their wives. But I want you to know that I've honestly appreciated your kidness and this is—this decision of mine—has nothing to do with my stay in your charming home."

"It just concerns Michael Copeland who is next door," Alice said, and there was a little smile about the corners of her lips. Carol forced a small laugh.

"It sounds silly, I know, but—yes. I—honestly can't bear him."

"But he's really very nice," said Alice. "Still I can see what you mean. In fact, I had a feeling that something was wrong between you last night." She patted a cushion into place and moved an ash-tray to another table. "Your faces looked—well, what shall I say? They looked *closed*. Not only closed against us—but against each other. I asked myself, then—'what's going on around here between these two kids?' " Alice's voice was light enough, but there was a different look in her eyes.

"If only Maxine knew how I *detest* Michael Copeland," Carol said suddenly, "she wouldn't feel that there was any reason to keep digging at me—any reason to feel jealous . . ." Overcome by embarrassment, her voice petered out.

"Maxine—*jealous*?" For a moment Alice's expression was incredulous and then she laughed. "Oh, Carol! Maxine isn't jealous of Michael. That I can tell you, for sure."

A passion of rebellious restlessness took hold of Carol and she felt something going on inside her which was like a formless prayer. "Please let me get away from here, before I say anything more." She strained herself together. "Well, anyway, that's beside the point. I hope you won't mind if I leave," she said lamely. "I'd rather, if you don't mind—at the risk of—hurting you."

"Well, my dear, what else can I do about it? If you 'gotta go', you 'gotta go'. Isn't there a song like that, or something? I can see there's a hard vein of obstinacy beneath that boyishly slender exterior of yours, Carol."

During the morning Alex Mason came back from the small block of offices at the Dam and drove Carol back to Laine's. Outside, everything was grey and the surrounding hills were thickly veiled with mist and rain. Fortunately, but for one very short patch, the road was macadamised because it was just running water. Everywhere evidence of the storm revealed itself in no uncertain manner. Small trees were washed down by the river and caught between boulders and beneath the bridge. Dry, uprooted grass and snapped-off logs had also collected there and they were causing the water to swirl around them.

"This is nearly as bad as London on a rainy day, eh?" Alex Mason laughingly set Carol's case down in the hall. "Now, don't forget, young lady, we're on the phone, if you need us or if you decide to change your mind. Takes a bit of getting through, that's all—if you don't give up."

Now that she was back she wanted to say, "I've changed my mind—I'm frightened," but she was also feeling the first attack of humiliation stirred up by her consciousness of having made herself ridiculous. She realised, too, that in spite of Alice Mason's agreeable expression, she had hurt her.

So much seemed to have happened since Laine's telephone call that she was surprised to find it was only morning tea time when Ramesh brought a tray into the living-room. It seemed much, much later.

Thoughtfully, Ramesh had put a match to the fire, so she took some magazines and a pile of fragile lingerie, which she was supposed to be embroidering—just in case Alice Mason turned up unexpectedly—and sat in front of the fire.

Before lunch she strolled out to the veranda and was overwhelmed to see how much the water had risen, but later, when she showed her concern to Ramesh, he only laughed. "That is nothing, miss. Nothing." They stood regarding the river and the completely silent banks.

"It looks to me as if the river is going to burst its banks," she said. "I don't know how you can say it's nothing, Ramesh."

"No, no, miss." He laughed again. "It often comes up like this. Especially in the summer, miss. We get hard rains, then. This was a freak storm because it is not the time of the year for storms. It must be the atomic bomb. Everybody blames the atomic bomb for the weather." He pointed to the bridge. "You see, there is a lot of stuff caught there. Once that moves the water will start flowing properly again.

"Well, will it move?" she asked.

"Yes, miss, it will move. You'll see."

She had her lunch, curry and rice, which was a specialty of the tea-room, but there were no visitors there today to enjoy its spicy heat. Then she put on a mackintosh and waded outside in the garden without her shoes on.

The birds, in their cages, looked bedraggled and drained of all their exotic colour, but what concerned her most was the fact that the cage occupied by Dorcas and Selika was quite a bit under water and the two cheetahs had gone to a slightly higher level and were gazing past her with translucent eyes, writhing back their lips in the manner peculiar to these animals. They appeared to be hating every minute of the splintering grey rain.

When Ramesh shrugged this off too, Carol found herself becoming exasperated with him, and fuming inwardly she whispered to herself. "He thinks he knows everything. One day he'll get a surprise!"

"Have you been out to the cages to see for yourself?" she asked.

"No, miss."

"Well, Ramesh," she turned to him, an angry light in her eyes, "how do you *know* that the cheetahs are all right?"

"I'll go out just now, miss, but I know there's no danger. Mr. Mulholland often says he should have built higher up the river—up that end," he gesticulated to a point higher up, "to save this kind of trouble, but it is still safe, for all that. Sometimes, down the coast, all the rowing boats get washed away when the rivers come down in flood and the River Tea Gardens are often under water."

She widened her eyes. "Whole buildings, you mean, under water?"

He gave her an unruffled smile. "No, no, not whole buildings, miss. I mean the gardens and sometimes the floors inside. The people, they just move everything, all the chairs and tables. That's all."

Because of what Ramesh had said she was aware now of a new unaccountable fear—it was the fear of danger, fear of floods, fear for the lives of the animals—not to mention her own and the lives of the staff.

When Ramesh informed her, in the early part of the afternoon, that he was going to Aloeberg in the Land-Rover to collect the post and to pick up several parcels at the railway station she said, "But you won't be long, will you?" She was reluctant to tell him that she would be nervous without his presence now that the idea of flood-waters was beginning to grow stronger in her mind.

Ramesh lifted his disciplined white-clad shoulders. "I can't say how long, miss, but I will be back as soon as possible."

"You won't get cut off, will you? That's what's worrying me." She was thinking about the bridge and the causeway which they had crossed coming to the Valley.

"No. The water is definitely not high enough for that."

"I see. Well, you'd better go, then, hadn't you?" she said half impatiently. "The quicker you go, the quicker you'll be back."

The tempo of the rain increased in the late afternoon, hammering against the windows and gurgling through the down-pipes. In the distance, the dam was just a grey sheet meeting the sky, and the river, more swollen now, carried with it all the debris which it had accumulated on the way —branches, rocks, stones and mud from collapsing banks.

With a weakening kind of terror Carol's eyes flew to the ramp of the bridge which was very close to the surface of the water moving beneath it, thickened by debris and mud, and she longed for Ramesh to get back, for it was getting dark so early. The fear that she had managed to arrest, after he had gone, mounted in her, and when the telephone rang her hand automatically flew to her throat before she pulled herself together.

"That must be Laine," she said aloud, to calm herself. But it wasn't Laine—it was Michael.

"Old Man Mason tells me you walked out on them," he said, and she could hear the displeasure in his voice.

"I didn't walk out . . ." she began, but he cut her short. "Are you out of your mind? You can't stay there alone. It's no place for a girl on her own. I'm coming over."

"Don't you dare! I don't need you," her voice was choked. "If you're under the illusion that—that I need— amusing, then you're wrong. As you said, there'll be more storms, more rain, more wind—and there'll be *Laine*."

"Yes, there'll be Laine all right," his voice was sneering. "It's a pity, then, that he's not on the spot now, where he should be, isn't it? Just when you need him."

"When I want somebody on the spot," she cut in, "it certainly won't be you, so you have nothing to worry about. Now will you get off the line?"

"Certainly," he replied, and she heard the receiver being slammed down at the other end. She lifted her shoulders in a gesture of despair. "Oh, Ramesh, where are you? I can't stand much more of this."

She went out to the veranda and her muscles tightened when she saw that it was almost dark now. In a short while, she thought, the water would rise until it covered the shallow steps and then came swirling across the veranda into the tea-room, curio shop and Laine's house.

The very first time she had seen all this water, she remembered, she had expressed the fear that the dam might burst and with it the river, drowning and washing away everything in its way. Her breath caught in her throat as she remembered the cheetahs and, not even stopping to think about a coat, she ran outside. The rain lashed and clawed at her face like a wild thing and her hair was whipped streaming across her eyes and clung to her cheeks. She was crying now, softly and desperately, as though each whimper hurt.

Past the aviaries and the cages where the monkeys hunched themselves upon their perches; down two garden steps to a lower level of the garden towards where Dorcas and Selika must surely be trapped.

This was the danger spot. "Fancy putting cages here," she thought above her frenzy. "How stupid can some people get?"

In her panic, she had forgotten all about the keys, and with a loud cry of despair she turned to run back, through all the water, past the cages and the aviaries, and as she ran she tried to remember where she had seen the keys. Then thankfully she recalled to mind that they were all on a specially designed board in the small office next to the curio shop.

It took several moments for her to find the light switch and then to trace down the correct key with the wooden name-tag attached to it: CHEETAHS.

To Carol's inexperienced eyes, the scene near the cheetahs' cage was nothing short of chaotic. On one shallow terrace, directly behind the cage, there was a subsidence and a torrent was rushing through the fissure with considerable force, and once the first horror of discovery was gone she accepted with resignation and almost with exultation that she would have to release the cheetahs.

Then she was plunging in water towards the cage. She was shivering and cold and her fingers slipped and fumbled and she was terrified in case she dropped the key. She unlocked the padlock and, in a suspended moment of shock, remained standing just where she was until the achievement she felt slackened into sheer terror. Then, with more fumbling movements, she removed the padlock, pushed the door in slightly and took to her heels.

At the foot of the veranda steps Michael stood looking through the greyness before wading across to meet her, then in three more water-clogged movements he was by her side, supporting her.

She looked like a boy in her pants and sweater which clung to her body, with only her hair to show that she was a girl. Holding her streaming hair back from her face with both hands, she said, through teeth that chattered, "What do you want here? I told you not to come. I don't need you!" and as she spoke, she tried to push him away.

"Don't be a little fool," he shouted above the wind which was suddenly out of all control. "What the devil did you have to come back here for? What the devil were the Masons thinking about? Come here." He made to pick her up.

"Just don't touch me!" She was breathless from running and shivering violently. She lashed out at his face. "Don't you ever touch me again, Michael Copeland!"

"And you just keep your hands off my face, Carol Tracey," he replied through clenched teeth. His own hair was whipped across his forehead and his tanned face streamed water. "Let me help you, Carol. It will be all right in the house. The river's come up a bit, that's all."

"A bit?" She laughed hysterically. "Isn't that the understatement of the year? Shouldn't *you* be on the spot? Talk about Laine! What about your miserable old dam? It might burst, you know, and you might have to control it—just like you try to control everything else!"

He lifted her up and, childlike, she fought him as he picked his way through the swirling water. In the midst of all this confusion she had the sudden desire to laugh, and found herself thinking of Laine as he had walked up the steps after tantalising Lisa and how she had thought he looked as though he was taking part in a film. At this particular moment she had the craziest sensation that all this couldn't be true and that she herself was taking part in some gigantic motion picture.

145

Michael closed the hall door with his shoulder, shutting out the sound of the rain, then he put her on her feet where, reduced to tears, she stood against the wall.

"You're satisfied now, aren't you?" she gasped. "This is how you love to see me. Broken and smashed and . . ." She pushed her hair back from her face and found that her teeth where chattering beyond her control.

"And wet . . ." he finished for her. His eyes flickered over her.

"I suppose you're thinking this will serve the silly little gold-digger from London right, aren't you?"

"Shut up," he said, "and don't be so childish. I'm not thinking anything."

"That's priceless," she stormed, "coming from you, after you've told me, not once but several times than I'm just a kid. I have reason to be childish. Well, Michael Copeland, for your information, the kid has grown up, the hard way, and that must give you a lot of satisfaction, mustn't it? There now, are you satisfied?"

"If this is how you've grown up," he told her, "I'm not sure I like what I see. I almost think I preferred the kid to this—this witch of a woman. Now, let's cut out this non-sensical talk, shall we, and you go and change? I'm taking you back to my bungalow. You might as well know it, but Alex Mason and Alice were fool enough to go up to Aloe-berg this afternoon, and they haven't arrived back yet."

"I'm not coming back. I'd rather drown here!"

"Oh, for Pete's sake," he was thoroughly aroused now. "Do I have to strip you and change you myself? You're shivering to bits. I've told you, you're not staying here by yourself—not while *I'm* around. What the devil were you doing outside, anyway?"

She remembered then—and lost colour. "I let the cheetahs out. Dorcas and Selika."

His face registered blank surprise. "You *what*?" His eyes explored her face. "What the heck did you do that for?"

"Because the cage was under water. The floor was full of water. I didn't want them to drown."

"What else did you let go?"

"Nothing." She felt the faintness which comes from excessive fear and thought she was going to slide to the floor, useless as a rag doll.

146

"Did you see them go?" he asked.

"No, I didn't see them go, but I pushed the gate open and ran. I've lost the padlock." She looked down at her hands in dismay.

To her surprise he laughed, and his laughter made her nerve-racking experience sound like some absurd frolic in the rain.

"You little fool," he said, sobering. "Do you realise what you've done, I wonder?"

"Where will they go?" Her hazel eyes searched his.

"Where do you think? Into the bush, of course. The nature reserve is just across the way. It will give the ranger something to do when the weather clears up. When you've changed into some dry clothing, we'll go." He went towards the living-room. "In the meantime I'll pour us a couple of drinks—and by the way, I think Ramesh is back. That means the Masons might well be back too and you will be spared the sordid experience of staying in my bungalow."

"You can go . . ." she started to say, but he cut her short.

"I'll be in the living-room. *Waiting*." He lifted back the sleeve of his mackintosh and looked at his watch. "I'll give you exactly ten minutes, Carol!"

She drew a long quivering breath and was going to say something, but instead she turned and left him. While she rubbed herself down and changed into dry slacks and a sweater her limbs shook with a private life of their very own, a trembling, dancing life over which she had no control. Reluctantly, she went through to the living-room, trying to ignore this form of physical weakness.

Michael had taken off his coat and was standing at the glass doors looking out to black nothingness, a glass in his hand. "Well, they've gone, all right," he said, not turning.

"Gone? What are you talking about?" she asked.

"The cheetahs. I went outside with a torch—the cage was empty. There was no sign of them." He turned to look at her. "Where's your toothbrush?" he asked.

"I'm not coming with you to your bungalow." She spoke with cool determination and felt a shaft of self-satisfaction at her new-found control.

"We'll see about that," he said, passing her a drink, and when she took it from him she nearly dropped the glass as her fingers brushed his.

"If Ramesh is back," her voice was unsteady, "then the Masons will be back too."

"If they're not back you'll stay at my bungalow." He lifted his glass with the ice-cold, golden liquid to the light. "I'm not in the mood to go begging for a bed for you from anybody else. Don't worry," he gave her a sarcastic look, "I'll supply you with a key. My only regrets are, of course, that I'm not in a position to lay on a future mother-in-law and a poodle. You'll be quite alone with me."

At that moment Ramesh, slightly aloof, relaxed, imperturbable as usual, chose to enter the room. "I'm back, miss," he said, and it was as though he permitted his facial muscles to turn on the appropriate expression at the appropriate time. "I am very sorry I am late, but I stopped to help a stranded motorist who had water in the petrol, but I am going to order a nice mixed grill for you now."

"Miss Tracey will not be eating here, after all," said Michael, dangling the ignition keys, "so you needn't bother."

"I see. Very well, sir."

The Masons' house lay silent and rain-drenched and the African servant spoke to Michael in Zulu. "He says the Masons were on the telephone, some time ago, explaining that they would be late. So we'll go to my place. I guess we can rustle up enough to feed another mouth."

"You don't have to put yourself out. I'll stay here," Carol told him, "and in any case I'm not hungry. I'm sick and tired of being parked here, there and everywhere until somebody else claims me like a parcel from the lost goods office! For your information, I am quite capable of taking care of myself—and if it comes to that, of pleasing myself."

With an explosive movement she put her bag down and walked towards the fireplace where a roaring fire was waiting to welcome the owners of the house.

"Don't be a little fool. Do you think I'd rest, knowing that there are two cheetahs at large, and you were here—alone?" She knew that he was laughing at her. He seemed to think it was amusing! Involuntarily, however, her hazel eyes widened and flew to the windows. He laughed outright like a young boy and then he said, "Carol! Oh, Carol!"

She coloured a little and turned her back on him. "Leave me alone," she said, and her voice was low and tense. "Just leave me alone, that's all I ask. I've hated you since you met me at the Marine Terminal. Do you play cat and mouse with Maxine like this? I came in handy after she left, didn't I?" She struggled to keep the jealousy that churned in her heart out of her voice.

"Do you know," he said, jingling the money in his pocket, "I took a jolly dim view of Maxine. The arrangement is *always* that *I* take her back to town. That is, of course, when she hasn't used the car which is always at her disposal."

Carol moved away in irritation, knowing that he was jingling his money and doing and saying everything in his power to reduce her to vexation and perhaps tears, even.

"I have no doubt *you* drove her away," she could not resist telling him.

"That's what you think! Anyway, do let's go next door to my place and have a bite of supper, shall we? We'll light the candles and see what else we can do to create just that extra little touch of subtlety. I know there's a bottle of Nederburg somewhere." He picked up her bag and took her hand, which was small and clenched and which she immediately snatched away.

Her eyes were wide and furious and she started to say something, but the words faded out before she could find the strength to utter them. Instead she sighed, and it was like a long shivering sob. "How long is it before you leave this Valley?" she finally managed to ask.

"Don't worry," he told her, his mood changing. "I'm looking forward to it just as much, if not more, as you are looking forward to seeing me go."

She followed him to the door. "I'm tired of arguing with you," she said wearily, and noticed that her teeth were beginning to chatter again.

His bungalow was exactly the same plan as the one occupied by Alex and Alice Mason (and the one next door to that, as it so happened), but it was furnished differently. A fire was burning in the lounge.

"Let me help you off with your mackintosh," he said, "and I'll relieve you of your bag. Then I'll tell the cook to shake a leg."

"I've told you, I'm not hungry."

"That's too bad, because I'm starving."

While she merely picked at the food on her plate Michael made a big thing of eating, and this too was only done to annoy her, she knew.

"Let's take our coffee to the fire," he said at last, and stood up ready to help her with her chair. Then he took the tray which the African manservant had placed on a small side table and carried it through to the lounge.

"Black or white?" he asked over his shoulder after she had joined him.

"White, please." She walked towards an easy chair, but when he had poured her coffee he put it on the long table, where he had been pouring it, next to his own cup and saucer. He patted the sofa. "Come and sit here," he said, "it's much warmer."

"I'm quite all right where I am, thank you." She left the chair to come for her cup, her skin burnished and glowing in the light of the standard lamp which was placed to one side of the sofa.

In one easy movement he was beside her. "Carol," his voice had changed. It was not bantering any more. "How many men have you known?" His eyes searched her face. "What do you know about love, a baby like you? Or are you such an old hand at the love game that you're sure of yourself with Laine Mulholland?"

She was terrified in case he could hear her quickened breathing and the thudding of her heart, and most of all, that he would be able to read what was there written for him to see—in her eyes. When she felt that she could trust her voice she said, "When are you going to stop torturing me? It must give you satisfaction to see everything going wrong for me, mustn't it?"

"Don't make a speech," he said, very softly. "Just answer my question." He looked into her eyes and then he said, "Carol, I'm going to kiss you," and when he said it she knew, in cold analysis, that it would happen again and again if she was going to be thrown into Michael's company, because she wouldn't be able to help herself.

With a look in her eyes that was partly anticipation, partly fear, she thought, beneath a terrible avalanche of despair, "I'm tired of fighting this thing," but in a small voice she said, "No, don't. Don't you dare insult me again!"

"I'm not doing it to insult you."

"What are you doing it for, then?"

"In case you want me to," he told her, and then when he bent his dark head, seeking her lips, she said, "No, Michael—no!"

He drew back to look into her eyes. "No two people say 'no' *together*, Carol."

At last, when the kiss ended, she lifted her lashes and their eyes met in a long explorative look. "How could you?" Her voice was broken. "You devil! I'm trying to understand what it is you're trying to do to me."

And then, while she cried as though her heart would break, he stood outside on the veranda, looking at the rain and the darkness, and he made absolutely no attempt to console her.

When she had calmed down a little she could see the red waves of his cigarette and then taking her bag she found her way to the bathroom and tried to repair the damage to her face.

Afterwards, she went out to the veranda. "Will you take me home, please?"

For a moment she thought that he was going to touch her again, but instead he said, "I'm sorry, Carol."

She took a long, shuddering breath. "Yes, Michael. I'm sorry too." She felt so unhappy she could almost die of it. "I'm so tired," she whimpered, shivering. "So tired." She felt weary, beyond all weariness and just a little sick. "Ever since I came to this country I've had nothing but— trouble." She sniffed, like a little girl.

"I know." He sounded like an older brother. "I know, Carol. I'm sorry."

The lights of a car swept upwards searching the sky, like a searchlight, and then there was blackness again. A little later a car door banged.

"The Masons are back," he told her quietly.

"Well, take me there," she replied. "In the morning Laine will take me home."

"Home." He spoke the word flatly. "Home? You're going—home, then, to Laine. To Mulholland."

"Yes." She watched him as he tossed the glowing end of his cigarette into the rain. It bounced once, on the soggy lawn, and went out almost immediately.

"Okay," he said, "let's fetch your case." It was a voice she hardly recognised.

CHAPTER TEN

In the latter part of the morning Laine came for her.

The rain had given way to a fine, misty drizzle and the newspapers, which came down to Imihlaba by van, were full of the storm which was termed as a "freak" because of the particular time of the year. They told of "widespread rains" which appeared to have ushered in the cold weather at last and reported the swelling of rivers which had poured their muddy devastation into the sea.

Carol allowed the stranger in her own body to submit to Laine's kiss, and when he lifted his handsome head to look at her she fought to keep her tone normal as she asked after his mother.

"She'll be all right in a couple of days. It's just a case of resting up. Maxine has been wonderful, of course. It was a blessing that she had this spot of leave due to her." His brown eyes searched her face. "How did you go in the storm? Were you terribly nervous! I understand Aloeberg and the Imihlaba area got the brunt of it."

"Well," she smiled apologetically, "I'd be telling a fib if I said that I wasn't scared! You see, I thought the dam might burst and the river would break its banks and drown us all. Anyway, I suppose I've been broken in now. The next time it won't be so bad."

He looked faintly irritated. "For pity's sake, child, I think I remember telling you there was nothing to fear in that direction. It happens sometimes that the river rises, but not often."

Alice Mason come into the room at that moment. "Hullo," she said bluntly. "How's your mother? Has she come back with you?"

"As a matter of fact," Laine's face was withdrawn, "she won't be coming back!"

"Oh?" Carol had the uncomfortable feeling that Alice's "Oh?" was accompanied by a strange expression in her eyes.

Laine turned away, and Carol felt rebuffed for Alice's sake. "This means," he said to Carol, "we'll have to hustle up our marriage."

She was careful not to look at him. "Well, in that case, we'll have a lot to discuss when we get back. I must thank you, Mrs. Mason, for looking after me. Thank you so much —and Mr. Mason too, of course."

"Yes, Alice, that goes for me too." Laine turned to Alice with his faintly twisted and charming smile. "You've been most kind."

A watery sun struggled, for a moment, through the mist, burnishing tiny blades of silver in his dark hair.

On the way back in the car he said, "It's quite true about having to hasten the wedding day. Mother has refused, point-blank to come back."

Carol looked out of the window, looking suddenly a little older.

"It wouldn't do to show lack of—prudent conduct," he went on, "and so I'm going to ask Mike to lock up the Taits' bungalow and put up at my place until I can arrange for a special licence. It's the only thing I can do."

She swung around and faced him incredulously. "You're going to ask Mike—Michael Copeland—to stay at your place?"

"Yes. It's the only logical thing," he said, and she felt a wave of tumultuous anticipation.

"Couldn't you arrange something else?" she asked in a low voice.

"I very much doubt it." He took her hand. "I suppose the garden looks a mess?"

"Er yes. Yes, it most certainly does. There was water everywhere—and mud," she told him, wondering how on earth she was going to tell him about Dorcas and Selika.

He took his hand away and looked at her. "How do you know?" he asked. "You weren't here!"

"I—came back—for a while." She realised, with dread, that they were nearly there—and that the time to tell him was nearly here. "I was worried about the animals," she explained. "You'll see for yourself that the water came up very high. It was an awful experience."

He parked the car and opened the door. "But I told you there was nothing to worry about," he said, before he stepped out.

"Mind the mud," he told her shortly, as he opened her door. "Where the devil is Ramesh?"

"Laine," she tried again, "Laine . . ."

154

"Why the devil hasn't somebody cleared up all this mess?" He was making his way towards the veranda which still appeared to be ankle-deep in frayed thatch, sodden leaves and even small snapped-off twigs, and she was almost glad to see that nothing had been done to move it away. This was the evidence she needed. Perhaps it might give Laine some idea of what it had been like—the danger—what she had been through. It would be easier for him to understand about Dorcas and Selika now.

He turned to look at her. "Don't fuss about your case. Ramesh will fetch it. Come and have a look around the place with me." She stood still.

"Laine, I have something awful to tell you. I let Dorcas and Selika go. I thought they were going to be drowned, so I . . ." When she saw the expression on his face she swallowed and stopped. This was going to be ten times worse than she had imagined.

"Go on," he said. "If you have something else to tell me, then for heaven's sake get on with it."

"That's all," she said, lifting her shoulders in a gesture of despair. "Isn't that enough?" She drew a breath. "I unlocked the gate and when I'd taken off the padlock I pushed it open and ran back to the house . . ." She broke off again as she saw his face freezing on an expression of shocked disbelief. "You *what*? You can't possibly mean this, Carol?"

"Can't you see, Laine? I was petrified. I didn't know where to turn. I thought of all these animals at the mercy of the floods——"

His lips flattened against his teeth. "Floods? What floods? The river was temporarily dammed by wash-away trees, caught between the boulders and beneath the bridge, and you call that a *flood*? Don't talk about things you don't understand. Have you taken leave of your senses? You were supposed to be at the Masons'. What were you doing back here—at the height of the rain? Ramesh knows how to run this show. What does a twenty-year-old girl, a Londoner at that, know about conditions here? Where was Ramesh, anyway? What was he thinking about?" He clapped himself on the forehead with the palm of his hand. "Do you realise what you've done, Carol?" She heard his breath explode from his lungs. "But no, how could you? Maxine was right . . ."

Even as he spoke he was moving in the direction of the cages and helplessly she watched him, then she began to walk slowly behind him in disgrace.

"Oh, please, God," she found herself praying, "*please*, I beg of you, I beseech of you, let Dorcas and Selika be back in their cages. Let somebody have recaptured them. Let a miracle have happened!"

The gate of the cage had been closed, presumably by Ramesh, but it was not locked. Carol watched with wide frightened eyes as Laine flung it open and then, stooping his head, he went into the cage—but they both knew it was hopeless. The animals had gone. One look had confirmed it.

He stood perfectly still, looking at the floor with a kind of anguish, his hands hanging at his sides, the fingers limp, and from where she stood Carol could see that he was breathing quickly, as though he was having difficulty. He rubbed a hand across his eyes before he came out.

"You little fool," he said quietly, in that slow perfect way he had of speaking. He presented a face that was angry, alien—without understanding. "What a stupid, childish thing to do. Do you realise what this means to me?" He turned away from her, scanning the other cages. "But of course you don't. How could you? I was a fool to believe you could ever understand." He wrenched off his cravat. "Exactly what happened?"

A huge exhaustion settled on her. "I thought I was doing the right thing. I thought I was *saving* them. You don't think I'd have done this on purpose, do you?"

He ignored her question. "And while all this—*saving*—was going on Ramesh was apparently providentially stricken with blindness—he saw *nothing*. He heard nothing. Where was he?"

"He had gone to Aloeberg—for the post." Because she couldn't help it, she began to cry into her hands.

"What the devil are you crying for?" he snapped. "It's too late in the day to start crying, Carol."

"But if only you could understand. If only you would *try* to see things the way I did!" She tried to touch him, but he flung himself away from her.

"Aah," he said, "let's not go on with it." He turned away and she stood helplessly watching him making his way towards the house, and she had a peculiar feeling that

156

she was going to fall apart. The violence of Laine's temper had stunned her.

At last she let her breath out through clenched teeth. "All *right*! *All right:* Well, Laine Mulholland," she said aloud, "you won't have to get Mike to put up at your place. You won't have to worry about lack of prudent conduct—because I'm leaving here. Now! This minute!"

She went back to the house and straight to her room where she immediately started to pack. In the background she could hear Laine's voice and then Ramesh as he tried to get a word in here and there. A little while later she heard the Land-Rover roaring off, and then there was silence.

When everything was packed she changed into a light, moonlight grey suit and checked the contents of her handbag, sorting her papers and her money and then she went out to the veranda. The car park for visitors was empty, but there was a light delivery van which had come down to Imihlaba with cigarettes for the tea-room. Ramesh was on the visitors' side of the veranda checking a document while the driver of the van sat at one of the small tables, a tray of tea-things and toasted sandwiches in front of him.

Carol went through the wrought-iron gates and walked over to Ramesh. "Where is Mr. Mulholland?" she asked him. "I heard him go out in the Land-Rover." She spoke quickly, tense with emotion.

"He has gone to the nature reserve, miss, to speak to the ranger about setting traps."

She felt inexplicably sick. "Setting traps? To—*kill* the animals, you mean? Dorcas and Selika?" Dismay darkened her eyes.

Ramesh laughed with light derision. "No, no, not to *kill* the animals, miss. To *catch them*!"

Something like hope came back into her face. "You think they will catch them, then?"

"I don't know, miss. If Mr. Mulholland has anything to do with it he will catch them with his bare hands. He is very cross."

She looked at him searchingly. "I'm sorry, Ramesh. I got you into trouble, didn't I? I heard him shouting."

Without looking at her he said, "It's nothing. It will pass. Don't worry, miss." He made to move away. "I must just give this to the driver of the van. Excuse me, please."

"Ramesh!" He turned at the tone of her voice and came back to where she was standing.

"How can I get away?" she asked.

His eyes took in her light woollen suit. "Away?"

"Yes. Can you help me? I don't quite know what to do. There are no buses, no trains—nothing! Do you think the driver over there will take me?"

"Where do you want to go, miss?"

"Well, anywhere. Where is *he* going?" She drew a deep breath and looked at him unflinchingly. "Is he going to Durban?"

"He has come from Durban, miss."

"Then please ask him, Ramesh. You see, I can't possibly marry Mr. Mulholland. I've written a note, so you won't have to explain anything. Just help me to get away!"

"There will be more trouble for me when Mr. Mulholland gets back," he told her, and she looked at him through a haze of anxiety. "Then you won't help me?"

He hesitated for only a second. "I'll ask him," he said quietly, and went to speak to the driver, who was young and lean, and had a typical "commercial traveller" look about him.

The young man listened, inclining his head a little and drinking his tea all the time Ramesh was talking.

Then, without looking up, he set his cup back in the saucer with a sharp porcelain-to-porcelain blow, fiddled around in his pockets for his cigarettes, lit one, and only then did he raise his head to look in Carol's direction. He stretched one dark, slimly trousered leg out to one side of the table. "Okay," he said across the veranda, "I'm leaving now—if you're ready."

"Thank you." She tried to smile at him, but she felt nervous of the young, sarcastic hostility about him.

Ramesh took her blue cases outside to the van and she followed him, but not before she had checked the room to see that nothing was being left behind. She did not want to leave any trace of herself in this room which Laine had prepared for her and which she hoped never to see again.

Outside, she said, "Thank you, Ramesh. You've been so kind to me. I'm sorry it has to be like this."

"I understand, miss. You are not for Mr. Mulholland. You are more for Mr. Copeland's type."

"Now why did you have to say that?" she asked sadly, but she was trying to smile through her tears.

The driver closed the rear doors of the van, shutting her luggage from sight. "Okay," he said. "You ready?"

"Goodbye, Ramesh."

"Goodbye, miss."

She got in beside the young man and Ramesh closed the door.

"I'm very grateful to you," she said, glancing at the bored young face next to her.

"Don't be," he said, "it's on the house. You don't have to thank me." He turned his head to look at her and a faint smile tugged at his mouth. "In any case, you might as well know that I'm actuated solely by selfish motives."

She flushed, and he went on, "I'd be a mug not to give a girl like you a lift, wouldn't I?"

Sensitive to everything, now that she was leaving, she was aware of the scents of rained-on earth, wet plants, the change in the light and the new strengthening of the sun as it tried to have its way with the low-lying clouds.

She told herself that what was happening to her could not happen again. She had glimpsed at something that would fade, like a snapshot, in the years to come.

The walls of Laine's home surged under her wet eyes and, in the distance, the dam tilted into the sky. She could not see the line of thatched-roofed bungalows, belonging to the Department of Water Affairs, but something told her that she would never think of them again without a never-absent heartache.

"You been on holiday down here?" The young commercial traveller drove fast; nervously, but well.

She came up for air. "I——" She looked at him, trying to get her thoughts back into some kind of shape.

"Running away, eh?" He grinned, not taking his eyes from the road, and she noticed his shining dark hair, cut in the latest style, his blunt eyelashes and the way he seemed to wear his face with the air of negligence which came from being sure that he was young and "with it".

She did not answer and, sensing her scrutiny, he turned to look at her. "Had enough?"

"If only you knew how miserable I am," she told him, trying to stop biting her lips, "you wouldn't joke about it. I've made such a—mess of things. I don't know where to turn."

"That laa-dee-dah accent," he said, "I like it. What are you—American?"

She gave him an impatient little smile. "Oh, for goodness' sake, do *I* sound like an American?"

"I don't know. That's what I'm asking you!"

"I'm from England."

"I had an ancestor from England," he told her, smiling. "What's he done to you, this guy? This Mulholland bloke. It must be him. Has he been trying his hand at cradle-snatching?"

They had crossed the causeway and had started the long climb. The Valley started to fall away like an enormous artistically crude canvas. "I have to give this old crate a burst to get up out of here," he said. "She's playing up—overheating."

Carol felt tired and shaken and was aware of a cold, shivering feeling in her back. Her head was aching slightly and it felt hot.

"Where are you going to in Durban?"

"I don't know," she replied softly.

"What I mean is—are you going to friends, ma'am?"

"No."

"Where am I to drop you, then?"

"Are you going near the Marine Parade? That's about the only place I know. There are hotels there, at least." She yawned, thinking how awful she felt.

"Baby, the hotels on the beach front cost money. Plenty of money. It's only fair to tell you. Have *you* got money?"

"I'm all right," she said, "although I haven't a clue about your money. I've still got to work that one out."

"It's easy enough," he told her. "Look, I could take you to my old lady, if you'd feel better—until you sort yourself out."

"Thank you, you're very kind, but honestly, I'll manage."

"Are you going to go back to England?" he asked.

"I don't know. I'm still in the planning stage, if you know what I mean. I might try to get work."

160

"What's your name?"

"Carol Tracey. I'm sorry, I should have told you." She tried to smile.

"Mine is Roger Thesen. I think I deserve a date, after all this. Don't you?"

Her smile widened. "I don't think I'd be very good company."

"Why not leave that for me to decide?" He turned again, so that he could look into her eyes, and she saw that his own were frankly admiring, but teasing.

She laughed softly, blinking her eyes in the slow way she had and shaking her hair. "Let me sort myself out, please." She became sober. "It's not just a case of off with one man and on with the next. I honestly have a lot on my mind . . . a strange country, strange money, funny languages—I don't know a soul."

"You know me."

"Yes." There was a small silence, and then she said, "You've been very kind to me, thank you."

He laughed. "Don't thank me—until there's something to thank me for. I haven't got you out of here yet." Then he braked suddenly, cursing madly, and she looked through the windscreen to see what it was that had made him do this.

Her eyes widened as she saw a huge bull, its rust-brown coat catching the watery sun, standing in the centre of the road, and then Roger swore again as the van stalled.

"If it's not ruddy goats, it's something else," he said, and then they both laughed as a rickety horse-drawn cart full of goats came round the blind bend just ahead.

He stopped laughing. "It's no laughing matter," he told her. "I didn't want the old crate to stall. Like I told you, she's heating and I'm going to have a job getting her started again."

She looked at the bull with a faint frown. "I can't say I'm partial to bulls. I hope he decides to move on."

"He'll move on if somebody chases him," Roger said. "Why don't you get out and do the necessary? I forgot to tell you, but I'm not strong. I've got a bad heart, or something." They laughed together, then he started to try the engine and the irritation he was obviously feeling had begun to work itself into his eyes. "She'll have to go in for a service," he said. "I've had this." He used a very bad word and Carol tried not to flinch openly.

"Are we stuck?" She was oppressed by a sensation of alarm.

"We aren't stuck, no, but she'll have to cool down. This is a difficult climb if you have this sort of trouble. I'll have a smoke." He settled himself and reached for his cigarettes. "You want one?" He held out a packet, shaking one out.

"No, thank you, I don't smoke."

He gave her a grin. "Well, how about that?"

A car passed them, hooting as it did so, then drew over to the side of the road right near the bull, and Carol was swept by a surge of dismay when she saw that it was Laine.

"Oh—oh!" Roger sat back, with his eyes half closed and his head tipped back, and started to blow smoke rings. "You're in trouble, girl."

"It looks like it," her voice was small. "What am I to do?"

They watched Laine get out and, completely oblivious to the bull who had now decided to lumber to the other side of the road, walk the few paces back to where the van was parked. He came round to Carol's side, and although his face was hard, his voice was cool. "What the devil do you think you're up to?" he asked. "Get out!"

"I won't," she told him. "I'm leaving. I left a note. Why did you have to follow me?" She glanced quickly in Roger's direction. He blew several smoke rings, but made no comment.

"Would you mind opening up the back? I wish to remove Miss Tracey's luggage." Laine's voice had risen very slightly.

Roger removed the keys from the dashboard and tossed them lightly in Laine's direction, and Carol tensed back as they flipped past her with a small, metallic sound. "Help yourself," the salesman's response came in a low, unruffled murmur. "Don't ask me to help—I've got a bad heart."

When Laine had gone round to the back of the van Roger said very softly, "What do you want me to do, Carol—although," he gave a short laugh, "I don't see what the blazes I can do. He's bigger'n me." He grinned at her boyishly.

162

She felt her strength flicker. "As you say, there's nothing you can do. I don't want to cause a free fight. I'll have to go back and face the music, and that's that. I suppose I was a fool to try to run away—I should have stayed to clear everything up between us."

The doors at the back slammed shut and Laine began to carry the blue cases, two by two, to his own car.

"I'm darned if I'll help him," said Roger, and she felt a little piqued by his apparent unconcern—and yet, she asked herself, what else could she expect of this compact young man, this stranger?

"I'll go now," she said, "before there's trouble. Thanks a lot for trying, anyway."

Laine was closing the boot of his car and then he came back to where she was standing in the road. "Didn't you think you'd caused enough confounded trouble and up-heaval?" There was a sarcastic twist to his mouth and she wondered how she could ever have thought it sweet. "Ramesh owned up, of course."

She made one last attempt. "Laine, don't you see, I can't come back. You don't have to worry about me. I have money . . . I'll do all the explaining to my father."

"Worry? Worry? You have caused me nothing *but* worry! However, for your information I have hopes of getting the cheetahs back—so there's no need for you to run away like the irresponsible schoolgirl that you are."

At this stage Roger Thesen got out of the van and came leisurely over to where they were standing. Laine looked up to stare belligerently at him, as though blaming him for everything.

"Why don't you leave her to go her own sweet way?" Roger said. "She'll be okay. Didn't you hear the girl say she doesn't want to go back, or are you stricken by deaf-ness?"

Laine's eyes were dark and intense. "You keep out of this, you insolent young pup!"

"Oh, please. Please! As she spoke, Carol thought that never in her whole life would she forget this senseless scene in the hills with the scent of the rain-saturated earth all about them. Once again she had the feeling that she was somebody else and the girl concerned taking part in some film. "Take me back, Laine. We can't argue here." She spread her hands. "It's all so humiliating!" She turned to

Roger. "It will be all right. Really it will. I'm so sorry to have embarrassed you. I'm terribly embarrassed."

"It takes a lot to embarrass me," grinned Roger. "I just want to save you from this guy, this cradle-snatcher!"

"Look, clear off, will you, before you go too far and I let you have it." Laine stepped forward, and Roger's eyes came back to Carol and he lifted one eyebrow. There was a lazy amusement in the expression of his face.

"I'd rather go back," she said, and the look she gave him was pleading. "I'm hating all this."

"Perhaps you'll think in future," Laine told her angrily. "In that way you might save yourself, and everybody concerned, a lot more embarrassment." He turned to Roger Thesen. "As for you, you insolent young devil—you haven't heard the last of this!"

"Who says?" grinned Roger, before walking back to the van in his leisurely way.

When it was all over and Roger had managed to start the van and driven off and Laine had turned the car in the limited space available, Carol sat back, sickened by everything that had happened.

She turned slightly and could see Laine's dark, smooth-shaven cheek and the upset little twist of his mouth, then he became a blur that rocked violently. She lifted her fingers to her cheeks to stop the tears before they rolled down so that he would not know that she was crying.

Crying again! It was strange, she thought, but ever since she had stepped off the ship she had experienced nothing but tension, and she could not even begin to count the number of times she had found herself giving in to tears.

"Quite apart from everything else, Carol," Laine said, breaking the silence, "something has gone wrong between us, hasn't it?"

"I—didn't mean it to—*want* it to," she told him miserably.

"You no longer want to marry me?"

The nets of what appeared now to be a fantastic nightmare began to seize her greedily, strong as chains.

"Oh, Laine, please." She was shivering again. "I don't know. I just don't know. I do—I do want to—only . . ."

"Only what?"

"There's been so much—so much. I feel quite sick."

"I'm not surprised," he replied sarcastically. "For that matter I feel sick myself."

Now that they were going down into the Valley he was travelling very fast, driving almost recklessly, and she thought about what Roger had said about animals always crossing the road so that a motorist would come upon them, quite without any sort of warning, on a blind bend.

"What's gone wrong between us?" he said. "You felt that Mother didn't like you. Well, Mother is out of the way now. I keep telling myself that I should make allowances for you—you're so young. I want you to know, though, now and for ever, that you are not to go near those animals again with the intention of interfering. I won't have it." He spoke commandingly and coldly.

"Why don't you just put me in a cage along with them, and be done with it?" she said miserably. Her thoughts were shattered. Laine spoke as though they were going to carry on where they left off. She tried to control her panic. Was she never going to get out of this? She gave him an agonised look.

"I would suggest that you try to pull yourself together and try to curb that childish little tongue of yours," he said coldly.

Some time later he said, "When we get back I'll be returning to the nature reserve. It was only by chance that I went back for something to find that you had gone."

"Are the animals in the nature reserve, then?" she asked.

With a kind of deep inarticulate sound expressing distress he lifted his hands from the steering wheel and then allowed them to fall back again with a small vibrating sound. Then he said, "What do you know about the cheetah, Carol?" and before she could even begin to answer he went on, "The cheetah is just about the fastest thing on four legs, did you know that?"

"No," she replied softly, "not really. I knew they were fast—I mean——"

He cut in, "A cheetah has been said to attain a maximum speed of sixty to seventy miles an hour—even ninety miles. These figures are, no doubt, exaggerated." His voice sounded tired. "Probably fifty miles an hour would be nearer the mark, however. For all its speed a cheetah soon loses its wind."

165

"But what you are trying to tell me," she said, "is that the chances of capturing these animals is slight."

"Very slight."

"Ramesh told me that traps would be set."

"Traps *have* been set," he told her, with a weary patience which made her furious. "What do you think I've been doing—arranging with the ranger? However, I had to give up and come chasing after you instead. I had to send word to Mel Crimshaw that I was going to be detained. Has it occurred to you, I wonder, that I need this man's help in more ways than one?"

"I've said I'm sorry," she sighed. "What else can I do? If I could catch them myself, I would."

"And I wouldn't put it past you," he said sarcastically. "However, at the risk of boring you, allow me to say that when you let those animals go you were merely acting in the interest of your own childish resentment. You were against the zoo right from the very start. Let's face it."

She turned on him furiously. "Oh, what rubbish you talk! Do you believe that I would be brave enough to let two wild animals loose just to satisfy some childish resentment? Do you think I calmly and calculatingly walked up to the cage and opened the gate and stood back gloatingly while they ran away? I acted on the spur of the moment. It was an act of fear, I tell you. I thought I was working in the interest of the animals. Afterwards, my legs shook so that I could hardly stand."

"Aah . . ." he said, as he had said at the beginning. "Let's not go on with it."

They began to cross the causeway, and on either side the water was clogged with the drifted accumulation of wreckage caused by the storm. Although she had not noticed it on her short excursion with Roger Thesen, because she had been so emotionally upset at the time, there was all the evidence that the causeway had been under water at some time during the storm. The tyres made sucking, rotating noises, then they were across and the unhappy journey back to Laine's home was practically at an end.

Her room was just the same. Nothing had been touched. Ramesh carried her cases back inside, then when she was alone she took a deep breath and was aware of her own perfume which still pervaded it.

During the next fifteen minutes or so Laine's voice could be heard, from time to time, then soon afterwards she heard the Land-Rover start up and she knew that he had gone back to the reserve without telling her.

After a while she went out to the veranda, where things were very much back to normal. Everything had been tidied up and all traces of the storm removed. She saw Ramesh at the tourist end of the veranda and, for once, the expression on his good-looking face had changed. Ramesh had the ascetic look about him that one sometimes sees in the faces of ministers. When he observed her, however, his face brightened and he bowed slightly, tipping his slender brown fingers to his immaculately draped turban.

During the day Carol's thoughts repeated themselves. What was she to do? Make a clean breast of everything to her father? Or, was she to try again and carry on from here? As her thoughts went round and round she felt the net closing about her again.

Light was a long time dying and then, towards dusk, Laine parked the Land-Rover and got out, slamming the door behind him.

The way in which he mounted the steps suggested an easy strength and sensing her eyes on him he turned, and the movement not only had a casual agility about it but also a sort of contained violence which she put down to all the hours of scheming and of anxiety which had claimed his attention in the reserve.

"I'm half out of my mind longing for a shower," he told her shortly, "so you'll have to excuse me. Tell Ramesh, when you see him, to put the tray with the drinks in the living-room and to see that there is a fire."

With concealed hope she asked, "Have you—had any luck?"

He continued walking and was already going through the door to the hall when he expelled air from his lungs with a gasp which sounded as though he had done so with great effort and which ended in a bitter laugh. "Luck? Don't talk to me about *luck!*" He came to stand where he could see her better. "The animals are exhausted—and so are we. Something's got to give, and it's got to be tonight. I won't be here, by the way, after dinner." He had removed the slouch hat and ran his beautifully shaped fingers through his hair. "I don't know just when I'll be back—but you'll be all right here."

A short while later, because it was almost dark now and because it was cold, she went into the living-room. Ramesh brought the tray of drinks across to a small side table near the fireplace where the fire was burning brightly.

Laine was in a vile humour and emerged from his shower irritable. She could hear him moving about the house in his espadrilles while he unnecessarily ordered the servants around.

When he was dressed in fresh khaki clothes he came through to the living-room and moved towards the drinks tray as though a magnet was pulling him. He poured her a drink and then poured himself a stiff whisky, with very little soda. Noticing this, Carol frowned.

"I'm played out," he said, throwing himself into a chair and cocking a leg over one of the arms. He looked at the panting blue, gold and scarlet flames and then sipped his drink experimentally. He did not look particularly played out, she thought, shivering.

Carol could hardly keep her eyes off Laine. His nervous energy fascinated and frightened her. Even though he was wearing casual khaki clothes he had tucked a deep tangerine-and-white cravat into the open neck of his shirt.

Dinner was strained, with not even the fumbling talk about mutual interest to ease the tension; at last he said, "Carol, before I go I have one or two things to say to you." He patted his lips with his napkin, gently, fastidiously. "And I speak from the soul. I have no wish to be made a laughing-stock again. You are not here to attack my way of living. You are here because you agreed to be my wife—and be my wife you will, make no mistake about that. Grant me the common sense, if you will, and the perception which influenced me to put the cages where and how they are, in the first place. We will just have to bury the conflict of the last few hours and go on as we had planned to go on. It was bad enough for me to have to go grovelling to Mel Crimshaw for help without having you walk out on me, just like that." He snapped his fingers, and she was trembling and shivering again. If only she could stop shivering! She kept her big eyes on his face.

"You will have to learn, dear girl, not to act as if everything is a calamity. I know what I'm doing here. Now, the

168

position is this. Your father seemed to think that *time—time*—was what we needed. Time for you to settle in—time for us to get to know one another—time for this, time for that. What a lot of confounded rubbish! I can't agree with him." He stood up, throwing his napkin down. "Looking at everything quite dispassionately I can't see what right your father has, at this stage of the game—after neglecting you since you were ten—in throwing down ultimatums. All he has succeeded in doing is to confuse you. Imposing parental discipline, at this stage, is, I think, just a little ridiculous. There is much about you that he doesn't realise."

She looked down at the cloth, not speaking. She was experiencing a sharp sensation in the region of her chest.

"Carol?" She looked up and her face was flushed. "Yes?" It was just a little dry sound.

"What are you shivering for?"

"Nothing."

"I won't have things go wrong between us, do you hear?"

"I didn't want them to go wrong," she told him. "I didn't want to make you, or anybody else, myself included, a—a laughing stock."

"I know what problems we have here—and the best way to cope with them," he told her. "Leave it at that."

She found her legs and stood up. "Have you quite finished with me?" she asked, and felt a wave of fury surging through her. "What you're trying to say, in a long, round-about way, is that you're going to break me in—*train* me—like you train your animals. Is that it?"

When he answered her his voice was soft, almost bated, in fact. "Precisely yes, Carol. If need be—*yes*. How dare you run out on me the way you did? Setting the cheetahs free was bad enough, humiliating enough—but to pack your cases and to get *Ramesh* to work in with you—I can't forgive that. I repeat, I will not be made a laughing-stock!"

"What if I—refuse to stay here and be trained?" Her golden face, with its flushed cheeks, was all planes in the candlelight. "What if I refuse, Laine?"

He came round the table and she was aware again of that lean, tanned vitality about him. "Don't speak like

169

that," he said, and his voice was soft now. "I believe we can recapture what we have lost."

She raised her eyes to him. "No—no, Laine!"

He pulled her towards him. "I intend to get it all back," he whispered, low and intense. "Don't leave me again, Carol." She felt the pressure of his hand on her chin as he turned her face upward beneath his own. Then he kissed her. The kiss seemed an eternity, and she felt herself shrinking and cringing from him. When he lifted his head her eyes sought his pleadingly, but the words she intended to say were stillborn when she saw the tormented look in his dark eyes. His face looked oddly naked and haunted.

"Don't leave," he said again. "I couldn't stand it if you left."

"All right." The words were wrenched from her, and as soon as she uttered them she felt that she had taken some fatal step into the fearsome unknown.

For one moment she wondered whether he was going to kiss her again, but instead he said, "Good. Let's see what develops, then."

His voice was back to normal now and there was a different look in his eyes.

The tormented look had gone. In its place the look was conquering—marked by victory.

CHAPTER ELEVEN

JUST after lunch the next day, Maxine arrived in an expensive-looking car, which as it so happened belonged to Dallas Mulholland.

Carol was in the garden, trying to get the feel of the sun, which had no strength in it now, into her bones. Laine, however, was out again. He had been out most of the night and most of the morning, returning for a quick lunch only to leave for the reserve immediately after the meal was over.

"Where's everybody?" Maxine's expression was unsmiling. She closed the door of the car and went round to the boot where she proceeded to remove several scarlet leather cases.

"If by 'everybody' you're referring to Laine," Carol said quietly, her eyes moving over the cases, "he's out." Automatically, she stepped forward to help move the cases to the side of the drive and then Maxine drove the car into the car-port, next to Laine's lock-up garages.

When she got out Carol asked, "Are those Mrs. Mulholland's cases. Is she coming back after all, then?"

Maxine's slightly slanted green eyes were almost emerald-like in her lovely face. "Actually, no. They're my cases." She spoke with deliberate slowness and then strolled round to the other side of the car, haughty and indifferent.

"Is anything wrong, Maxine? Has—anything happened?"

"Nothing's wrong and nothing has happened. Dallas has hired a nurse to look after her, that's all. She insisted that I hand in my resignation and come down to the Valley to Laine's. So I won't be going back to town to nurse the old dame. Somebody else has taken my place, so I'm free to do as I like."

Carol felt a sudden sense of having been affronted. "You're going to stay here, then—not at your aunt and uncle's?"

"That's right. Dallas is not coming back and she has sent me in her place. That's why I've given up my old job. You can't stay here with Laine by yourself, or hadn't you thought of that?" She began to walk towards the house, but turned slightly to look over her shoulder. "Will you get someone to attend to my bags?"

Maxine was wearing an exquisite three-piece suit, the colour of wet moss, which was slim-fitting and chic. Her hair was a swirl of red silk.

"I'll get somebody," Carol replied stiffly, looking at all the cases. Maxine seemed to have moved in for good. She still wore an offended air as she followed Maxine's elegant and departing back.

Maxine went straight to Mrs. Mulholland's room, and when she came out she had changed into velvet tights the colour of Parma violets topped by an antique-green, heavy-knit silk sweater. She was provocatively beautiful and acted as if she knew it. Her green eyes bored deliberately through Carol.

"Where did you say Laine was?"

"As a matter of fact, I didn't say—but he's in the nature reserve."

The cigarette Maxine held was still unlit in her hand, and then she put it between her lips. "Is he visiting Mel Crimshaw, for Pete's sake?" The cigarette bobbed around as she spoke, then she dropped her lovely gauzy-green eyes and held a match to it.

"He—hasn't gone visiting, exactly. He has gone to try and catch the cheetahs—Dorcas and Selika." Carol had coloured a little.

Maxine crossed to a low table where, stopping a little, she flicked a small coating of ash from the tip of her cigarette.

"What do you mean—he's gone to try and *catch* Dorcas and Selika?" She straightened up and her eyes raked Carol, who found herself shivering again.

"They escaped into the nature reserve at the height of the rain."

"They *escaped*? How, for Pete's sake?" Maxine crossed the room to stand before a gilt antique mirror where, with an exacting eye, she inspected her beautiful face.

"They got out, Maxine, after I had undone the padlock and opened the gate to the cage." There was an edge to Carol's voice.

Maxine swung round with excited green eyes which widened in disbelief. "You what? Say, what's going on around here that I don't know about? What on earth are you talking about?"

Carol stared at her for a moment, then went to stand next to the tremendous sliding glass doors and looked out. She felt too tired to speak. All the clouds had gone now, she noticed, and in the innocently new winter air the hills were sharp—every bush and the metallic leaves of the trees standing out like brush-strokes on an excellent painting. She found herself thinking that it was strange that not all the trees lost their leaves in the winter months.

"Would you mind answering me?" Maxine's voice was harsh.

Carol turned slowly. "I'm sorry," she said. "I was just looking at the weather."

"Well, look at it some other time. I want to know what happened to Dorcas and Selika. I'm waiting."

"During all that rain, I thought that the animals were in danger, Maxine. The water had risen considerably," Carol explained.

She heard Maxine's angry intake of breath. "You little fool! What did you have to do that for? The animals were perfectly all right. What did you have to interfere with Laine's zoo for? It's his whole life. Do you know that?"

"I do know—I should know. I've been told often enough."

"You don't belong here, Carol. You don't belong in Laine's Valley. Let's face it—if you lived to be a hundred you would never fit in here and you would never understand Laine." Maxine always spoke as if *she* did.

"You don't have to tell me that, Maxine." Carol's voice was soft. "Don't I know it? Why do you think I tried to escape yesterday? This time yesterday I was on my way out of Laine's Valley. I'm only back here because he caught up with me and brought me back."

Maxine blinked once and then looked at Carol searchingly. "Are you trying to tell me that you—ran away?"

"If you can call cadging a lift with a commercial traveller running away—well, yes. Unfortunately for me, his van was heating and it stalled on the climb up. Laine discovered, in the meantime, that I'd gone—he followed us in his car and," she shrugged, "here I am! Back along with all the other caged things!"

Maxine sucked a quick breath through her teeth. "So Laine went after you? He brought you back?" She swung round and her eyes glittered with rage. "And you allowed him to bring you back? Like a lamb! Oh, you little fool!"

"I came back because a scene was developing. I think Laine would have hit Roger Thesen eventually. I had no option. I couldn't involve an innocent party."

"And now you're supposed to be back where you started—you're back here as the future Mrs. Laine Mulholland?" The ash dropped from the cigarette Maxine had forgotten between her fingers.

"I'm supposed to be, yes," Carol replied, with a curious mixture of resignation and defiance.

"Are you or are you not? Do you intend to carry on with this crazy thing?"

"Maxine, I can't get out of it. Don't you *see?*" Carol's voice rose.

"You're not in love with Laine?" Maxine's breath was fast.

"No." Carol made a wide deprecatory gesture. "No, no, no!" Her voice broke. "I don't quite know how I'm going to bear it. I—don't want to belong to him."

"So you don't want to marry Laine?"

"Leave me alone, Maxine! Stop torturing me, will you? All this has got nothing to do with you. Just because you're on such good terms with his mother it doesn't entitle you to cross-examine me like this." Carol went to the windows again. "I'll have to stay," she said. "In his own way, I suppose, Laine is in love with me."

"He only thinks he loves you," Maxine said furiously. "He only *thinks* he loves you."

Carol turned and their glances clashed. "A man of forty-two? He should know what he wants by now—and he happens to want me, even though I don't want him. I made the big mistake of my life getting involved with him."

"It was only your youth that attracted him. He was madly flattered. It appealed to his—his self-opinionatedness, because, of course, Laine suffers from self-interest, let's face it! I'd be a fool to be blinded by him. But that is Laine. I accept him for what he is."

"Oh, Maxine, stop it, please! I can't stand it. I've had enough." Carol had spent most of the night sitting huddled on her bed, only to fall into a troubled sleep towards dawn, and she felt like sinking through the floor.

Maxine was lighting another cigarette and for a brief moment her face was hidden by a pearl-grey cloud of smoke. Then she said, "Carol?" Her green eyes were cold and glittering. "You've got to leave here." She came towards Carol, moving with all the smooth easy motions of a cobra.

"All this time I've been wondering how I could get you away from this Valley," Maxine was saying, "and all the time I didn't know that you would leave it of your own free will." She laughed. "Imagine, all this time I've been agitating to get you away from the man I love, and short of kidnapping you against your will I didn't quite know where to begin. And yet here it is, everything is so simple, because of course you'll come away—of your own free will. It's as simple as that." While she spoke she moved about the room with her beautiful walk. "In other words, I'm going to get you out of this Valley before Laine gets back."

Carol gave her a helpless look. "Oh no, Maxine. You seem to imagine that you just have to make your own plans and I'll fall in with them. Do you imagine for one moment that I want to go through everything again?"

"Oh, for goodness' sake, don't stand there making speeches! Don't argue with me. We've got to move fast, before Laine gets back. We'll both have to pack. Fortunately, I hadn't unpacked much. I was going to do that tonight. But first I must have a quick drink."

As Maxine poured herself a drink and cradled the glass in her hands Carol saw that her hands were shaking.

"I'm the only one who can help you get away, can't you see that?" Maxine's voice was a throaty, excited whisper. "Laine hates to be made to appear a fool. For that reason alone, he'll never let you go."

"I can't do this, Maxine. I've caused such a lot of trouble as it is. Can't you see that?"

"If you'll leave everything to me there'll be no trouble. I'll do all the explaining—Laine won't want you back by the time I've finished. You'll be free of him."

"I don't feel like having my name painted more black than it already is," Carol said with a helpless, half-tearful expression.

"What's your name got to do with it—when your whole life is at stake? Do you want to end tied up to a man you don't love?"

"No."

Maxine gave her a cold impersonal look. "Well, then? Take my advice and get moving. All this serves two purposes, don't forget. You're helping me and I'm helping you. To stand and argue like this is nothing short of madness."

After that, things began to happen. Maxine spotted Ramesh and called out for him to come into the living-room. "Ramesh," she spoke quickly and urgently, "I'm taking Miss Tracey away, and you are not to interfere, no matter what orders you've had from Mr. Mulholland. Is that clear? Miss Tracey doesn't wish to remain here."

Ramesh lifted the palms of his hands and opened his mouth to speak, but Maxine cut him short. "Listen to me, will you? This will have nothing to do with you because you've seen nothing, heard nothing. So far as you're concerned I didn't arrive here today. Do you understand?"

"Yes, miss, but . . ." Ramesh looked as if his holding-power of amazement had long since been exhausted.

"No 'buts', and you're not to let Mr. Copeland know that I've been here either. I *particularly* don't want you to get in touch with him. I don't want him to get the scent of this."

Ramesh's shoulders lifted in a delicate movement. "I'm not here to interfere, miss, but I must point out to you that I have been in constant trouble with Mr. Mulholland—since—the last time." He glanced at Carol.

"Oh, shut up, and get me Mr. Mulholland's mother on the line, will you?" Maxine told him, then turned to Carol. "And you go and pack. I have something personal to discuss with Dallas on the phone, *if* you don't mind."

"Maxine?" Carol felt completely drained, and realised that she was shivering violently. Her head felt hot and yet inside she felt cold. "Maxine, please . . ."

"Go and pack! Time is going on. Laine will be back before we know what's hit us."

"I feel sick, Maxine. You've got to believe me. I feel so awful that I doubt whether I would be able to—travel. Apart from that, I have nowhere to go."

176

"Oh, rubbish! You're only sick because you can't face up to anything in life."

Carol clenched her teeth and said nothing. Somehow she felt that Maxine's thrust was too near the truth to be treated with resistance.

As she packed those things which she had taken out of the cases which had already been packed for her previous flight Carol could hear Maxine speaking in a low, urgent tone on the telephone, and soon afterwards she came into the room. "Well, are you ready?" She looked at Carol. "Because *I* am."

"Yes, I'm ready, Maxine."

Ramesh and one of the waiters were in the room gathering her cases. "Those blue cases," she thought, "with my 'London glad-rags' in them. There they go again. Out one door and in another."

"I think, perhaps, before we go, I'd better have an aspirin or something. Maybe a—hot toddy."

"A hot toddy?" Maxine's lips were determined and ruthless. "For Pete's sake! What do you want a hot toddy for? You make me sick, Carol. Come on!"

"We'll have to go like the hounds of hell," said Maxine, "because, quite apart from Laine following us, it's getting late."

"It's terribly cold," Carol murmured, holding her elbows with her hands. She closed her eyes.

A little while later she said in a flat, little voice, "You were always so worried about the man you love, Maxine. Why don't you get married?"

"Why do you think I want to get *you* away?" Maxine answered.

"In a way I think you'd like *both* of them, wouldn't you?" Carol's teeth were chattering and she felt herself slipping beyond all hope of every getting warm again.

When Maxine's hand startled her some time later she realised that she must have been saying something. She felt Maxine's hand on her forehead. "This is just the last straw," Maxine was saying. "*You sick?*"

"I *told* you I was sick. I tried to tell you, Maxine." Carol sank back in a spasm of shivering confusion.

When she awoke again the car had stopped and Maxine was shaking her. "Here," she said, "drink this. Dallas

177

always keeps a little whisky in the car, in case of accidents. I don't know why I didn't think of it before."

Carol clenched her jaws.

"Drink this, Carol, and stop clenching your teeth before I force your stubborn little jaws open and pour it down your throat. Now, come on!"

"Now, get a grip of yourself," ordered Maxine, slipping the bottle into the glove compartment and starting the engine. "Do you often get fevers like this? But of course you can't. You can't possibly have malaria. You haven't been in this country long enough—and besides, Imihlaba isn't in the malarial belt. So what's your case?"

Carol struggled to sit up. "I think it's a chill. I got very wet. I'll be all right in a moment, but we seem to have been an age on the road, Maxine."

"Well, Laine's place isn't quite what you might call on the outskirts of town," Maxine's voice was sneering. "I've been going as fast as I can."

"We're running into lights now."

"We should be. We're nearing town. I wanted to phone some place for you—a boarding-house, or something, until you can make plans to get back to London. I know you have money, because Laine told me about your father's arrangement, if the marriage didn't work out."

Carol was feeling slightly better, but not much. "You don't have to worry to phone," she said, her dislike for Maxine reaching its peak. "Just drop me in town. Any taxi-rank will do."

"Where will you go?" The relief in Maxine's voice was completely undisguised.

"I—I—have friends." Carol grieved for herself. *Where would she go?* What a plight she was in, but she would rather sleep in the gutter than have anything more to do with this red-haired devil of a girl at her side. "It's quite simple, I'll just phone my friends." "Who am I," she thought, feeling the desire to giggle hysterically, "that I can't invent a few friends now and again?"

"Where do your friends stay? How can you possibly have friends in this country when you've only just arrived here?"

"These friends are from London. They're madly rich and they're going to open an exclusive antique shop in Durban. I have their address. You don't have to worry,

178

Maxine. You can get back to—the man you love—and good luck to you. For that matter, good luck to him, too—he's going to need it. By the way, he has quite a brand of kisses, hasn't he?" No sooner were the words out than Carol regretted them, appalled and shrivelled up at the cheapness of them, and she closed her eyes against the tears—remembering. "Why did you do this to me, Michael?" her heart cried. "Why? Why? What am I going to do without you?"

"As soon as we get on the outskirts of town you can get out," Maxine's voice was hard, "and good luck to *you*—and to your madly rich friends and their antique shop."

"I've read about girls like you," gritted Carol, "but I never thought I would ever meet one."

"I've read about girls like you, too, if it comes to that. Out for all they can get!"

Nothing was making any sense now, and Carol tried to focus her attention on the last lap of the journey. The lights were coming faster and thicker now and she found her eyes swivelling against their yellow glare and knew the fresh pangs of fever.

"There's a taxi-rank down near the theatre," Maxine was saying, concentrating on the hectic traffic. "You say you're going to phone your friends. Well, I'll drop you just outside the theatre. You'll find a telephone booth there. If your friends decide to come and pick you up you'll be able to wait just outside the foyer. If, on the other hand, you have to take a taxi—well, all you have to do is to phone for one and in two shakes of a nanny-goat's tail one will be on its way across from the rank. It's not far—the rank, I mean. Just across from the theatre."

"You're so kind," Carol said bitterly. "So thoughtful, Maxine."

Soon after that Maxine slowed down and stopped. "Shall *I* phone for you?" She sounded faintly worried.

"No, thank you."

"I'll help you with your luggage, then."

"Thank you. Just—sling it in the gutter over there. That will do." Carol was aware of the unfamiliar harshness in her voice.

"There's no need to be nasty. I think I've done my best for you." Maxine got out and closed the door with her shoulder.

Carol busied herself trying to open the door. Her body felt racked with aches and pains.

When Maxine came round to her side she said, "Oh, you have, Maxine. You have. You've done your best all round."

Carol stepped out and felt the sudden violence of the wind as it tore at her hair. Quite suddenly she wanted to laugh. "If only I *had* a bed," she thought, half-tearfully. "Oh, if only I had a bed right now!"

"The theatre people are beginning to come out now," Maxine told her, taking the last case from the boot, "so you won't be alone here. There's life going on all about you. And there's the telephone booth, right over there, and the taxi-rank across the way." Her manner was nervous. "The number will be in the book. I can't make out the name from here. Perhaps you can? Those neon lights there, going on and off? Can you?"

Despite anything she could do Carol began to laugh hysterically, doubling over a little. "Oh, Maxine," she gasped, holding her chest, "who are you trying to reassure? You—or me? Please, please—just get lost, will you?"

Maxine started to say something and then, suddenly' with her mouth open, she appeared to think better of it and was silent. Then she turned and got into Dallas Mulholland's long, expensive car, and in another moment she had started the engine and had driven off.

And then, when she was gone, Carol stood staring at nothing and shivering.

CHAPTER TWELVE

PEOPLE were moving around her and there were shining cars pulling away from the kerb and the parking area. Luxurious cars taking people home to luxurious beds, with padded headboards, where hot water-bottles would be keeping warm between sheets and blankets. Homes where hot toddys would possibly be waiting . . .

She turned away from her luggage in an effort to see the telephone booth, then when she saw where it was she was aware of a great distance dividing her from it and she could not find her way across that distance.

"Excuse me, but are you all right?" The voice filled the pavement with its vitality.

The owner was a well-dressed woman who was, perhaps, in her eartly fifties, and as her eyes searched Carol's face Carol, sick as she was, felt strangely embarrassed.

"I—I think perhaps I'm going to be ill. I'll be all right once I get into bed with a couple of aspirins and a hot water-bottle."

"Are you waiting for someone, then?"

"No. Only a taxi." Carol looked at the woman through queer sickening whirls and had the feeling that she was in orbit.

"Oh, so you've phoned for a taxi?"

"No, not yet."

"Look, my dear, do allow us to take you to wherever it is you're going! It's so cold, and you don't look at all well. Where are you going?"

"Well, quite frankly, I don't know. It will have to be somewhere on the Marine Parade, though."

"Why, dear?"

"Well, because I don't know any other place."

"Where are you from, then?"

"London, actually."

The woman gave a faint smile. "You're a long way from home, aren't you?"

"Yes, I suppose I am, really."

"Simon? Look, this child is obviously sick and a long way from home. London, actually! I suggest we take her home with us and get Sargasso in to have a look at her. What do you say, darling?"

"I don't like the idea of getting ourselves involved to that extent, Vicky. Quite the most logical thing to do would be to run her straight down to Casualty," the man called Simon answered shortly, and his wife turned away from him with something like irritation. "Look, my dear," she said to Carol, "have you *anybody*, anybody at all, who is expecting you? I mean, you haven't just come from London—plop! Like that! Have you?"

"The only friends I have now are—*invented* friends, to be quite truthful," said Carol.

"Oh, Simon, for goodness' sake, that settles it. The poor child is half delirious. Bring the car and let's get going and ask questions afterwards."

"I am ill," Carol thought, and then once the first horror of this discovery was gone she accepted with resignation that her cases were about to be carried through yet another door.

"You're so kind," she mumbled. "I can't tell you how —awful—I feel." She allowed herself to be helped into the car and suffered acutely over her impotence. "What an awful thing to have happened," she kept repeating.

"I'll sit in the back with you. Just tell me one more thing—what is your name?"

"It's Carol. Carol Tracey."

When they were in the car she said, "You aren't taking me back to Laine Mulholland's Valley, are you? I don't want to go back to Imi—Imihlaba."

"She smells slightly of liquor," Simon was saying, over his shoulder. "You realise that, of course, Vicky? Frankly, I think we're making a mistake. The child should quite obviously be put in the hands of the welfare people."

"Oh, rubbish! She's sick and she's in trouble, and that's all that concerns me. She's beautifully turned out." Vicky spoke as though Carol wasn't there.

Liquor—the word throbbed like a scar on Carol's mind. Finally she managed to say, "Maxine gave me whisky in the car—to warm me up."

In a way, Carol thought vaguely, the house was very much like Mrs. Mulholland's house. She even had a feeling that it was the same well-to-do suburb. There was the same kind of long drive to it, flanked at intervals by converted gas street lamps which were all lit.

The drive ended in a courtyard, in the centre of which was an illuminated pool containing fish and pink water-lilies. There was a spectacular elegance to the hall with its wonderful crystal chandelier and its flowers.

Her feet sank into soft carpets and her luggage was taken care of, even at this time of night. Upstairs in a bedroom, which had its own bathroom and balcony, Vicky, whoever she was, seemed to be doing an awful lot for her, she thought in despair. "I can manage my panties," she found herself whimpering. "Vicky, I can manage those— and my stockings. Please!"

"You poor little thing! I'm only trying to get you into bed before Simon—Mr. Chalmers—gets through to Dr. Sargasso. You'll be all right, darling. You don't have to *invent* any more friends. You are with friends. Will you remember that? Will you try?"

"Yes." The tears were beginning to fall now. "But— it's all so—humiliating."

"Not at all. If one woman can't help another—well, well. Where would we be? And here is that water-bottle you've been craving for."

"Oh, thank you." Carol looked up from behind fever-shrouded hazel eyes. "Did you manage to get a lemon?" she began to say, and then broke off thinking, "I'm wandering. Oh, heavens, I'm wandering!"

Some time later she was awakened from a nightmarish sleep by the doctor who made a quick examination. "She's got pneumonia all right, and she's obviously been under some sort of strain. She's suffering from exhaustion. You're set on keeping her here, then?"

"Quite set. Nothing would make me move her."

Carol allowed them to tuck her up again, and a long sigh escaped her when she heard the wind outside hurling itself with shuddering thuds against the window panes and she recognized her thankfulness.

"Anyway," she piped up, "I've got a bed. That's the main thing. And a hot water-bottle . . ."

The night became, for her, a succession of confused faces. A face here one minute and gone the next, but it seemed to be mostly Vicky's face hovering in semi-darkness.

183

"I'm a nuisance," she said. "Aren't I?"

"You're not a nuisance, dear." The voice might have come from a disembodied soul.

All through the night there were whimpers and gasps for breath, which Carol knew were made by herself. She was aware of shivering channels of fever somewhere at the end of which she heard herself shouting Michael's name, and then there were great shuddering noises from the wind outside.

She began to feel hot instead of cold and wet and tried to kick the blankets away from her body. Desperately she saw visions of vast white refrigerators and icebergs and snow; then she found herself shouting incoherently about the snow on the Berg and telling Michael that she loved him. She knew she was doing these things and saying these things, but she could not stop herself.

Time and place and principle of order were blotted out. There were pains in her chest now which seemed to go right through to her back, the kind of pains that advanced and withdrew in a sequence of sharp and regular waves with each labouring breath. Every time she took a breath it was as though knives were being thrust into her and she felt herself sobbing and calling Michael's name.

Morning was heralded by the wan light of a dull and dismal sky; Carol did not resist when she felt arms about her and she submitted to being changed into fresh pyjamas.

Somebody else seemed to be in charge of the nursing situation now. Somebody who was brusquely kind with a deep voice and who was obviously Scottish. Sick and weak, Carol could do nothing but try to do as she was told.

There were flowers in the room now. Flowers reaching out and catching the light coming from the bedside lamp. It must be night again, she thought, looking at the petals, so confident of their flawless sheen, then two hands encircled the white vase and the flowers were gone. Gone for the night. They always took flowers away at night in a sickroom.

The wind was blowing harder, by the sound of things, rattling the jalousies outside the windows. She began to experience intervals of calm lucidity, but these intervals, as yet, did not last long enough for her to identify what was happening about her.

At one stage she mumbled, "I'm sorry. Desperately sorry," and a dim figure in starched white emerged from a chair near the bed. It was the Scot's voice. "But what on earth for, lassie? You've no need to be sorry."

Carol frowned as if seeking some elusive memory. "For being such a nuisance," she said, feeling weak and helpless.

"You've been awfu' sick, but you're well over the worst now. You're no' to bother your head about a thing."

Before she dropped off to sleep again Carol felt more refreshed and more aware of her surroundings than she had been during all the labouring hours that had gone before. Her eyes took in the rose carpet, which stretched away to the cream walls, the gilt Venetian furniture and the exquisite curtains to match the carpet. Merely to be in such a room generated healing power, she thought comfortably.

The faces were clear today. She saw Vicky Chalmers and the nurse, who was wearing her cape, which meant that she must be going off night duty. To the man in the dark suit she said, "You must be the doctor. I vaguely remember seeing you about." She smiled shyly. "You've been very kind." Her eyes went from face to face. "You've all been very kind."

The doctor smiled from behind thick horn-rimmed glasses, accepting the tribute casually. "You're feeling much better, eh?"

"Much, much better. I—even feel quite hungry!"

"Well," the elderly Scottish nurse went towards the long line of cream-and-gilt built-in cupboards, "I must away and catch my bus, so I'll say cheerio." She opened a door and took her bag from the shelf. In the space below Carol could see her blue suitcases mocking her.

CHAPTER THIRTEEN

As soon as Carol was allowed up Vicky Chalmers insisted that she did her the favour of not mentioning the immediate future until she was fully recovered and until after the fund-raising mannequin parade which was being held in her home was over.

Money spilled its evidence everywhere in the Chalmers' home. It was a magnificent setting in which to recover, and gradually Carol found her shattered spirit pulling itself together.

The days were now filled with the preparations for this big occasion, which was to include a buffet supper and dance. The servants went about rearranging furniture and abusing each other with good cheer while Simon, coming home early from his offices only to be jostled about by Vicky, coughed over his drink, swore and then apologised to Carol. When Vicky discovered that Carol had done modelling in London she asked Suzi Sullivan, who ran a charm school, to include her as the guest mannequin on her list of models. And then, miraculously, by nine o'clock on a comparatively mild evening, all the tension was over and Vicky's charitable function was going strong. People had been arriving since about eight o'clock and were making a deafening volume of talk.

Two glass-fronted rooms, of tremendous proportions and opening directly out to the lawns, swimming-pool and garden had been set aside for the purpose and the ceiling to floor sweeps of sliding glass led the eye outwards towards the floodlit garden and pool.

Lighting was flattering and discreet to the many beautifully groomed women whose gowns suggested exciting backgrounds of flagged terraces, smooth architecture and vast crystal-blue swimming-pools. There seemed to be a lot of glamorous girls about with young men who, with their skimped and narrow suits, looked as though they had just walked off the pages of *Esquire*. Champagne foamed all round and a small dance orchestra was playing soft, prim music over the babble of noise.

Into this scene, on the stroke of nine-thirty, came the first mannequin, and there was an excited rustle before people quietened down and the number which the band was playing died to make way for piano music.

The model stood, just looking around, not moving an eye-lash, then the voice of Suzi Sullivan, speaking above the piano and the last minute chatter, was describing a "costume for high noon to evening in the season's new colour".

The models, all startlingly beautiful, in a dramatic way, came and went, and then Suzi was saying, "And here is lovely Carol, our guest mannequin from London, wearing a ravishing gown, drawn with an extravagant pureness of line. Flowering lamé whorls about the body in a single great petal, closing to one side."

So much had happened to shake Carol's confidence in herself that for a moment she stood, breathless and hesitant, until Suzi said in a soft, amused voice for everyone to hear, "Go on, Carol—they won't eat you!" There was a tiny amused murmur of laughter, and then Carol knew that she had herself under control and was walking in the old, brisk, faintly aloof stride of the model.

The next time she began to enjoy herself, moving from table to table with ease and supreme surety, turning from time to time in a gorgeous flourish of colour. There was a refreshing lack of flamboyance about her confidence and her hands moved only when necessary.

She turned at one table and stepped forward—then she suddenly lost self-assurance, her hand automatically flying to her throat, because sitting at the table was Michael Copeland. She saw the lift of his eyebrow, the faint quirk of his mouth and the deepening of the ripple in his cheek, and she realised that there was something she didn't know —something she hadn't been told. For a moment they gazed at each other and the room was filled with silence for them, even though the piano was playing and people were softly discussing the fashions. Then she moved on.

In the powder-room Vicky was waiting for her. "Carol," she said, "I'd like a word with you. In my office," so Carol followed her down a carpeted corridor into the office with its lime-green carpet which was tipped by burnt-orange curtains.

Vicky walked over to her black penthouse desk and picked up an antique letter opener, with an ornate silver top to it. Then she perched on the arm of her chair and crossed her legs. "You've seen him, of course," she said.

"If you mean—Michael Copeland, yes." Carol's voice was taut.

"I invited him here. You must have guessed that. I mean, it's just too much to ask you to believe that it was a coincidence."

"Might I ask—why you asked him, Vicky?"

"I think you know the answer to that one, Carol!"

Carol tried to rise from the awful humiliation she was feeling. "You shouldn't have done this, Vicky," she said, in a hard little voice. "I remember vaguely, of course, calling for Michael when I was running a very high temperature. What amazes me, though, is how you could have taken any notice of these—these ravings, on my part. Michael Copeland happens to be in love with Maxine Mason—the girl who drove me to Durban." She gave Vicky an agonised look. "How—did you know where to find him? We've never spoken about this."

"It wasn't hard." Vicky put down the letter opener and stood up. "You mentioned Laine Mulholland's Valley and the dam, and while you were so ill you spoke about the floods and the zoo. The rest was easy. I got in touch with this man on the telephone and he told me the rest. It was he who put me in touch with your Michael Copeland. It was then arranged for Michael to present himself when you were well enough. We decided that tonight would be a good time."

"I don't know how I'm going to bear going back out there," Carol said. "I feel so embarrassed."

There was a tap on the door and Simon came in. "Monty Jacques and his wife have to leave," he said. "Will you come and do the necessary, Vicky?"

It seemed useless to create a scene, so Carol allowed herself to be led from the office; then when she was changed she joined some people at one of the lavish bars which was laden with cold cuts and salads. She took a heaped-up plate of turkey, chicken, ham and potato salad and accepted a cocktail from somebody, which she didn't know what to do with, but she was too upset to know what she was doing.

She would have to leave Durban, of course, she thought. It was possible that Michael's work at the Valley would be over now and he would be back in his flat in town. Their paths had crossed and would no doubt do so again.

When he came to stand beside her she felt the blood drain out of her face and her fingers were clamped around the glass she was holding. They looked at each other silently and gravely, then he said, "Let me take that glass from you." She watched him putting it down, loving him, and then he was saying, "I've been half out of my mind with worry over you."

The area in which they stood seemed to be full of people, ringed by more people, and waiters had to edge sideways through the crush with their silver trays.

"Michael," she said, "why didn't you tell Vicky Chalmers about you—and Maxine? If you'd had any feeling for—any feeling *at all*, you would have spared me this embarrassment by not coming here tonight."

They moved apart to make room for some people who wanted to pass through to the ballroom beyond, then when they came closer again he said, "I've told your Vicky Chalmers all there is to tell about Maxine—and what I *think* of her, incidentally."

They were jostled apart again, and taking her arm he said, "Let's get out of here." She made no resistance until she discovered that they were in the ballroom, when she took her long skirt between her fingers, as though preparing herself to run from him.

"We'd better dance," he said, and Carol stared at him with wide, hurt eyes while he took her into his arms and guided her to the floor where, with her body against his, they were soon lost in the dancing crowd.

"Carol," he said, tilting her face, "Maxine might have used my shoulder to cry on, but we were never in love. Maxine has never appealed to me—and she never could."

"Oh, don't," she begged, smiling a crooked, wounded smile. "*Don't:* After all, I've pulled through. If that was Vicky's idea she got you here too late. She should have got you to come to the bedside when I was delirious and raving. Because it was raving—nonsensical raving! Frankly, Vicky surprises me!"

"Talking about Vicky Chalmers," he said, "she appears to have quite a reputation for organising things all round."

"She enjoys this sort of thing, I understand." Carol took her hand from his and made a small gesture. She was trying desperately not to let the nearness of him disturb her.

"It was because of this ability of hers to get things organised," he went on, "that she sorted the Mulholland-Mason problem out. Laine and Maxine were married four days ago!"

Carol had the feeling that she was spinning into space. "Laine and Maxine?" she repeated stupidly. "Married? You're making it up. I don't believe you!" She raised her eyes to his. "Is that why you're here? Because Maxine has—jilted you?"

He drew her closer. "I'm here because I love you. I've loved you since I saw you standing at the Marine Terminal with that damned photo of Laine in your hand."

"It doesn't make sense!" Her eyes searched his. "You —often you were—insulting. You actually seemed to *enjoy* insulting me."

"When a man behaves in the manner that I behaved it's usually because he loves a girl." He lifted her hand to his lips and her eyes followed his movement.

"Vicky Chalmers has asked me to convey a message to you," he said. "She said to tell you that your father is making plans to be with you as soon as possible. She's been in touch with him. She got his address from Laine."

A cold wave washed over her. "*My father?* Coming here? To *South Africa?* Oh, what has Vicky been up to? My poor father must be beside himself with worry over me!"

"He's coming here because he wants to. Vicky has explained everything to him."

All she could see was a blur that rocked crazily. "I feel as though I'm—falling apart," she told him, smiling—but she was biting her lip.

"Well, don't," he said tenderly, "because I want to marry you. Not because Vicky Chalmers wants it but because *I* want it. I've wanted it for a long time now."

She did not answer and he said, "Carol?" then she looked up and he grinned. "This is a heck of a place to propose—on a dance floor, and I can't take you outside because you've just had pneumonia." She could feel his heart and she felt like melting into him.

"I've wanted it that way too," she told him shyly, "but I've never allowed myself to think of it."

He drew her closer. "Only one thing worries me," he said, placing his fingers just beneath her chin.

"What is that?" She looked back at him with troubled puzzlement.

"I feel so *nervous*," he said. "I wonder what your father will think of the 'stand-in'?"

Her lips curved against his chin. "Oh, he'll *love* you, darling. He just won't be able to help himself. Isn't that supposed to be the correct answer to a question of this nature?" She looked up at him. "You see, I remember *everything* you've ever said to me."

The music stopped and they stood until the polite clapping had ended. People were starting to walk from the floor. "Let's go and find Vicky," he said. "She'll want to start organising the wedding for us."

He smiled down at her and she put her hand in his. "And then let's find a place where I can kiss you." The intensity of his tone made her blush.

THE END

Readers rave about
Harlequin romance fiction...

"I absolutely adore Harlequin romances!
They are fun and relaxing to read, and
each book provides a wonderful escape."
— N.E.,* Pacific Palisades, California

"Harlequin is the best in romantic reading."
— K.G., Philadelphia, Pennsylvania

"Harlequin romances give me a whole new
outlook on life."
— S.P., Mecosta, Michigan

"My praise for the warmth and adventure
your books bring into my life."
— D.F., Hicksville, New York

*Names available on request.